ADVANCE ~~PRAISE~~
PARASITE LIFE

"Victoria Dalpe's stellar debut novel suggests that sometimes you consume the ones you love. The prose is tough and unsentimental, yet evocative in its depiction of the cancerous nature of abuse. *Parasite Life* battens down on you—insidious and predatory."

—Laird Barron, author of *Blood Standard*

"How do you breathe new life into the YA vampire novel? If you're Victoria Dalpe, you do it by wrapping a refreshingly humanistic interior and an incredibly compelling narrative voice in the Gothic, primal, atavistic horror that made the children of the night sing tous in the first place."

—Orrin Grey, author of *Painted Monsters & Other Strange Beasts*

"All relationships are parasitic. That's never been truer than in *Parasite Life*. A visceral and tempestuous ride through a genuine teen hell, *Parasite Life* is a beautifully written, gothic tale about that give-and-give-and-take in all kinds of love—familial and romantic—that slowly drain us dry even as they feed us. In *Parasite Life*, Dalpe tells a fine *damned* story."

—Susie Moloney, author of *A Dry Spell*, *The Dwelling*, and *Things Withered: Stories*

"A dark and stormy read! *Parasite Life* is the kind of book that makes you want to lock the doors and draw the curtains just so you won't be interrupted. Victoria Dalpe is such a charming woman that it's surprising to realize she has such a dark and macabre imagination—a classic tale whose Gothic roots run deep throughout the story."

—Adrianne Ambrose, author of *Fangs for Nothing,*
Confessions of a Virgin Sacrifice, and the
"Betty and Veronica" Archie Comics

"In Victoria Dalpe's compelling debut, seventeen-year-old Jane DeVry shares a house in a small New Hampshire town with a mother suffering from a mysterious condition whose symptoms include mysterious wounds and sudden bouts of screaming. When the friendship of a new student at school awakens new desires in her, Jane sets out to learn who she is, beginning an odyssey that takes her first into her mother's old journal, and then to the art scene in contemporary Manhattan, in search of a father she has never known. Smart, gripping, and possessed of real emotional depth, *Parasite Life* invokes the traditions of the Gothic while taking the form boldly into the twenty-first century."

—John Langan, author of *The Fisherman*

"Already trapped in a claustrophobic life which forces her to play caretaker to her own mentally ill mother, teenaged Jane is finally forced to confront the secrets and lies which surround her when her attraction to Sabrina, a new girl at school, awakens hungers too violent to ignore. Victoria Dalpe's *Parasite Life* is a coolly sensual slice of darkness that reads like Anne Rice for the post-*Twilight* age."

—Gemma Files, Shirley Jackson and Sunburst Award-winning author of *Experimental Film*

"*Parasite Life* is a totally unique spin on the vampire genre. This dark and blood-soaked coming of age tale haunts and intrigues as the secrets of Jane's past are revealed."

—Abby Denson, author of *Cool Japan Guide* and *Dolltopia*

"Sensual, moving, and sometimes grim, Parasite Life explores the tough questions: what would you do for love? What would you do for need? And who would you betray to survive?"

—Nancy Baker, author of *Cold Hillside* and *A Terrible Beauty*

"Visceral but polished, grim but lush, and ultimately optimistic. A coming-of-age story in more ways than one."

—E.L. Chen, author of *The Good Brother*

VICTORIA DALPE

PARASITE LIFE

Distributed in Canada by
Fitzhenry & Whiteside Limited
195 Allstate Parkway
Markham, Ontario L3R 4T8
Phone: (905) 477-9700
e-mail: bookinfo@fitzhenry.ca

Distributed in the U.S. by
Consortium Book Sales & Distribution
34 Thirteenth Avenue, NE, Suite 101
Minneapolis, MN 55413
Phone: (612) 746-2600
e-mail: sales.orders@cbsd.com

Library and Archives Canada Cataloguing in Publication Data

Dalpe, Victoria, author
    Parasite life / Victoria Dalpe. -- First edition.

Issued in print and electronic formats.
ISBN 978-1-77148-446-6 (softcover).--ISBN 978-1-77148-398-8 (PDF)

    I. Title.

PZ7.1.D35Pa 2017   j813'.6   C2016-905902-2
                                               C2016-905903-0

ChiZine Publications
Peterborough, Canada
www.chizinepub.com
info@chizinepub.com

Edited by Sandra Kasturi and Samantha Beiko
Proofread by Leigh Teetzel

Canada Council   Conseil des arts
for the Arts   du Canada

We acknowledge the support of the Canada Council for the Arts which last year invested $20.1 million in writing and publishing throughout Canada.

ONTARIO ARTS COUNCIL
CONSEIL DES ARTS DE L'ONTARIO

an Ontario government agency
un organisme du gouvernement de l'Ontario

Published with the generous assistance of the Ontario Arts Council.

Printed in Canada

PARASITE LIFE

VICTORIA DALPE

Contents

PART I: Ars Moriendi   13

PART II : Imago   161

PART III: Memento Mori   315

PART IV: Epilogue   333

A scorpion approached a frog sitting at the edge of a river.

"Would you carry me across?" it asked the frog.

The frog was hesitant, naturally fearful of the scorpion.

"You will be safe, I assure you, for hurting you would only drown us both."

So, the frog allowed the scorpion to climb on its back.

When they were midway across the river, the frog felt a terrible pain; the scorpion had stung the frog.

With its last breath as the frog began to sink, it asked the scorpion, "Why?"

The scorpion replied, "Alas, it is my nature."

And the two sank beneath the waves.

—animal fable originating in the 1950s

Loneliness will sit over our roofs with brooding wings.

—Bram Stoker, *Dracula*

PART I: Ars Moriendi

Pain wanders through my bones like a lost fire;
What burns me now? Desire, desire, desire.

—Theodore Roethke, "The Marrow," ll. 11–12

I.

Fast breathing, twin mouths, horses galloping, their hooves tearing up the ground. Thump, thump, thump, thump, as regular as a heartbeat. Faster and faster, louder and louder. Rippled muscles gleamed on shining oiled backs, mouths frothy, eyes wild and spinning. Thump, thump, thump, thump, the footfalls echoed my heart, possibly were my heart . . .

I sat up in the early dawn, confused. Pulling back the canopy bed drapes I squinted at the clock, it was nearly 4:00 a.m. Out the window, the sky was still a starless night-black. I wondered what woke me. My mouth tasted sour; my eyes were bleary.

I stood up, swaying, and caught my reflection in the vanity. I looked terrible: my skin drawn, my eyes wet and feverish, bloodless lips pulled back to reveal blunt teeth. I tried to swallow but my throat was dry as parchment. I headed to the bathroom for some water. My hands shook so badly that I barely got the glass to my mouth.

For a fleeting moment, the water was a welcome relief. Then it hit my stomach and immediately came back up.

I found myself staring at the swirling bile in the basin of the toilet. Once it was gone, my bearings returned to me and

I returned to bed. I crawled back in and pulled up my coverlet. My skin felt like it was crawling with insects, my head like it was trying to split open from the inside.

I rolled into a fetal position and focused on my breathing, my heartbeat, before nodding back off.

The horse was there, waiting for me, still and serene in a wide open field, the sky a pure cloudless cerulean. As I drew near, it backed away, over and over. I never got closer; it was always out of reach. It was always moving farther toward the horizon. The sky darkened, and as it did the horse blended into the shadows, its gleaming hide winking in and out. The dream shifted in the way of dreams, and I was waist deep in warm dark water, and the horse was gone. Instead the water was filled with large wriggling fish, red as rubies, hard bodies bumping against my bare legs.

The next time I woke it was to a shrill keening. It had to be an animal injured and wailing out in the yard.

Then my eyes adjusted and I realized, no, I was not in my bed, but my mother's. I sat up quickly, disoriented. My mother was awake, her eyes wide as she stared at me. And she was wailing. In terror? In pain? I couldn't tell.

I must have sleepwalked. Did I do that?

"Mom! What happened?"

She just went on with that strange and horrible sound.

Then I noticed the smell. The air was rank with human waste. As I pulled up her nightgown to check, I was surprised to see a rosette of red sticking the cotton fabric to the skin of her inner thigh.

"What the hell, Mom? Did you do this?"

I sucked in a breath at the sight of the fresh wound. It was a deep half circle. Red and fresh. I felt woozy looking at it. Its tinny scent coated my mouth and throat and filled my lungs. I could feel bile rising, hot and acidic.

I left the room, grabbing the first aid kit from the medicine cabinet in the en suite bathroom. As I cleaned and dressed my mom's wound, I forced my mind to go blank. To go to black. To take me away from my present moment.

Once she'd calmed, I changed my mother's diaper and nightgown and settled her back into bed. Her breathing had slowed and the panicked gleam in her eyes had faded.

Later, I stood trembling with exhaustion, staring at the pink water in the sink, her bloody nightgown floating around in bleach. My reflection in the mirror stared back at me as I scrubbed at the stain. Why was I in her room? What did she do to herself? I must have heard her crying out and come to her without realizing it. It was messed up to do things you didn't remember doing.

I woke a few scant hours later and trudged blindly through my day, the bad dreams and interruptions to sleep covering the day in a fog. Though if I was being honest, it felt like I'd been walking through that particular fog for two years. All my days blurred and overlapped, as did the weeks and months. Every November felt the same, and the November of my senior year was no different.

The air had a bite to it as I stepped out of Ronald James High School. I pulled my jacket closer. Three dirty school buses idled in the cul-de-sac in front, the portly part-time drivers talking quietly while waiting for the bell. They periodically stamped their feet or blew into their hands. I was the first out. I had a tendency to move quick.

Behind me I could hear the rest of the student body flooding out into the crisp air. Most of them would file onto one of those buses. Gossip and chatter their way home. My house wasn't far, barely a mile, so I walked it. And after a long day of being crowded in school and herded by teachers it was nice to be alone.

My house sat so far back off the road you'd probably never notice it if you weren't looking for it. It was the last house before the road narrowed from crumbling asphalt to dirt and the woods crowded in on the sides. There was a tall stone wall with an ornate rusty gate that I had to shake and lift to get open. The aged tar driveway had surrendered to the earth below and was breaking apart into chunks, letting the dirt and roots through. I loved to stare at that broken asphalt, at the hidden things under it, pushing up to the surface.

The large front yard was overgrown, dried grass and flowering weeds reaching to my chest. In the summer, with the window open, it was near impossible to sleep: all the creatures that lived down there, hidden away in the grass, would sing and scream, all night long. It was like a secret city in my very own front yard, hustling with its own life. Bursting with activity, oblivious to a larger human world above them. Microcosms upon microcosms. Living and dying, never understanding the finite nature of it all, their fragility. Hunters and hunted.

But in the fall, it all went silent. The bugs either died off or nestled deep into the earth to wait for spring.

I'd never seen the house in its glory, but looking up at the three-story Victorian with the sharp turret and wraparound porch, it wasn't hard to envision: pink, with crisp white trim. It had the bearing of a gaudy old woman, all dolled up, but time had crinkled her face and yellowed her clothes. The porch had caved in on one side long ago and heavy vines consumed it. The peeling paint fluttered in the wind and all the windows were dark. If someone drove by, they'd assume the house was abandoned.

Growing up, my mother had been neurotic about locking the doors, the windows, everything. But I didn't see the point. Who'd want to come here?

Inside, I could hear the radio and smell the wood in the fire. I shuddered a bit; that meant my mom was awake.

My cat, Tommy, sauntered out of a dusty shadow and dragged himself along my shins. He was ancient and looked and smelled it. A fat old tomcat with orange stripes and loose skin. I scratched his head and ventured toward the sound of the music.

The kitchen was at the back of the house, and the only room with any light on. The old radio was perched on the windowsill. Billie Holiday crooned at a low volume. A can of soup was open on the counter. My mother sat at the table with her head down, her hands pooled uselessly in her lap. Around her the table overflowed with unopened mail, mostly past-due notices, and miscellaneous crap. Mom was asleep, snoring softly.

They were twins, my mom and this house. Both of them had an air of the lost, of the haunted, giving clues to the grand creatures they had once been, before time had worn them down.

I reached out and touched her arm. She started awake and blinked up at me. Her milky eyes took a moment to focus. She smacked her gums together wetly.

"Did you get enough to eat?" I asked.

She was slow to respond, but finally gave a single shaky nod. It was more than I got on most days. I had to make sure she was eating. If I didn't stay on top of it, she wouldn't eat at all. Every morning before school I set out a breakfast and a lunch for her. If she wasn't in bed by the time I got home from school, I'd make her dinner too.

Today I had left soup and a sandwich. She seemed to be wearing the majority of the soup on the front of her nightgown.

"I'm going to run a bath for you, okay?"

She shrugged indifferently.

Upstairs, I stopped up the tub in her bathroom and filled it with warm, rose-scented water. She'd always loved the smell of roses.

I brought my mom up the stairs very slowly. Everything I did with her was at a creaking pace. Mercifully, her bedroom was the closest, being at the top of the stairs, facing the back of the house. By the time we got up into the bathroom, the tub was full and at the perfect temperature. This was all so routine.

She stood staring at nothing as I slid her nightgown off and helped her into the water. Soiled laundry under my arm, I turned on the radio that was balanced on a shelf above the pedestal sink. Soft, benign jazz filled the room. I kept radios in all the rooms she went into. Music soothed her. Even made her smile on occasion.

She was so small in the big mound of bubbles. Her body so skeletal, it was painful to look at. Her dark, circled eyes were vacant as she sat there, staring at the tile wall, completely oblivious to the world around her.

I left the room to finish the rest of my chores. I threw a load of laundry into our rusted old machine in the dank basement, banging the side of it three times to get the water flowing. Back upstairs, I washed the dishes in lukewarm water. I dried and placed them back in the cupboard. Plates first. Then cups. Then silverware. Same order every day.

Once that was done, I headed into the parlor at the front of the house to tend the fire. It was still warm from that morning, the kindling the wood stove fed off all day no more than glowing ash. I stuffed a few logs in. The fire came back to life. Comforting, that.

Then the final piece of the routine: I sat back in the worn leather chair and closed my eyes. Just for a minute . . .

It was always at that moment, dancing between sleep and wakefulness, that I felt the pronounced hunger for something to change. The hope that if I opened my eyes, I would be somewhere else entirely, someone else even. The routine of my days felt like a prison. The entirety of high school had been much the same day in and day out. I'd outgrown the shape of my confinement, which seemed like it was for a smaller, more naïve version of myself.

That minute of rest turned into twenty. I must have dozed off. Not good. I jumped out of the chair and then almost fell immediately back down again. My head was swimming. I pinched the bridge of my nose. Squeezed my eyes shut. Willed the wooziness away.

I was probably coming down with something, again. Lately it took all my strength to do just the basics: keep us fed, keep us warm. As the feeling of light-headedness receded, I ran up the stairs as fast as I could.

Mom was exactly the way I'd left her. She'd made no attempt to get herself out of the tub. Instead she'd opted to sit in the tepid water, shiver, and stare off at the tiles.

I eased her frail, shaking body out of the tub. She was all knobby knees and loose skin shaking in the cold air. As I toweled her off, it was impossible not to look at her disfigured body. It was mottled with scars: puckered white and pink indentations, oblong welts, half-moons, some smooth, some rough-edged to the touch.

Even when my mother was well and I was really young, I remembered those strange marks all over her arms and legs. I'd always assumed they were lesions or rashes, but I wondered now if the marks could have been self-harm. I lifted her forearm, looking at an old scar that was an oval, the skin raised and pale. I reached out and stroked her arm, her skin thin and silky as a baby's. She allowed me to do this, unaffected, her eyes cloudy and distant. Looking at her, what I thought was: How can this woman be only forty years old?

I slid a clean nightgown over her head and an adult diaper up her legs. She'd become incontinent over the past few months. Yet another dimension to her care that I was loath to take on, but what other choice was there? I shuffled her to into bed, pulling the blankets up to her chest.

I suddenly had to lean against a bedpost. The headache that had been threatening all day had gotten meaner. A spike of pain stole my breath, left me immobilized for a moment. The whole world throbbed with pain and sharp light.

When I looked up again, I was surprised to see my mom staring directly at me. She was frowning, and if she were anyone else I'd have said she was concerned for me. I smiled weakly at her, and her eyes darted away. Her lucid gaze faded as if it had never been there.

I dragged myself to the opposite end of the hall to my bedroom, fingertips pressed to the wall for balance. I opened my bedroom door and sighed in relief. Here was my sanctuary, the one space in this big old house not taken over by dust and strangers' memories. My room guarded me from all that.

The tall windows faced the long, overgrown front yard with its metropolis of insects and critters. I had a spacious walk-in closet connected to a private bath, all kept meticulously ordered and touched only by me.

The four-poster canopy bed had been my grandparents' bed. This had in fact been their bedroom. The walls were pale violet damask wallpaper, iridescent in the light, the heavy drapes a faded retro brocade. There was a small white vanity and a large velvet chaise worn to the springs. It was fussy and old-ladyish, but I loved it.

I stumbled to the bed, as if I'd walked miles to get there. I pulled the canopy drapes shut and I eased myself into the soothing darkness. No energy for schoolwork, and frankly, no desire either.

I just needed to rest. My last thought before falling asleep was: This is my life.

Seventeen years old, teetering on the cusp of adulthood, and I was already dead and buried.

───◦◦◦◦───

That was all I remembered, until I woke up in my mother's room to her keening and strange wound. I staggered back to my bedroom—I had to get some sleep before school, but two scant hours later, my alarm forced me up. The prospect of going back there for one more day before the weekend was excruciating. But even worse was the idea of being stuck at home all day with my mom. I dragged myself up. I showered. I dressed. I wound my long thick hair up into a bun. Routine. Routine. Routine.

I headed to my mother's room and found her awake and gazing out the window. I pulled her up, harder than I knew I should, and changed her. I led her down the stairs and plopped her in her chair in the den near the fire.

"You want to talk about last night?" I asked as I coaxed toast and some very watered-down coffee into her. She remained distant, eyes glazed over. I gave up and prepped her soup and sandwich for the day.

I knew I'd been rough with her, and had been loud when getting ready. But the stunt early this morning with the wound and the mess had put me in a sour mood. I grabbed my things and left. I stomped down the drive without looking back, kicking the chunks of tar that got in my way.

My walk to school was hunched, my teeth clenched until my jaw ached. It wasn't as if something was different about this morning, compared to the hundreds before it. My mom hadn't spoken in years, and she was often wounding herself. But this morning I was haunted by the night before, by my dreams, the sleepwalking, and the need for something to change. It was painful to admit, even alone with only a flat gray November sky to listen. I hated my life. I prayed for something, anything, to change.

Just like someone who'd made a deal with the devil at the crossroads, later I'd really wish I'd been more specific.

II.

Ronald James High School was a large gray building, dark and institutional, a gold glow from the windows the only brightness it offered. I resisted the urge to turn around and go home, and pushed through the double doors. The silence outside was replaced by the cacophony of teachers and students, the heady scent of people and life, of body odor, burnt coffee, and a hundred perfumes. The fluorescent lights buzzed and sneakers squeaked along the mirror-buffed floors. My senses were strained by the onslaught.

I came in just as the homeroom bell went off, slipping into my classroom without a minute to spare. Neither Mr. Henderson, the ruddy-faced science teacher, nor my homeroom advisor bothered to look up when I passed. Henderson had stopped talking directly to me some time ago. I sat down hard in my chair. I fumbled through my textbooks and worked to get as much of my homework completed as possible before classes began.

It took a second for me to notice the silence in the room. I looked up to find my teacher and the majority of my classmates staring straight at me. I blinked and they looked away. I went back to my homework. The first period bell chimed and everyone got to their feet.

I'd just stepped through the doors when a wave of dizziness hit me. I leaned hard against the doorframe, halting the exiting students behind me. A few grunted.

"Miss DeVry, are you all right?" Mr. Henderson asked, his voice gravelly.

I nodded, eyes watering at the astringent alcohol smell on his breath. I stepped into the hall, keeping close to the wall. Mumbles and snickers followed me. I arrived at my first class, head filled with cotton. My eyes were so heavy that I dozed through the lesson, nestled in the back of the classroom. The class was relatively full, but the neighboring seats were all vacant. But I liked my space. If I had a mother who spoke, or any family at all, they'd probably be worried by my complete lack of friends. I didn't have the energy for them, anyway. Sometimes I felt like a ninety-year-old British lady instead of a teenager.

Back when she still speaking, I would talk to my mom all the time, ramble on and on, about anything and everything. Vainly thinking she would care what I was doing and how my life was going. But she didn't, even back then. She told me as much.

"I do not care to hear about your life," she actually said, once. Nothing like having your crazy invalid mother give you those two cents as you washed her and fed her and took care of everything else she needed.

When she stopped speaking, I kept on with the talking for a while. I figured maybe it would help. Give her something to hold on to. Some voice outside her own head.

Then one day I stopped that too. Since then, it had been short exchanges and the radio to fill the silence.

Strangely I could remember the last real conversation we'd had. It was at the kitchen table, over a meal. The summer balmy and humid, fabrics felt damp, the wood everywhere sticky and the wallpaper curling. Crickets and peepers filled the night, and large moths and June bugs batted against the door screen. And us at the table, soup and salad. I'd been proud of the salad, vegetables julienned, a homemade dressing, all from a cookbook I'd found. My mother had been unimpressed though.

"Maybe I could be a chef, someday. I think cooking is kind of fun."

She'd just glared at me, pushed the plate away. "It's no good. Nothing you touch is any good. You spoil things." And then she never spoke again.

In some ways it made it easier, my mother being silent. At least the endless vitriol had stopped. Truth be told, I hadn't much liked her when she was an actual person. Mercifully, I could barely recall the sound of her voice, it had been so long.

While I was growing up, she'd spent most of her time locked up in her attic studio. I learned if I wanted to eat regularly, I'd need to shop and prepare things myself. She couldn't be bothered, too busy working on whatever new series of paintings had her entire focus.

When I was in elementary school I asked her about art, begged her to teach me and include me, even though I'd never been artistic, barely able to connect two dots, let alone understand shading and dimensions. But I wanted to have something to share with her, so I tried and tried, filling sketchbooks with my attempts. She'd been up and mobile still, though even back then she'd need long naps and got frequent flus.

When I showed her all my hard work, she'd flipped through it. "You don't have an artist's eye. The drawings are fine, they're a child's drawings after all, but they have no soul, no heart." She weighed me down with a stack of art books to study and sent me to my room and back up to the attic she went.

Invitations from friends weren't exactly forthcoming, but I didn't care. I learned to focus on my schoolwork, and filled what little time I had with books and television. One more year and I'd be done with school anyway. I kept below the radar mostly, except for a brief moment my sophomore year when I'd briefly attracted the attention of an exchange student, Javier. He'd been kind to me, and maybe even interested, and the jocks had teased him mercilessly—so mercilessly that he'd ignored me the rest of the semester. It hurt, losing Javier after just a taste of friendship, but it also taught me to toughen up. The "normals" couldn't see where I was coming from; they couldn't understand. I'd always be a freak at school—if any of them spent half the time I did cleaning up after my mother's accidents or binding her bedsores every day, they'd feel the same. It was better to keep my head down, better to not care at all.

When I was younger, I thought maybe I smelled, or was ugly. Teachers only called on me for the sake of fairness, no one picked me for groups or sports. My report cards were filled with notes about being withdrawn.

My mother, when she still functioned, always had an answer for them: I was just shy.

Annoyed at my own thoughts, I tried to focus on class and put the melodrama in my head away. I took a deep breath, louder than I meant to, and a few heads turned. The teacher, Mrs. Cox pursed her lips disapprovingly. I ignored everyone and stared at the board. She resumed her lecture.

"You're all familiar with Lyme disease, I'm sure, growing up in these woods. Because of their diet, ticks are a carrier for at least twelve different diseases. Ticks satisfy all of their nutritional requirements as ectoparasites, which are parasites that live on the exterior of their hosts. They are obligate hematophages, which means they feed only on blood to survive and move from one stage of life to another. While they can fast for long periods, they'll eventually die if unable to find a host."

I was nearly asleep again when the door opened and a girl walked in. She handed the teacher a folded slip of paper, an obvious newcomer. The girl was medium height, a little heavyset around the middle, and stood nervously, gnawing at her lower lip. Her dyed blue-black hair was pulled back in two pigtails, her eyes painted up like a pharaoh. She wore a black lace top and an old oversized army jacket, the cuffs rolled to reveal a ring on each finger and chipped black nails. She fidgeted, shifting from foot to foot in scuffed black boots, under the eyes of a curious and judgmental class. The teacher appraised her with a sour face and gestured at the room.

"Find an open seat. You'll have to share a book for today, and I'll get you a textbook of your own after class. Everyone, this is our new student, Sabrina Karnstein. Please make her feel welcome."

The class erupted into whispers, and I slumped down farther at my desk, wanting to go back to my nap. A rustle of fabric and the scent of cigarettes and vanilla perfume made me look up. The new girl loomed nearby, eyes expectant.

"Mind if I sit here?"

I glanced around, a bit surprised, before realizing there were no other open desks in the room. I nodded, unsure if I should say anything, and then sat up, sliding my book her way. She shimmied her desk closer and pulled the book half onto her desk, balanced precariously. The room was silent, all eyes our way. She didn't seem to notice.

"Thanks, by the way. This new school thing totally sucks. I'm Sabrina." She stage-whispered this, waiting for my response.

"Jane," I replied, my voice hoarse with disuse.

We read together, nearly forehead to forehead. Sabrina was, in a word, distracting. She chewed at her lip almost constantly, breaking occasionally to put a strand of hair in her mouth, moistening it like she was threading a needle. She also picked at her nail polish, leaving flakes of black on the desk. Her lower body had a dance of its own: toe tapping, crossing and uncrossing her legs with a random kick to my shins with her heavy boots. She was incapable of stillness, and I wondered if I made her anxious or if she had something wrong with her. She made me very aware of how little I moved around. I was a rock to her surf. Ten minutes before the end of class she turned to me, her eyes hazel with flecks of green and gold.

"Do you know where the gym is?"

I nodded about to respond, but she continued, "I have PE next class, which is really just insult to injury at this point."

"You can follow me." When the bell went off, I waited in the hall while Sabrina was issued her textbook. She bounded out of the room and we headed down the crowded hall together.

"No offense, but this school is so rural. I literally feel like I'm in the middle of nowhere. I mean, I threatened suicide about a hundred times to my parents, but we moved here anyway. In my senior year. My dad transferred here for work. And my mom writes trashy romance novels so she can do that wherever, but she's wanted to get out of the city practically forever. So it's me and my little brother, uprooted and forced into a new school in the boonies. I mean, this town totally sucks. No offense, but there's nothing to do here. What do you do for fun?"

I walked beside her, but it took all my energy not to cringe at the direct question, or recoil at the sheer mania coming off this girl. She'd talked more to me in the last ten minutes than anyone had in months. Sabrina waited for me to answer, her large eyes on me.

"There is absolutely nothing to do here. I watch TV, read, and sleep."

"Wow. Fun."

Together we shared a disgusted sigh as we passed through the double doors into the gym. I bit the inside of my cheek to keep from smiling, enjoying the company. The gym had a big red and white court, the mascot—an anthropomorphized cardinal with a muscular chest—painted nearly two stories tall on the back wall. Sabrina surveyed it, then looked back at me with a snort. I giggled, surprising myself.

We snaked along the wall, toward the locker room. Inside there was plenty of commotion as girls talked, laughed, and tried to dress as fast as possible. I headed to my locker, Sabrina at my heels. She looked around the dim change room, grimacing.

"It stinks in here."

"You don't have to hang out in the locker room. You don't even have gym clothes." I replied.

"Better in here talking to you then being ogled as a new student out there."

I slid on my gym shorts and fished out a T-shirt. I was standing on one foot putting on a sneaker when another wave of intense vertigo hit me and I leaned back into the lockers, almost falling. Sabrina yelped in surprise and reached out to steady me. Her hand felt hot on my arm, almost scalding. I frowned, seeing twin Sabrinas, one overlapping the other. I didn't remove her hand until they'd merged back into one.

"Are you okay? You looked like you were gonna keel over!"

"I'm fine. Just got dizzy all of a sudden."

I rested my head against the cool metal of the locker door, catching my breath, centering myself.

"Thanks for not letting me fall."

Sabrina nodded, watching me closely as we went back to the gym to sit with the rest of the class. She didn't have to participate, and instead sat on a bleacher, headphones in, fiddling with her phone. For all of my inactivity, I did like to run, and normally enjoyed the feeling of my body in motion. Today I was too weak and afraid I'd pass out. I dropped my pace back to a trot. I was still ahead of most of the class, who barely even jogged, making a show of how unhappy they were to do even that.

I could feel Sabrina's eyes on me, and when I looked back at her she would stick out her tongue or wave. It was strange how quickly she'd decided we were friends. Did I even want any friends? Friends were work after all, they needed things, they wanted things. But I had to admit that having someone to talk to, someone who was not my mother . . . it could be nice.

By the end of gym class, I decided to be open-minded about Sabrina. I went to the locker room, rinsed off, and dressed.

She was waiting for me by the gym doors. I knew she'd be there and it was a strange, comforting feeling. She slumped against the wall, snapping a piece of green gum. It was lunch period, and as we walked along the hall to the cafeteria, all eyes turned to us. Big news to be a new kid in a small school. Bigger news to be the new girl hanging out with the school freak. The cafeteria was loud and raucous, but we found an unoccupied end table and sat down. I had no appetite, so I just watched as Sabrina pulled out a rumpled brown bag and started peeling a cheese stick like a banana.

"So what's the story with you? Sitting alone in the lunchroom, slinking along the halls. No close friends, no boyfriends?" She said this as she scanned the room, her mouth full of cheese.

I shrugged, indifferent.

She scrutinized me, nose scrunching up, the wheels turning behind her raccoon eyes. "Mmm, I don't buy it. I don't buy the whole super-loner thing. You were nice enough to me from the get-go, so it's not like you're a bitch. You dress weird, but it's more quirky than lame. And you're like model tall. I don't get it."

"I guess you're a special case."

"I'm special?" She pressed a hand to her chest, teasing me.

"Okay, not special . . . persistent. I mean, most people don't go out of their way to talk to me. And frankly, I just don't have time to care." It like felt Sabrina had me under a microscope.

"Why don't you have time to care?" she asked in between bites of sandwich.

"I didn't realize you were my new . . . therapist."

We sat quietly while a group of football players entered the room hooting and hollering, their girlfriends in tow. When they caught sight of us they barked like dogs and laughed.

"Dickheads." Sabrina crumpled up the cheese wrapper, folding her arms. "All I'm saying is that it sucks being new and you seem pretty cool. Anyway, thanks. I mean, if you don't care so much, I can leave you alone."

Despite the blasé way she said it, there was fear in her words. I might not care much about being alone, about being friendless, but she did. I had a feeling it terrified her. Her clothes, her personality, everything about her screamed "look at me, pay attention to me." I knew she wanted to see a kindred spirit in me, another spooky loner.

I wasn't trying to be anyone. But Sabrina was different. Maybe she was so blinded by her own need to be part of a twosome, or a unit, that she was willfully ignorant of whatever strange membrane separated me from most people. Or maybe she was immune to it. Or—crazy thought—maybe there really wasn't anything wrong with me besides being shy. It was strange how spending a few hours with this girl was already forcing me to question my identity.

Sabrina waited for a reply. A huge part of me, the coward, just wanted to dismiss her so I could go back to staring at the wall for the next twenty minutes. You asked for change just this morning, I reminded myself. And I felt a connection. I really did like this girl.

"You aren't pestering me, and you're welcome to sit with me. But if you're looking for a good gateway person to help with settling into this school, I'm not your girl. You'll be branded an outcast from now on."

She surveyed the room and curled her lip in disgust.

"Fuck those guys. I can find jocks and mean girls anywhere; cool people are a much rarer breed."

III.

The rest of the day was a blur. Sabrina wasn't in any of my afternoon classes, which was kind of a relief, because I needed the peace. Her presence was confusing. Honestly, I think it scared me. I was so used to being perpetually alone.

The sky was steel gray as I stepped out of the school, and a frigid mist of rain blanketed the parking lot. I started walking home, hands in my coat pockets, wishing I'd remembered to bring an umbrella and gloves. The ground was mucky, and by the time I got to my sagging front porch, my shoes were squelching with the wet and I was shivering. The fire had gone out, obviously hours earlier, and the house was cold and stale. Sighing, I picked through the woodpile and dragged an armful of kindling inside and relit the fire, turning on a few lights as I went, Tommy winding around my ankles.

Although it was midafternoon, the house was very dark. I found my mother sitting at the kitchen table, wearing her soup down the front of her nightgown again, dozing. It was practically a repeat performance of the day before, and the one before that. At least today I wasn't as bone-weary as yesterday, so I tidied her up with a bit more energy. I even felt like talking, a side effect of Sabrina, I'm sure.

"I made a friend today," I told her as I pulled off her nightgown and wiped her mouth and chest with a washcloth. I wanted to sound casual, but it came out rushed and excited.

She remained still as a statue; the only movement was the rapid spread of goose pimples along her heavily scarred, emaciated frame.

"She's a bit annoying, but seems nice enough. Chatty, kind of crazy, and for some reason she wants to be my friend. It was nice having someone to talk to."

I pulled a clean flannel nightgown over my mom's head. Handing her a glass of water, I worked a soft brush through her hair. I watched her hand slowly, unsteadily, lift and she sipped some water. It was so rare for her to move in front of me that it was notable. I stared at the way her fingers clutched the glass like a claw. The sleeve of the oversized nightgown bunched up at her elbow revealing the scars, standing out brightly against her blue-veined forearm.

"Why do you do this to yourself?" I whispered to her, reaching out to touch one of the old scars.

The glass exploded. Her body, ramrod straight, hand still reaching out, fingers curled in. Glass jutted out of her palm, blood and water dripping pinkly down onto her lap, onto the floor, onto the chair. I gasped, surprised that she was physically strong enough to crush the glass in her hand. She turned and looked at me, her eyes wild, feral even. Her hand trembled terribly. I could hear the blood dripping onto the linoleum.

I bent to gather the larger pieces of glass in my shirt, but as I got to my feet, I couldn't stop staring at her palm, the crystalline glass, glistening, embedded in the meat of her hand. The blood had welled up and was slowly overflowing, running down her wrist to drip off with a pat, pat, pat. I felt my body moving closer. My heart fluttered, my mouth dried. I was leaning in, reaching my hand out for hers when a wail sliced through the room. I stared at her, startled out of my fascination. She pulled the maimed hand to her breast, staining the flannel with splotches of vibrant red.

I made my way up on wobbly legs for the first aid kit. Again. In the bathroom I splashed some water onto my face, hoping the chill would wake me up. It took a moment to recognize my reflection—my cheeks were so gaunt, my eyes dark, wild looking. My lips were chalky, nearly colorless; I scowled and poked at my whitish gums, vaguely remembering a health class anecdote about anemia. Maybe I needed vitamins, maybe the well water was poisoned, maybe mother was infectious, maybe it was genetic. Sighing, I dragged myself back upstairs to her room to fetch yet another change of clothes.

I found myself staring at a picture of her hanging on the wall of the second-floor hallway: Mother's coppery hair thick and lustrous, eyes bright, her smile infectious. She had on a leopard-print dress, with red platform shoes, and sparkly eyeshadow.

"I was a club kid," she'd explained when a younger me asked about her wild outfit. I wish I'd known that woman. With her crazy looks, interesting friends, and overflowing creativity, I wanted her for a mother.

Among the many topics we'd never talked about back when she was talking was my father. She never mentioned him once.

As far as I knew, I was a test tube baby or an immaculate conception.

Mooning over her and the mystery of her past wasn't improving my own health or my mood. My head throbbed, another migraine rearing up and clawing at my eyes. I'd had headaches as long as I could remember. Real head-splitters. And they were getting worse. So bad recently that my fingers would go numb and my stomach would knot up.

I was losing weight too. Long and lanky to begin with, I needed all the meat I could get. My ribs and hipbones were poking out. A voice in my head had started whispering cancer. As my complexion grew waxier and I got weaker, I had to admit this wasn't just some flu.

What if cancer ran through my father's family as well? For sure, early death was in mom's genes. Both of her parents had died in their late fifties. I'd be absolutely blown away if my mother made it to that age.

God, if she made it to fifty, I'd be twenty-seven. I wondered what was more horrible: wishing that she would die sooner or wishing that she'd live on for years in a state of perpetual decay?

If I put her in a home, I'd lose the house. I'd end up in foster care for at least a year and I'd have no money. My mom's paltry disability check and the remainder of some dwindling trust were the only things that kept us in bread and hot dogs as it was. No white knight was coming to save us. This was no clichéd fairy tale. Or if it was, it was a pretty damned bleak one.

For a random second, I pictured the smiling happy faces of my classmates on the school buses. Trundling away to their clean homes and normal parents who might not really care but could at least pretend. They'd never know the fear that lived inside of me, of coming home to my mother dead. Or my house burning. Or being taken away from her, forced to live with strangers.

～◦⊱◦～

Mother still sat, rigid, with her bleeding hand clutched like a baby bird to her chest. Her eyes were lucid though, and tracked me into the room. Frustrated, I dropped to my knees and reached for her hand. She didn't want to give it, so finally I yanked it free. She keened, and I glared at her. The urge to yell "shut up" was heavy on my lips. My withering stare was enough to finally quiet her.

Swallowing my anger, I slowly picked the glass out of her hand. My mother stayed very still through the process. Once done, I swabbed the area with alcohol, watching her face for any reaction. There was only a quivering in her mouth, but she didn't pull her hand away. I spread iodine over the cuts and wrapped gauze, then a bandage around her hand. I yanked off the now soiled nightgown, revealing her scrawny shivering frame for the second time, and quickly tugged on another.

"The whole load of laundry is going to be bloody nightgowns if you keep this up," I muttered.

Now that she was dressed and tidied, I quickly, if a bit roughly, finished brushing her hair, then plaited it down her back. I settled her in her parlor chair, placed a clean blanket on her lap, and turned the television on. The sound and brightness was jarring in the dark room. It was sad that there was more life in the syndicated game show than in this entire house.

I returned to the kitchen to finish cleaning up and to calm down. My mom's nearness made me tense, my spine in traction, pulling me tighter, straighter, creaking. I swept up the remaining bits of glass in a towel, and shook them over the trash. A few pieces were tangled in the weave of the cloth and I pulled them out, staring at my mother's blood covering my fingertips.

Without thinking, I put my fingers to my mouth.

The metallic, briny taste was strange on my palate. Almost smoky. I ran my tongue over the ridges at the top of my mouth, and over my teeth to catch the last of it before it was swallowed. All my senses receded to the background, only my mouth existed.

I snapped out of it and looked around. Horrified, I dropped the soiled towel into the sink as if it were covered in bugs and stepped back, rubbing my hands along my thighs. I looked back at the parlor, to where my mother sat, and couldn't bring myself to go near her.

I fled to my bedroom and tried to focus on my homework. The words were hard to read. They swam across the page like microorganisms under a lens. I pinched the bridge of my nose and tossed the book aside.

The room felt small and tight suddenly, so I walked into the hall. The house itself had shrunk in my duress; I needed to get outside, get fresh air. Get out. Unsure of where I was going, I ended up throwing on my coat and walking out the front door. By the end of the driveway I'd committed to going to the general store, I glanced back to see Tommy's feline outline in the window, the only sign of life in the big old house.

IV.

Hob's Valley felt like a forgotten town. Barely more than a smudge on a map. A few roads that led nowhere and then vanished back up into the hills. I'd lived here for my entire life and hated it for just about as long.

It seemed like it was always dark. The old trees were tall, the forests dense, and it was hard for sunlight to make its way in. The town was cold, raw, and achingly quiet—barely a thousand people lived here. Main Street boasted a school, a town hall, and a general store. An entire life could be lived here in three or four tired old buildings. The town hall was also the police station, the town clerk, the mayor's office, the library, and the fire station. The general store was also the liquor store, the pharmacy, the gas station, and carried dusty DVDs that no one rented.

I always pictured the town nestled like an egg in the center of a mountain range, the horizon a craggy black outline of mountains and tall sentry pines in all directions, isolating us from anything else. It didn't seem like there were any roads leading out, just paths deeper into the woods. It seemed almost impossible that someone like Sabrina had found her way in here.

The seasons were the only thing that ever changed. I loved those scant few weeks of fall, of explosive color and crisp weather, a time when the Colonial homes seemed not oppressive but quaint, decorated with corn husks and pumpkins.

Fall was like life, though; it ended quickly. The leaves flipped to golds and reds and then they were gone. Off the trees, brown and dead, waiting for snow to blanket the valley for months.

⚜

Mercifully, my mother received that small disability check each month, which she started collecting four or five years ago when she'd still had the wherewithal to worry about such mundane things as food and money.

My grandparents died before I was born, and she was their only child. They'd been quite old when they had her and hadn't been particularly healthy. She'd moved away to attend art school and had lived in the city for years before coming back here. As she'd told me bitterly on numerous occasions, she'd had a good and vibrant life in the city. She'd been a painter. Up and coming.

"I could have been one of the greats," she said frequently. She liked to remind me she'd been Someone in the city, an artist on the rise, and she'd sacrificed that great life to raise me in the sticks.

Now my mother's dusty canvases filled every available space in the house not already occupied by my grandmother's accumulated hoard: a hodgepodge collection of precariously stacked old furniture, towers of moldering books, and discolored boxes of old clothes. The only space free of the clutter was the attic, which had been converted into my mother's painting studio. It was the only part of the house I was expressly forbidden from entering, and its door was always locked.

Years back, I'd found a flyer that advertised a gallery show of hers tucked away and forgotten inside a book, the show's dates from a year before my birth. I'd kept the flyer in my nightstand, and looked at it often. I'd wanted to ask her about it, but then lost the nerve.

When my grandfather died, he'd left my mom a small amount of money. Though it wasn't a lot, it had held up through the years and kept her from working. Though I doubted she'd ever had a real job. When she stopped driving, she also sold the car. But all that money was long gone. The disability checks barely covered the basics: utilities and food. I really only left the house to go to two places: school and the store. Both I could walk to, though the walk would grow increasingly unpleasant as the fall ran into winter. I often wondered what it would be like to have a family that wasn't so poor, to be able to buy new clothes and fancy foods, guilt free.

It was dark, the few sporadic streetlights providing islands of orange light. I stumbled over the rocks on the side of the road, walking as fast as I could between one patch of light and the next. The general store was a little over two miles walk from my house, with the high school as a midway point. At this time of night there was little traffic and it felt like the town was holding its breath, waiting for the other shoe to drop. Unseen eyes peeped out from behind the curtained windows. The houses looked vacant except for the smoke wisps escaping the chimneys. There was a prevailing sense of fear and foreboding. Isolated people living sealed-up lives.

It was a strange sensation to be unwelcome in your own town. Like a force field separated me from everyone else. I imagined it was how ghosts felt.

Finally, I arrived, tired, cold, and uncomfortable, stepping into the bright halogen light of the general store parking lot. There was more activity here than in the rest of the town combined. Cars getting fuel, a few kids sitting on a picnic table out front, dressed in school sport uniforms under puffer coats. Locals returning from work in neighboring towns, grabbing last minute things for dinner and the requisite six-packs.

My attention went straight to the kids. They were classmates of mine. Their conversation ceased as I passed, the silence so abrupt I felt as if I'd gone deaf. In a moment of bravado, I spun back and faced them, challenging them. There were three total, two sitting on the bench, one standing beside. The standing guy was Brent, tall with shaved blond hair. He laughed, but wouldn't meet my eyes. I glared at him, at all of them. Cowards. Bullies. They had everything but that wasn't enough, they needed to make sure you knew. I marched up the worn wooden steps to the store.

With my back to them, they started talking again, either thinking I was out of earshot, or not caring.

"God, she's freaky. I swear I almost pissed myself!" said Brent.

"I know, right? I heard she's like a witch or something. Always thought it was bullshit, but up close . . ."

"Yeah, it's her eyes . . ."

Frowning, I pushed into the store. A part of me, the part that was being suffocated by this tiny town and its tiny people was tempted to walk back out to them and yell, "Why? Why are you scared of me? Why do you avoid me? I haven't done anything to anyone. And what the hell's wrong with my eyes?"

A blast of food-scented warmth scattered my thoughts, helping me remember why I was here. I took a basket from the stack at the door and started my rounds of the shelves. It was the exact same list, always the same: adult diapers, cat food, toilet paper. The cans of soup, the loaves of cheap white bread, tuna fish, pasta, rice. Milk. Processed cheese slices. The food of poor people, the food of vouchers, subsistence. Barely enough nutrition to sustain us, packed with enough sodium and preservatives to last in bunkers through an apocalypse.

I was nearly finished when I decided to stop at the butcher's counter. The butcher, a heavyset older man with bulldog jowls, turned to me. His jovial expression chilled, but his customer service skills trumped his dislike of me.

"Do you have liver today?" I asked.

"Sure, what kind are you looking for?"

"Beef."

"You gonna do a liver and onions or something?"

"Yes, I, uh . . . My mother likes it."

"It's good, an acquired taste, but good. And good for you, packed with nutrients."

"Yes."

He puttered around and produced a bloody dark brown mass wrapped in plastic. We barely had enough money for the basics but at least twice a month for as long as I could remember, my mother insisted on us having liver for dinner. I didn't care for it, but I still bought it when we could afford it. I smiled, thanked the man, and headed for the cash register.

The small DVD rental section was to the right of the butcher counter, and as I passed it I noticed a familiar dark shape slinking around. I was surprised to see it was Sabrina. When she looked up and saw me watching, she smiled wide and came toward me.

"Hey! What's up? Doing some shopping?" She looked down at the basket of food and toilet paper. The large hunk of meat balanced on top felt shameful there and I couldn't explain why.

"I needed to get out of my house."

"I hear that. Who even rents DVDs anymore, right?" She kept talking, something about a fight with her mother, and her brother being annoying. My attention drifted as I glanced at the butcher, noticed him eavesdropping. I mentally steered back to Sabrina. She wore an oversized hooded sweatshirt, striped scarf, and the same scruffy boots as before. The outfit would've looked masculine on anyone else, but her face and pigtails added a soft girlishness. Again I was struck by the theatricality of her makeup. She was certainly going to be memorable in a small town like this.

"Hellooo, Jane, are you listening to me? Am I boring you? Well I'm bored, that's for sure. I was going to rent a movie, but everything they have here I've seen a hundred times or is total shit. Besides, I can download newer stuff. I have my mom's car, want to hang out? I thought about calling you, but never got your cell or your email, and I couldn't find you online. God, I sound like a stalker. Anyways, we should definitely exchange numbers, either way." She stared at me expectantly.

"I have to get these groceries home to my mother, and . . . uh . . . get her to bed . . . She's unwell."

"Oh, yeah I get it." Sabrina visibly deflated. I felt a pang of guilt. She was as lonely as I was. She was reaching out. Why are you so scared of her?

"If you want to give me a ride home to put away my groceries, maybe then we could . . . hang out after." She brightened immediately, clapping her hands together.

"Awesome. I was going to go home and slit my wrists if you said no. Not really though, God, that sounded so pathetic and psycho. Just ignore me."

I felt little bursts of euphoria behind my eyes. I was, weirdly, having a good time. Sabrina's stream-of-consciousness mouth was very entertaining. Her energy was attractive. Even being near her made me feel more aware. Being seen, being talked to, was starting to make me feel more substantial.

I stepped up to the counter as Sabrina walked away to call her mother.

The sour-faced cashier rang up my items quickly, and then we were out. I was envious that Sabrina needed to call someone to check in. As we exited the store, the same boys were lingering on the bench. Their conversation petered out and stopped again as we passed. This time I didn't bother to look at them when they stared. Sabrina did though, spinning, incensed, and calling out to them.

"What the fuck are you staring at?"

"That's what we're trying to figure out."

One of them chuckled, braver than the others. The blond one, Brent.

I reached out and took Sabrina's arm. It was like an electric shock, the touch. She felt it too, and turned to me, startled, her penciled eyebrows up high.

"Just leave them be. There's no point," I said.

She nodded and we walked away, shoulder to shoulder. Suddenly she spun around and flipped off the boys with both hands. I laughed in spite of myself.

We arrived at a sensible maroon sedan. I had expected Sabrina to drive a big glossy old hearse, or a giant Bondo-colored Cadillac. Something big, rude, belching smoke. But this boxy, efficient vehicle just screamed "Mom's Car." Looking at it, I raised my eyebrows and Sabrina huffed and flipped me off too, and pressed the fob to unlock the doors. Instantly the general store behind my back stopped weighing on me, and the boys on the bench barely registered. It was amazing how just one person who actually saw you changed the world.

We slid through the night. "Wow, you live pretty close to me. I'm down the street at 55 Elm Grove," Sabrina said as she drove. The darkness was so different from inside the safety of a car.

Sabrina had the radio on loud, a band she seemed to know well, singing along off-key. The synthesizers and guitars were mashing away together while the vocalist shrieked. I liked the intensity and the newness of the sounds. An altogether different feel than what I usually found listening to the radio or my mother's old albums. When we pulled up to my ramshackle house, I got out to open the rusted gate.

"Jesus, this is like if the Addams Family house had a baby with Strawberry Shortcake or something. I love it."

I looked up at my house, trying to see it through Sabrina's eyes. The car bumped and dragged up the driveway to the front. We finally stopped with a lurch and I quickly went for the handle. The house took up the horizon, a dark shape skewering the bruised night sky. When I looked at it, all I saw were flaws: the drooping porch, the broken windows, the crooked, amethyst-tipped lightning rod jutting off the ostentatious turret. The qualities I found shameful didn't faze Sabrina at all.

"I'll be right back."

I grabbed my grocery bags from the backseat. Sabrina shut the engine off and was standing beside me when I turned, laden with my purchases.

"No way, I have to come inside. Your house is amazing."

"It's not really . . . guest friendly, and my mother's quite ill. We don't have people over."

"Pleeeease?" She clasped her hands and batted her heavy, mascara-coated eyelashes.

V.

"So like I said, it's just me and my mom, and she's very sick. We don't have any money, and I'm a terrible housekeeper. You're the first person I've ever brought here."

As I opened the door, a blast of musty, wood-smoke-filled air hit us. Sabrina followed on my heels into the foyer.

I tried to see it through her eyes: the grand curving staircase, the chandelier, the stained-glass windows. Or was she distracted by the mounds of magazines, books, and debris, the clothes and shoes piled on the stairs? The rugs covered in cat hair. At the back, the dingy kitchen, and to the left, the parlor. The small wood stove provided the only light.

My mother's figure outlined by the scant firelight in her usual chair was like something out of a horror story. Sabrina looked around, eyes wide. In the kitchen, I quickly put the food away.

"Should I go say hi to your mom?" she whispered.

A million nasty replies bubbled up in my mouth, but I pushed them down. "Don't worry about it. I'll let her know that I'm going out for a bit. She's not much of a talker. She probably won't even look at you."

I finished putting everything away, unsure if I should just drag Sabrina back out the way we came, or show her around. She was poking around the dimly lit kitchen, noting and recording every detail. I couldn't quite gauge how I felt about her being here, besides a mild anxiety.

"I just love creepy old houses. Please make this girl stuck in a new, ugly subdivision happy and jealous and show me around?" I was surprised by the word "jealous." The idea that anyone could be jealous of my life seemed absolutely insane.

"Well . . . this is the parlor. My mother spends her days here since it's the warmest room in the house." The walls were stacked high with bookshelves, and two worn club chairs faced the small wood stove, which was settled haphazardly inside the flue where the old original fireplace still stood.

Sabrina noted the artwork as we went up the stairs and into the hallway. I pointed to my mother's room: the large brass bed, the faded velvet drapes to keep out the chill and the light. The threadbare Oriental carpet. Her bedpan, her walker, her adult diapers. Sabrina could see all of this from the doorway and could probably smell the stink of sickness absorbed deep into the fabric.

On the hallway wall outside her bedroom door was a cluster of photographs, the largest one showing a smiling child with a shock of red hair and not a care in the world. Sabrina walked over to look closer at the photos. In particular, one from when my mother was a teen. She had just aged out of the gangly, awkward phase and was transitioning into the woman she would become. It was a birthday picture, fifteen according to the cake, and my mom smiled at the camera demurely, more aware than in her younger photos. Her proud, beaming parents stood on either side of her.

"She was so beautiful." Sabrina reached out a finger to touch my mother's face. I watched a film of dust come off on her fingertips. "You don't look much like her, or your grandparents."

"No." I stepped back into the shadows of the hall. I turned on the light. "Apparently, I look like my father."

Sabrina didn't follow me, instead she flipped through the canvases littering the hall, releasing an explosion of dust.

"Did she paint all of these? They're really cool."

I glanced back dismissively and nodded, then took her into my room. It was a strange feeling watching her cross the threshold into my sanctuary, a trill of fear at literally letting someone in. This was the only place that was solely mine. I realized I was holding my breath, and forced it out as Sabrina came farther into the room.

"I love the curtains around your canopy bed. Reminds me of A Christmas Carol, actually."

I nodded, feeling helpless and awkward.

"Any ghosts peep in the curtains at you while you sleep?"

I shook my head.

Sabrina walked the perimeter of the room. I had never entertained, per se, but even I knew that this behavior was odd. The way she was studying every detail, like she was casing the joint or something. When she'd completed the circuit, she came to the small desk with my schoolbooks, touched my few childhood toys, flipped through the library books I was reading, then turned to me.

"Your house is a strange place. Like you and it are something out of a fairy tale."

I flinched a little. But there was no malice that I could see. She meant it to be a compliment. I shrugged, which apparently was one of the few things I could do to communicate, and eased myself onto the bed. Sabrina mirrored my move and sat beside me.

"So what's wrong with your mom, exactly?"

I stopped myself from shrugging again, looking out the window into the night beyond.

"She's just sick. Only forty and she looks like an old woman in a nursing home."

"Forty? Wow. Who else takes care of her? Do you have a nurse come in or something?"

I shook my head, hands limp in my lap.

"It's only me. It's always been me."

"That's crazy. What do the doctors say?"

My pulse sped up; I could feel myself becoming defensive. "I don't know. She stopped going years ago. It's all so pathetic, huh?"

"No. It's just sad. What if something happened to her?"

"I just need to keep her well until I turn eighteen and graduate. It's not too far off. Then I'll have some options . . ."

I tilted my head up at the ceiling, tracing the veiny cracks in the plaster, the water stains blossoming in the corner from the leaking roof. The whole house felt fragile.

"Not that there's much to lose."

I said this quietly, almost as an afterthought. I felt unbelievably vulnerable. Sabrina was quiet. I could almost hear the cogs turning behind her heavily made-up eyes. After a pause she lay back on the bed, hands over her head.

"That is some heavy shit, Jane."

My heart sank. Was it too heavy a burden for a new friend? But Sabrina simply laughed and rolled over to face me and without a second thought, changed topics.

"So, Jane, do you like anything from this century? Like what kind of music do you listen to? I've been into this very synthy German Darkwave band lately. And I love this smutty fantasy series, Helix One—you ever read it?"

I'd heard of none of them, and she promised to share them with me. When I confessed I read mostly art books and pulp mysteries (because it was all I had in the house), she wrinkled her nose.

"You could go to the library. I know Hob's Valley is basically a street, but they do have one of those." She went on to tell me about her old life in Boston. "It's way better than here obviously—there are restaurants and you can take the train, and go do stuff. But my school was terrible, all stuck up bitches, and when they go after you, they really go after you." She got quiet, thoughtful. "Like a dog with a bone. Better to get the fuck away from all that, get my GPA up." She told me she wanted to go to Emerson, that she wanted to be a graphic designer. Then she moved onto food: she loved Chinese food (of which there was none in town) and she hated tomatoes. My head swam with the deluge of information. I let her talk, appreciating having someone to talk to.

Eventually Sabrina stood. "Can I have a glass of water?"

"Sure. I can get it for you."

PARASITE LIFE

"Nah, it's fine. I'll grab it myself." She went downstairs, taking her bag with her. A few minutes later she returned, giddy. Rooting around in her giant shoulder bag, which resembled a pillow case covered in skulls more than anything, she produced a small bottle of whisky.

"Where'd you get that?" I asked, but I knew.

While drinking was the favored pastime of most kids in my school, I'd never tried it. Most of my knowledge of alcohol was PSA-related, honestly: teen pregnancies, DUIs, and social media bullying. I could vaguely recall my mother occasionally sipping some wine or an amber cocktail that smelled medicinal and was full of ice when I was very young. But not often, and while I'd passed the dusty bottles in the cabinet a thousand times, I'd never thought to drink out of one of them. I was shamefully out of my depth.

"I found it in your liquor cabinet downstairs. So, what do you say, hmmm?"

I thought of the large ornate credenza in the rarely used dining room. The rows of dusty old bottles there and Sabrina stealing something. I was conflicted, afraid of being drunk, afraid of losing control. Afraid of her.

"Oh, loosen up, Jane. I can put it back if it's that big of a deal. Just thought it would be fun!"

Sabrina went over to my stereo, griping over the album collection around it. She found an old CD of my mother's and soon early 80s new wave filled the space.

"Well?" She waved the bottle back and forth until I finally nodded. Grinning devilishly, she cracked the bottle open and took a long, aggressive swallow, recoiling instantly with disgust after swallowing it. She made a face, eyes streaming, before putting a fist to her mouth. "It's really strong," she choked out. Sabrina held it out to me, eyes red, wiping her chin with her sleeve.

I looked at it with distaste. "You're really not selling me on this."

"Oh, come on. Just a sip. Just one! Come on . . . you know you waaaaant to . . ."

It was clear she wouldn't stop offering, so I took the bottle from her and our hands brushed. An electrical current seemed to run between them. Her hand so warm, compared to my cold one.

I put the bottle to my mouth, smelling both the sharp fumes of the alcohol and the vanilla from Sabrina's lip gloss. I took a tentative sip. The liquid burned down my throat, scalding my stomach. But as the burn faded, the heat remained, the warmth soothing me. It seeped into my limbs and face. I felt more aware of the blood in my body than ever before. I laughed aloud at the sensation, handing the bottle back to Sabrina.

She was spinning in my rickety desk chair. After her second, nearly gag-inducing drink, she slid off her boots, revealing pink socks with polka dots. Her nervous energy was being smoothed away by the alcohol. She sang along to the CD and fingered all the items on my desk in an idle way. I wanted to ask Sabrina more about herself, to make her talk about her life and her hopes and dreams, her desires for the future. She noticed me watching her and raised an eyebrow.

"What's your family like?" I said.

She took another drink, this time with ease, "My family is pretty boring. Not fucked up like yours. But, I guess they're happy. I'm still barely speaking to them because of this move. I mean, it's crazy. And social suicide. But they don't get it. They were, like, king and queen at their prom. The fucked-up thing was my parents actually thought this move would be good for me. Because I didn't really have a lot of friends at my old school, and there were some jerks who were always teasing me, like online and in class. It's not like anyone was really sad over me leaving or whatever. Anyways, I don't want you to think I was a loser. I just fooled around with this guy and it became this whole thing. I'm sick of mean girl bullshit, you know?"

She swayed a little in her seat and I could see the alcohol now, looking at me through her eyes. She took another pull before handing the bottle back to me. The whisky made her vulnerable too.

"Was he your boyfriend?" I asked carefully.

She groaned and spun the chair, covering her face and peeking out through her fingers, "No, I liked him, had for a long time. Thought he was out of my league y'know? But then one night I see him at this party. I normally wouldn't have gone, but I did, and he was there and we were drinking and smoking out on this porch. Like all night. I thought we really connected." She sniffed. "Anyways, we fooled around, and then at school Monday, it was a big joke. He'd told everyone, made fun of me. It sucked."

"I'm sorry." And I meant it. Sabrina's tough exterior hid a pretty sensitive person. I'd only known her a day and even I could see that. "I know what it's like to be on the outside looking in. To not get the joke or whatever."

"I noticed that here, actually, how people like . . . I'm trying to think of how to say it that doesn't sound totally horrible . . ."

"Just say it."

"They aren't making fun of you, more like they're freaked out by you or something. It's like they're scared of you."

I was sitting on the bed pulling at a loose thread in the comforter, my fingers working of their own accord.

"It's always been that way, even when I was a kid. Most people want nothing to do with me. Even my mom, honestly. It's why I thought it was strange you wanted to be my friend."

"Huh. I don't know, you seemed cool and weird. I'm cool and weird, and I would prefer to hang out with a cool outcast than a bunch of bitchy girls. Anyway, all this maudlin shit is bumming me out, and you too. We talked about what I want to do, but what are you going to do after high school?"

"After?"

I just let it hang there. Not wanting to admit that I didn't know. The entirety of high school I had just told myself to graduate, turn eighteen, and then I'd be free. But that didn't mean anything, that wasn't enough.

"Yeah, like college?" I couldn't explain to her that I was too scared to really think about my future. I couldn't tell her that the idea of leaving my mother and my house terrified me as much as staying with her, trapped forever. She couldn't possibly understand that this was a house where dreams died and hope was for other people living other lives.

The silence stretched between. Finally, I just shook my head.

My heart felt heavy and the first tingles of anger stirred. I just wanted to have a nice night with a friend. But who I was made it hard to keep things light.

Just then, the song changed to something faster and Sabrina leapt up excitedly and turned up the volume, bopping across the room to shut off the overhead light, leaving only the bedside lamp to light the room. She started dancing and singing to the song, loudly and off-key, without restraint. I took a few heavy gulps of whisky.

Cheeks flushed, she stuck her hand out for me to join, dangling her ringed fingers with their darkly polished nails my way.

Feeling like I was in someone else's body, I stood. The alcohol was making me braver. My vision had soft edges and there was a distance between my body and my reluctant mind. I also noticed an absence of the fatigue that had been plaguing me for so long now. The subtle throb of an impending migraine that normally resided behind my eyes, as well as the chronic ache in my jaw, were gone.

I was standing, while Sabrina flitted and jumped around me. She reached toward me again and this time I accepted her hand. The skin to skin contact caused my pulse to race, my breath to hitch. The sensation amplified as our fingers intertwined, our bare forearms wrist to elbow pressed together. Waves of energy pulsed through every inch of skin that made contact. She swayed her hips, tossing her pigtails, head thrown back and eyes closed.

Objects in my room shook and clinked together. I tried to mimic her, because I realized I had no idea how to dance, settling on an awkward rocking from foot to foot. Sabrina stopped, breathless, to take a drink, singing and dribbling liquor down her shirt. She'd broken contact to peel off her sweatshirt and I longed for her touch; my dancing stilled as she stepped farther away, a coldness seeping in.

"Don't you want to dance?" she asked, concerned by my sudden stillness in the middle of the room.

I shook my head no and took the bottle from her, the heat having less and less impact with each sip. A comfortable numbness was spreading all through me. My brain was foggy, strange, my limbs felt limber and well-oiled. I wanted Sabrina to be close to me. I wanted to be able to touch her.

The alcohol allowed me to just want; with each drink the narrative in my skull quieted and simplified to a whispered mantra, over and over, until I said it out loud: "I want . . . I don't know how to dance," I said to her.

She laughed and stepped close, swiping the bottle, and moving from foot to foot. "It's easy, Jane, everyone can dance. You just need to feel the music, and move however your body wants to move. There are no rules."

The song ended, and the next began. This was a slower number, sad and ballad-y. I'd listened to the album a hundred times, but never truly listened, trying to find a beat that would synch with my body. Sabrina held out her hand, timidly, and I placed my hand in hers and she then placed the other on my waist. The contact nearly made my knees buckle. I pulled her closer, relishing the way our stomachs slid along each other, the press of our breasts. I stood a few inches taller than her, my chin at her ear. She stiffened, and a wave of panic surged in me that I had overstepped, that I was being weird. She pulled back a little, but didn't break the hold.

"Isn't this how you slow dance? Or am I doing it wrong?" I asked. It came out as a whisper in her ear, we were still that close.

She craned her neck to look at me and she stuttered a bit, stumbling for words.

"No, this is good, it's just . . . a little, uh . . . I mean, I'm not . . ."

"Are you uncomfortable? We could stop. I don't want it to be weird or anything . . ."

I gave her the out. I didn't want to, because I was terrified she would take it. I loved the way her body felt against mine, the heat she gave off, warmer than the whisky, warmer than I had ever been. Safe. And alive. It made me feel real, made me feel like a person. For once I was not a ghost haunting this old tomb of a house.

"Do you need to check on your mom or anything?" Sabrina asked.

I'd completely blocked out that my mother was still here, downstairs in the dark, in the den. No doubt she could hear the music blaring through the floor. I should put her to bed. I should do a lot of things. But the whisky plowed through those thoughts like a wrecking ball.

I should be dancing and having fun. I deserved it.

The darkness and anger deep within me woke then, coiled like a slick black snake, slithered up my spine and into my brain. "I'll leave her down there all night, in the cold. I deserve a night off to have fun. Fuck Mother. She can rot down there for all I care." The thought surprised me, but once it was out and floating, actualized, it felt good. It felt wild. The song's tempo picked up and Sabrina absently moved her hips to the beat. I brazenly leaned into her, my hand still in hers, my other arm bringing her close, with no space in between us.

She stepped back a bit, the fog lifting slightly, surprised.

"I, uh . . . think we're both pretty drunk." Sabrina laughed nervously, but my arm was still around her so she couldn't break away entirely. Did she want to leave? I felt a pang of anxiety. I studied her face: there was doubt and indecision all over it. She was intrigued by this closeness—I could read it in her body language, almost in her scent. It was a strange revelation to realize I could sense her attraction to me, and I didn't know what that meant, but I knew I didn't want it to stop.

I took the whisky from the table and took another deep drink. The bottle was now half empty and I handed it back to her, a lopsided smile plastered on my face.

"Yeah, but I'm having fun. You're amazing, you know. I don't think I realized how lonely I was. I'm really happy you moved here."

Her eyes on the floor, she smiled a sweet, grateful smile. I knew how lonely she was, I knew how ashamed she'd been of being betrayed and vulnerable at her old school. Being drunk was changing my personality. I could feel it as if watching from outside myself. Ordinary Jane was passive, she did everything for her mother, she wanted or got very little. Drunk Jane wanted. Drunk Jane wanted Sabrina to stay, urgently. Alcohol was a funny thing. Brain to mouth, brain to body. Sabrina leaned in and embraced me.

"I'm happy I met you too, Jane."

The hug caused synapses to fire in my brain, the supple skin of Sabrina's neck and face close to mine. I could smell her soap, the acrid cigarette smoke in her hair. I let my nose run along the soft spot between her neck and shoulder, feeling the quickening pulse there. She felt my face against hers, the intimacy of the contact, and she pulled back, fighting her own curiosity. She was breathless, her inhibitions knocked down by drink, but her fear was trying to override it. She swallowed loudly.

"Are you, uh, hitting on me, Jane? Because I like you as a friend."

She said this nervously, her normal confidence gone. What I said next would either change our friendship, or kill it. The drunkenness and my desire for her made me brave, made me honest.

"I don't know how I feel. All I know is I really like being near you. . . ."

Sabrina's breath caught as I pulled her closer, and without a thought at all, I touched her lips with mine. It was the most intense sensation I had ever felt. The heat of her mouth, combined with the slightest wetness. She stiffened, but didn't push me off. I leaned forward, desperate to get her mouth back to mine. She gave in, and her body lost all of its tension and melted into mine.

I wrapped my arms tightly around her, and she did the same. She opened her mouth and my tongue slid inside, tasting the whisky in her saliva. She sighed as I moved against her, bringing us even closer to each other. Our hips grinding together to the rhythm of the song. I walked her backward to the bed and when the backs of her knees hit the mattress, she froze, breaking the kiss and putting some space between us.

"I'm not . . . I mean, I'm not gay, I'm just wasted."

I simply stared at her puffy, bee-stung mouth, her disheveled makeup, her indecision. I had done more talking than I had in months today, and I didn't want to talk anymore. Something inside me, that slick, black snake, was looking out through my eyes and it was a selfish thing.

I want, I want, I want.

"I don't care what you are. All I know is that this is an evening of firsts. First friend to come over to my house."

With that I moved closer again, closing the gap between us.

"First time I've ever drank." I inched closer still. "First time I've ever danced with someone." I took her hand, and her eyelids fluttered, drunkenly. "And my first kiss . . ."

She stared at me for a moment, desire shining in her face. "I'm just . . . scared, Jane. I don't know what any of this means . . ."

"It doesn't have to mean anything. It feels good; it gets us out of our heads. Why does anything have to be more than that?"

We were nearly nose to nose now. She closed her eyes. A voice inside was urging me on. The whisky had awoken a part of me I had never known. A lifetime of being denied had fattened it. The black snake was possessive, controlling; it wanted. Sabrina's indecision kept me from her, and that made me want to take control.

In a bold move, I slid my arms around her and leaned forward, knocking her onto the bed. She was surprised as I landed on top of her. She didn't squirm away so I kissed her.

My hands snaked underneath her shirt. I luxuriated in the explosive heat of her skin, like a cat in a patch of sunlight. I heard her breathing, loud and jagged as I explored her breasts, first with my hands, then with my mouth. She moaned as I slipped a hand into her pants. It was searing hot inside. And all along I kept thinking: I was not in my body, I was someone else. I did not seduce drunk girls.

And yet I was. Sabrina's shirt and bra were gone somehow, as if they had just dissolved. Her pants were off too, her body gloriously pale in the soft lamplight. I was naked, our bodies sliding the length of each other, warm and smooth.

My mouth was everywhere. I was kissing her, greedily sucking at her lips. I migrated to her throat where the pulse hammered along my tongue's path. My mouth dripped with saliva. I licked at her skin, salty on my tongue, and then I bit. She was breathing very fast, and I could feel the beginnings of the spasms deep in her belly. I allowed my teeth to sink deeper into the skin of her throat. It was surreal how easily the flesh parted. My mouth filled with blood, hot and meaty, complex and alive. I was lapping it up as it flowed out of the wound, mindlessly, greedily. She was gasping for breath. I felt powerful and free, and there was nothing else but the fast, birdlike beat of her heart, her panting, hot and moist in my ear, and my throat, swallowing and swallowing.

VI.

$\mathcal{I}$ woke in the morning unsure what was real and what had been a dream. My mouth tasted sour and metallic. I was lying on my stomach with one arm over something . . . warm . . . and breathing.

I struggled to sit up. Disorientation at first, but then vague memories slowly returned, the whisky, the dancing, and the kiss. In shock, I looked at Sabrina, who was dead to the world, tangled in my sheets, her face turned away from me. I touched my mouth and looked around my bedroom, confused. The bedside lamp was still on, the radio was still on, my mother . . .

"Fuck!" I jumped up, threw on a T-shirt and sweats, and dashed down the stairs to the frigid den. The fire had gone out in the night and my breath plumed in the chill air. My mother was slumped in the chair, her head on her chest. Her skin was cold, and I felt tendrils of the old horror creeping in. But then she moved, slowly, creakily, and looked up at me with sleep-addled—but otherwise clear—eyes. What she saw there caused her to moan, loudly, and she turned away from me.

"I'm so sorry for leaving you here all night, Mom, you must be freezing." Guilt like a noose around my neck, I eased her up out of the chair, rubbing her trembling limbs. Upstairs, I changed her and put her in her bed to warm up. Once she was tucked in, I scurried back downstairs to relight the damned stove. I started some coffee and oatmeal, falling into my standard routine. Poor neglected Tommy yowled and hopped on the counter, no doubt angry for closing off my room to him all night. I kissed his head and opened a can of cat food for him.

I couldn't stop thinking of Sabrina, which inevitably led me back to thinking about last night. It was still foggy, but I remembered the feelings—the joy, the freedom, dreamlike and blurry. I remembered the way her body moved under me. I remembered how I'd enjoyed it. But there were huge gaps, and I was shocked that it had gone down that way in the first place. I had never been a particularly sexual person. I never thought much of marrying, or having kids, or boyfriends, let alone girlfriends. In the pale morning light it was shocking and somewhat shameful to think of myself as the aggressor, as the seducer. Regardless of who I'd been last night and what whisky had woken, I felt fantastic, probably the best I had ever felt. My body felt strong, alert, and alive. Smiling and humming under my breath, I brought a tray of food to my mother and some coffee to my room, eager to see Sabrina.

My good mood deflated as soon as I entered the bedroom. I hadn't noticed when I woke earlier, but now I could see the stains on the pillowcases, and the sheets: brownish red smears everywhere. Sabrina was standing to the side, hunched over and watching me, sunken eyes wreathed in smeared black makeup, face pale. She recoiled as I came in, wrapping her arms around herself.

I raised the coffee and forced a smile. "I brought you some coffee and aspirin. Sure glad it's Saturday. Can you believe I was drunk enough to forget my mother downstairs in the parlor last night?" I chuckled as I walked toward her. Sabrina glared at me and scrambled away as I came near. I put a cup on the desk where she could reach and stepped back. She was unsteady on her feet and she eased into my desk chair, putting her shoes on with trembling hands.

"Are you okay?" I finally asked when I could take her silence no longer.

I liked her warmth and her chatter. This pallid, somber Sabrina made me uncomfortable.

"No, I am not okay." Her pale hazel eyes brimmed with tears.

"What's wrong? What happened?"

"Where to start?! First you . . . take advantage of me . . ."

"What?"

"Then you fucking bite me!"

"Bite you? What are you talking about?"

"My blood is all over this bed! Look at my neck!" Angrily she pulled down the neck of her shirt, revealing her bruised and ravaged throat. It was an angry wound, each tooth represented in a neat circular mark. I staggered back from her, nearly missing the bed as I sat down. She was crying, shoulders shaking silently, fat tears that streaked her makeup even more. She swiped at her eyes with her sleeve and continued gathering her things.

"I don't know how you could gnaw on my neck like that without me even noticing. I must have been fucking wasted, or else maybe you slipped me something. I guess I know why everyone is terrified of you. I learned my lesson."

"Wait, Sabrina . . ." I croaked, feeling scooped out and hollow. Her hand was on the doorknob, her back to me. Her head was down.

She craned her neck back toward me, no longer the bubbly, smiling girl from yesterday. On her face was the cold, fearful stare that everyone else in the world gave me. I had to hold in my breath so I wouldn't let out a sob.

"Have you even looked in a mirror this morning?" She hissed this as she yanked the door open. I stood and glanced in my vanity, and froze. My mouth was outlined in crusted brown. I scratched at it and it flaked away. With dawning horror, I realized it was Sabrina's blood all over my face. Which meant she was right, and I had bitten her. What was wrong with me? Why couldn't I remember? I turned to her beseechingly. But she was gone. A minute later I heard an engine start, followed by the sound of her tires peeling out of my driveway.

My chest ached as if it had been pierced. I slid onto the floor, bundled myself into a ball, and did not move for hours.

VII.

It was midafternoon before I was able to rouse myself. I checked on mother, bringing her up some lunch and her medicine in bed. She watched me and I did my best to ignore her.

Later, in the bathroom, it took all my willpower not to smash the mirror. The face that looked back at me belonged to a stranger. What the hell had happened? Was I losing my mind? I hated to admit that while my heart ached at the loss of Sabrina, my body still felt good. Strong, even. The physical renewal didn't overcome the dread or the confusion about last night. If anything, it complicated things. My stomach flip-flopped. Why would I hurt her? Why did I want to? Obviously something was wrong with me, and for the first time in my life, I felt dangerous.

I turned the shower on blisteringly hot and stepped in, gasping in shock and pain. Good, I thought to myself, as my skin flared pink from the heat. When I could take no more, I turned the temperature to a more comfortable setting and scrubbed myself vigorously. Once clean, I sat in the tub, letting the water pelt me. I replayed the evening in my head, trying to focus on the fuzzy stuff. Round and around I went, seeing her at the store, getting in her car, letting her in. Taking a drink. I'd wanted to touch her, craved it as if starved. But as soon as I could get close, I'd bit.

And I'd known what I was doing, maybe not consciously, but I'd known I was seducing her. The guilt blossomed. The guilt and the horror. Was my mother right? Was there something so horrible and wrong with me that I spoiled everything? Was I so deviant that I was incapable of loving or being loved? There were so many questions. The worst and most problematic: why didn't I regret it?

After my shower, I dressed in warm clothes, changed my linens, and bleached my sheets. I checked on my mother, whose lunch sat mostly untouched. She tracked me through the room like I was going to steal something, and for a moment, an insane moment, I was tempted to tell her about the night before. But I couldn't. Her withering stare—and if I were honest, the fear of some awful truth—clammed me up. So instead I retreated to my room. And I just sat there, staring, trying to not think about anything as the sun set. But the more I tried not to think, the more thinking I did. Sabrina's smell was everywhere and the sweetness had turned noxious. I remembered her lying on my bed, smiling, and my stomach squeezed like a fist—shame and lust, the ghostly memory of a mouthful of tinny blood. My gorge rose.

I needed to move, I needed to be doing something. In the hallway, my eyes caught the paintings stacked along the walls. I hardly saw them anymore, passing by them hundreds of times a day. But Sabrina had seen them, and had moved some to take a closer look. I reached behind me and turned on the hallway light. The bulb cast a dusty yellow glare. I traced my fingers along Sabrina's fingerprints in the dust at the top of one canvas, evidence that she had been there, and I nearly sobbed. Kneeling, I pulled the paintings apart and spread them out. Really looking at them this time, trying to see them from her eyes.

The one that caught my eye was a strange self-portrait. It was the same painting my mother had used on the flyers for her last art show in New York, the flyer I had stashed away in my nightstand. In the painting, my mom was both young and old, each face overlapping. The only thing that each face shared were the eyes, her eyes, painted a vibrant blue and staring out, confrontational. It was an expression I had never seen my mother make. It was so dominant, so strong. I was amazed by the amount of skill it had taken to paint those photo-realistic portraits. Each face looked like a ghost, perfectly rendered but layered transparently, superimposed on top of one another.

There was something haunting about the portrait. My mother had painted it before I was born, but it looked like even then she knew something was wrong with her. The more I studied it the more distressing it became. The oldest face was uncannily accurate compared to how she looked now.

My mother was in her bed, covered in wounds. Wounds that looked so similar . . . No. My mind closed shut like a bear trap. My mother painted pictures of her youth fading. My mother had answers that I needed. I flipped the painting forward, its back revealing a title printed in neat blocky handwriting:

"The States of Being" V. DeVry. The rest of the paintings in the stack were similar in style, portraits and portraits. All of her.

I stood and wiped my dusty hands on my pants, feeling uncomfortable and unwelcome. I fought the urge to stack all the paintings again, turn off the light, and forget everything. Go back to grilled cheese sandwiches, banal TV programs on mute, being alone.

But I couldn't go back. The night before, Sabrina had wakened something in me, something violent, and I needed to know why. The only person with answers was the architect of this sad life of ours. I needed to know my mother, about her history, about my history. These paintings didn't answer my questions, they created more. Who was this woman I'd lived with for seventeen years? Hell, who was I?

I couldn't ask my mother; she hadn't truly spoken more than a few words this year, and honestly, I couldn't bear to confess to what had happened with Sabrina. Not yet. But maybe this house, her living shrine, could help me. At least it would keep me occupied, get me out of my own head and into hers.

～❀～

The bedroom next to mine was filled nearly to the ceiling with my mother's things. Paintings of course, but also her clothes and books. I found boxes of housewares: dishes, a beautiful blue vase, some awards for art she'd won in high school. A shoebox of notes in childish bubble handwriting, filled with the crushes and drama of junior high. Peace sign earrings, a worn old bear, a pearl rosary in a blue felt box. All these years the boxes had been moldering one wall away, but I'd never once felt compelled to root around looking for my own history.

Had my mother planned to unpack, display, and incorporate all this stuff into the house? Before she gave up and sequestered herself in the attic to paint, or before she fell ill? Or perhaps she'd never intended to stay here.

Night fell. Clicking the lamp on, I rummaged through the boxes with more vigor. There was a person-shaped puzzle being pieced together, and each friendship bracelet and bookmark, each photograph and memento, contributed another piece. If only I could understand why this seemingly ordinary, albeit artsy and eccentric, girl went sick and mad. How much of this was caused by her health and how much her mind?

I rubbed some dust out of my eyes and sifted through a box of photos. They were mostly of my mother when she was young, even some of her as a baby with my grandparents. At the bottom of the box I found a newer-looking picture album with a plain black cover. Wiping the grime off the surface, I cracked it open. There was my mom, right on the first page, looking young and hopeful.

In the photo she was in her late teens, possibly early twenties. My fingertips traced her face without meaning to. Her hair was vibrantly red, curly and long. She was standing on the stoop of an apartment building, wearing a paint-smeared T-shirt hanging off one bare, pale shoulder, and very short cut-offs. She was beaming, her skin unscarred and flawless. She squinted in the sun, her hand waving at the unknown photographer. Next to her was a curvy brunette, her hair heavily feathered with a few bleach-blonde streaks. She also had a big smile and her arm was around my mother. The friend was pointing at the address plaque on the building. I flipped the photo over: Moving Day! Viv and Gina.

I couldn't take my eyes from the photo. The two good friends, their hands paint-splotched, their smiles filled with so much hope and possibility. I felt a pinch in my chest, a deep non-specific sadness. I'd never known the woman in this photo, but I would have liked to. I dug through my memories, back as far as I could, trying to blend the image in my hand with the one barely alive in this house. When my mother was a sentient person. But even then she wasn't this picture-woman, so happy, so bright.

In my earliest memories she was anxious, paranoid, even cruel. She didn't want me to play with other children; she was always worried about strangers. I spent hours locked up in this house while she furiously painted in the attic, coming down only to eat at random hours. Sandwiches and canned soups, things you could buy in bulk that would keep indefinitely. My mother would only go out for supplies in spurts, stocking up as if planning for the apocalypse.

Those visits to the neighboring town's box stores were my only memories of leaving the house growing up. Holding onto a cart, amazed at how big and bright it was, and how many people were there. But we never dawdled, just got what we needed and left. I was sent off to "play" and my mother would head back up to her attic lair. I was never allowed up into her studio. "It's not for children, it's Mommy's place," she would say when she would hear me on the stairs. In consolation, I would play at the bottom of the steps, waiting for her to come down.

Was she sick because of me? I hated to think that motherhood, and my existence, had consumed her mind, her body, her passions, and eventually would usher her into a hole in the ground.

There was a life crammed in here. If all my mother's stuff were destroyed, no one would remember she existed at all. And with her gone, there would be no one who knew me either.

I searched for another hour or so. More photos, many, many sketchbooks, even old report cards. More puzzle pieces creating an idea of my mother, but some large and very important pieces were absent. Everything in this room projected normalcy—it all spoke to the life of a pretty red-haired girl with loving parents. She had friends and boyfriends, in-jokes and good grades; her college years, with their yellowed essays, collections of band flyers, and concert tickets. But nothing told me why my mother came back to a place she hated. And nothing told me who my father was, or what was wrong with me.

This room had been here my whole life, unlocked. And like a lightbulb over my head it dawned on me: there was still only one place I was expressly forbidden to go—the only place that was my mother's space and hers alone, that was literally locked. The attic studio.

It seemed silly that I hadn't gone there first. But even now I felt that ingrained taboo. I stepped into the hall. I forced the child in me back down as I stared at the swinging pull chain to the attic stairs, and the padlock that attached the trap door to the ceiling. I was owed some answers.

I found bolt cutters in the basement. I balanced on a stool and I cut the lock off. It fell with a loud and damning clunk, releasing a plume of dust.

I pulled the chain.

VIII.

The sound of the stairs unfolding and hitting the floor triggered an explosion of memories. I'd heard it nearly every morning of my childhood when my mother went up to her sanctuary. The stairs to the attic were narrow, paint splattered, and rickety. I realized staring up into the cold dark hole in the ceiling that I was frightened. Mercifully, Tommy the cat had trotted out of the guest room and was looking up at the attic, equally curious. With the cat at my heels, I carefully climbed the stairs and popped my head in. The room was nearly black, with only the weak light from the moon through the slats in the shuttered windows to guide me. I felt along the wall for a light switch and when I couldn't find one, wandered around flailing my arms for a pull chain, my heart hammering in my chest the longer I shuffled in the unfamiliar dark. When I felt something cord-like brush my hand, I yanked it like a lifeline.

Canvases upon canvases were stacked everywhere. The space was plastered with drawings, barely an inch of the walls visible underneath. I walked from piece to piece, surprised by how many of them were self-portraits. The painting style seemed more refined than her normally frantic, energetic brush strokes. The endless books on art appreciation Mother had foisted on me came back to me as I looked at her work. The paintings in the attic reminded me of "The State of Being" painting downstairs. But where that one had lightness in the young woman turning old, these felt much less natural.

The paintings were tortured, overworked, attempting to document the nuances of her face down to the individual pore, to capture flesh. Each successive painting depicted her wasting away more and more. What were probably the earliest, stacked closest to the walls and floor, showed her younger, like the photographs and my early memories. Serious, pretty. In one, she was pregnant, topless, holding her belly in one hand. The face looked haunted, glancing to the side, as if waiting for someone. The later paintings showed her scars, or bandages covering wrists, throat, and a menacing shadow in the background. In others, which I guessed were most recent paintings, the shadow had more form. As she withered, and became more indistinct, the shadow in the back grew more corporeal. I'd only recently read The Picture of Dorian Gray for English Lit and it was impossible not to draw the clichéd comparison.

I reached out and touched what had to be the last painting in the series. It was unfinished, still set up on the easel. In it, my mother looked almost as she did today: sallow, hunched, old, her hair thin and gray. The shadow figure at her shoulder was nearly in focus. I leaned closer to look and realized that the shadow was me. Meticulously painted, a creature made of darkness, I loomed behind her, staring directly out at the viewer, eyes like two gleaming black buttons, doll-like.

My facial expression alien and utterly cruel.

My legs turned to jelly. I stepped back, wanting to be as far from the picture as possible, yet unable to look away.

How could my mother hate me this much? My head ached. I'd been slaving to take care of her all these years. Giving her my childhood, giving away any chance to have a normal life, to be a real person. I wanted her love so much I could taste it. But I was filled again with the crushing despair of knowing that I would never have it. I was stuck living in this glorified hovel on canned soup, changing her shitty diapers. And all the while she had been up here, spending all those healthy years, all the years she could have been talking to me, teaching me, being a mother to me. But instead she had been painting.

The injustice of it was choked me. I hated her. Once the word was at the surface of my mind, it couldn't go back down. Hate, hate, hate. She was a cruel and selfish person. My eyes burned with unshed tears, my fists tight. I could barely breathe, rage like a walnut jammed in my throat.

On shaky legs, I stood and walked to the painting and kicked the easel, knocking it down. With a cry I stomped on it. The easel snapped into kindling, the painting's stretchers cracking, pulling the staples from the back, paint flaking off. I ripped through it with another kick. Cathartic.

I was breathing heavily as I threw the remains of the canvas aside, grinning victoriously.

I picked up a box cutter sitting in a box of tools and brushes, and went to work. I stomped and slashed, tearing the drawings from the walls, ripping them to confetti. My spree lasted until my muscles ached, eyes burning from dust. I looked around the dingy attic at the destruction, and only then, looking at my mother's life's work shredded and destroyed, did tiny tendrils of guilt touch me. This was all she had. And it was gone. I'd taken it. What a sad small world.

I hadn't been a bad child. I couldn't think of anything I could have done to have caused her so much pain. I righted a stool I'd knocked over in my fit and sat down. From this angle I could see out the small octagonal window, facing the backyard where I used to play. I would've liked to think my mother sat up here and kept an eye out for me, but I doubted it. I stared at my dirty hands, remembering my mother's blood on them earlier. The strangeness of tasting it. And then Sabrina.

As my gaze trailed off, I noticed a piece of the windowsill was loose, and as I leaned in to investigate, I saw the binding of a book jammed inside the wall. The hiding spot looked intentional. I pried the book out and shook off the layer of dust to reveal a leather-bound journal.

Opening it, I saw the paint-y fingerprints on the pages and the familiar scrawl of my mother's handwriting. I was looking at my mother's diary. I stared at it almost reverently—this was the kind of thing I'd been searching for.

My thoughts in a jumble, I stood. Tommy finally crawled out from where he'd stashed himself during my rampage.

I turned off the light and slowly went down the ladder, clutching the journal. I wasn't ready to open it yet—my fear of its contents was too large. Instead I tucked it into my night table drawer and went to wash up. I felt both elated and intensely guilty just thinking about the violation of going into my mother's space, touching the last vestiges of the person she once was. Not only touching, destroying.

I brought Mother her dinner in bed. She was sitting where I'd left her hours before, bundled up, the bathroom radio keeping her company. She stared at the wall, eyes fogged, lost in thought. But I didn't quite believe she was entirely unaware. There was a tightness to the skin around her eyes, a tremble in her lips that made me think she was a little more lucid than she was letting on.

When dinner was cleaned up and her blankets pulled up to her chin, I turned to go, but was shocked to feel my mother's hand on my wrist. She had moved much faster than I thought she could. Her eyes were clear, intense even. I couldn't recall the last time I'd seen so much of a person looking out from those eyes.

"What, Mom? What do you need?" I whispered, afraid.

She blinked a few times, eyelids fluttering as a few thick, slow-moving tears slid out. Her mouth moved as if to talk, lips shaking, dry tongue snaking out to moisten them. She took a rattling breath, and I could feel her pulse racing through her hot hand. It burned my arm, as if feverish.

"I'm listening, Mom. Please . . . what is it?"

I didn't want to sound so desperate, but it had been years since she'd actively spoken. Years of nothing but wheezes and moans. She stared at me, another tear streaking down, and then the lights went back out behind her eyes. Her grip loosened and slid away, her eyes took on a cloudy, faraway look, and she disconnected. I hadn't realized there were tears in my eyes, until I blinked. I rubbed at them angrily as I turned her light off, and stomped out of the room. I couldn't go on this way. I knew I was going to lose myself in this house, lose my mind, hurt her, or end up another object tucked away in a box.

By the time I got to my room, my hands itched for the journal in the drawer. I needed to read it. I bundled up in blankets, Tommy jumping up and curling himself at my side. I absently petted him while staring at the nightstand.

I had to be brave. I refused to turn into one of those pathetic adult children who ended up drowning an invalid parent in the tub or starving them to death, pushed to their breaking point.

I had to be more than that.

I took a deep breath and pulled out my mother's journal. The leather was brittle. I traced the fingerprints of paint on the outside. I opened the book to the first page and started to read.

IX.

June 1st

Well, this is the first page of my journal. It's been sitting on the shelf for a few weeks, taunting me. I don't write—always found writing hard—tripping over my words. I feel like I'm never able to say what I mean. I wish writing was like painting. And I'm sure there are plenty of people who feel the exact opposite. Anyways, ramble over, and now the page has some writing on it. Gina gave me this journal as a graduation present. It's beautiful, thoughtful. She'd wanted me to use it as a sketchbook— and I thought I would, at first. But I have hundreds of sketchbooks. The luxury of the binding, the supple leather, all of that seems too fine to sketch in—you can't even rip out the pages. It's too much pressure. Sketches are supposed to be spurts, exercises, nothings that sometimes become somethings. But in a book like this? Well, let's just say I had performance anxiety.

So after two weeks of the book taunting me, I decided, fuck it, this book will be a journal, my memoir. I haven't really lived an exciting enough life to have a memoir, but it who knows, I may from here on out.

There. Page one is filled.

June 15th

I had this idea that if I committed to the journal it would help me with self-improvement or understanding myself. Or I could go back when I'm old and gray, when I'm a superstar painter with a super handsome, successful husband. I'll look back at this record of my early twenties and think fondly on my shitty apartment, shitty roommates, all of it.

It's so annoying living with a couple. Technically, Kyle doesn't live here. He has some mythological apartment somewhere. But since he sleeps here every night and eats all my food, I doubt it exists. And as glamourous as sharing a railroad apartment is—and listening to them fight and fuck all the time—I would love to get my own place. Or maybe they'll move out together and I can get a nice, normal roommate who isn't a messy sculptor, with dust and debris everywhere from making a ten-foot-tall vagina tree while her poser boyfriend "collages" shit.

I mean, I don't want to sound like a snob—but it's my journal, after all—and their work is terrible. Gina is my friend, don't get me wrong, I love her as a person, but her art? It's gotten too Judy Chicago feminist. It's derivative. And Kyle is a poser, always scheming, always schmoozing. And I know all he sees is potential contacts. Kyle's dad is some bigwig professional artist and professor at Pratt. Kyle's mom is some old money socialite type. Gina could meet the right people, get in anywhere. It's depressing, the whole system is depressing. Between working at the restaurant all hours and then coming home and trying to paint—when exactly would I have time to schmooze?

I'm trying not to lose the dream. I know I just graduated and it all takes time, but how much time? Best to work on my paintings. I feel like I'm really on to something amazing—so I'll just keep at it. And if it's good, good things will happen. Or, worst case scenario, back to art school for my Masters and more loans! (Joke—sort of.)

Anyways, enough whining for one night. I hear the roommates in the hall. Have to go be social . . .

June 20th

Okay, so something weird happened with Kyle. Can't talk to Gina about it, or any of our other friends, really, since they all know Gina and have big fucking mouths . . . but this could be major.

So, the other night I was at home. I actually had the night off. I've been really into this new series I'm working on—my poor bedroom's so jammed with canvases it's pretty much a fort in here. So I'm working on the big Red one, no title yet, but this whole realist/futurist thing. Anyway, I'm in a painting frenzy, music loud, in the zone, when Kyle comes in.

Now first off, I didn't know he was home. Second, I didn't hear him come in, or even knock to come into my room. Yeah, the door's open, but that's not an invite. On top of that, I'm in my usual painting attire, which, if no one is home, is just an oversized man's shirt and undies. So there I am, in my underwear, in my room, and Kyle comes in, and he seems a bit nervous. Finally, I ask him what he wants, and he's all cagey at first—making weird pleasantries, and in my head I'm just begging for him not to hit on me or do anything weird.

Finally, I say something to that effect, and he blanches and gets all defensive. Eventually, he spits out that he met a gallery owner and art dealer that was interested in my stuff. Which is weird, since I hadn't sent any galleries my new stuff . . . then he says that he took the liberty of photographing them and showing them to some of his parents' associates.

Now, this is fucked for a couple of reasons. The main one being: why behind my back? Kyle says he was worried nothing would come of it—didn't want to get my hopes up, but that feels like a lie. Finally he confesses that he didn't want to piss off Gina, whose work won't sell. Ha! Vindication.

It all seems weaselly, but at the same time, it's nice he believes in the work, right? And as much of a slime as he is, it's still a bit flattering that he wants to help, that he believes in me. So I agree, and he's excited.

Anyways, he tells me about the gallery that was more than just interested. Apparently, it's in Chelsea, and has a small but solid reputation, but the director's a bit off. This is all so fast—I feel like this series is unfinished. Kyle says he'll put it all together, contact the gallery, and in the meantime, I should be painting like a maniac and getting together a statement, titles for all the pieces,

I keep stepping back and looking at my paintings. Especially the Red one, which is my baby at the moment. I don't want to brag, but it's amazing. I can honestly say that. Its scale, the vibrancy, and the portraits of myself within it are really . . . uncanny. I think it's good, but good enough to show? Good enough people would want to buy it?

Ugh. What have I done? I hate to admit how excited I am, but I am. If I can get a show, it will be so major. It'll show everyone that I wasn't just wasting my talents trying to make a hobby into a career. Mainly it would show Dad that I'm doing it and he can be proud of me. And I'd dedicate the show to Mom—she always believed I could do this. If she were still alive I'd be telling her all of this instead of writing it in a stupid journal, and she'd be ecstatic.

Better get working. Kyle will check in soon.

June 25th

So things are moving fast, and I had a minute and figured I should scrawl in the damn journal so I have a record of this shit. (How many times have I jokingly done something crazy "for the memoirs.") Anyway, the gallery director scheduled a time to come and look at my paintings. I want this so bad. I look at this dump, imagine him clomping up the four spindly flights of stairs to our cramped little garret. He'll look at our curb-find furniture, the sickly plants, the dust bunnies perpetually fluttering around. Oh God, and he'll have to walk through Gina's crummy sculptures and track footprints from the goddamn plaster into my room.

And, since we're at this stage in the game, I had to tell Gina. And she was not happy. I mean, I think she'll talk to me again someday. She's a chatterbox, and I think would physically die if she was unable to talk to someone. So I just need to wait her out, really, and let the anger fade.

Kyle on the other hand, he's not her favorite person in the world right now. I don't know if she dumped him per se—I think it's being defined as a need for "space." But she knows her boyfriend has been talking me up all over town and not her. She'll get over it, in time. Maybe she'll even swallow her pride and come to my show.

Okay, now I'm really getting ahead of myself. There is no show right now. The gallery owner could walk in here, shake his head, and walk out. He just agreed to take a look at the paintings based on the photos he saw. He's a businessman. I can't let my hopes go off the rails. I need to stay in reality. I did tell my dad about it, but he seemed . . . well, the way he seems about most things these days: indifferent. I mean, I could hear him trying to be excited for me, but his heart just wasn't in it. I worry about him up there in that big house up in Hob's Valley all alone.

But if I have a show, he could come down. He could stay for the weekend—well, no, between all the stairs, my lousy neighborhood, and our lumpy vintage sofa, I doubt he'd be comfortable. But, maybe a nice hotel room. He could come down, see some sights, go home with the bragging rights for coming to my gallery show. It would be good for him.

Okay, gotta run. I have to clean like my life depends on it, and it does, since this guy is coming tomorrow.

June 27th

I feel like I'm on a rollercoaster, ticking away the last few seconds before the track drops and we plummet, screaming.

In a good way, I think.

So, yesterday morning was my appointment with Mr. McGarrett to look at my paintings, in the flesh. His assistant set it all up, official like. I was penciled in.

So, I cleaned and Gina sulked, shuffling around, sighing and plopping down in random chairs to stare vacantly out windows, constantly asking if I thought her art was good.

Obviously I said yes about a thousand times. That it was just too conceptual for most people, they lacked vision, were too repressed to really see her work. Or something pacifying like that. I finally got her dressed and out of the place.

About an hour later, I'm sitting in the apartment, fidgeting, dusting, trying not to run and change for the thousandth time. I decided on my black dress. It's off the shoulder, a little edgy, probably inappropriate. I looked good. If nothing else, I could say that at the end of this ordeal. The gallery owner might hate my art and be visibly disgusted by my apartment, but I still looked good.

I was practically crawling out of my skin with nerves. I sat on the edge of the sofa because I didn't want to wrinkle my dress. I was sweating. I could feel a trickle running down my back— half nerves, half the result of living in a hot as hell fourth-floor walk-up in summer.

Finally, finally, the buzzer rang. It was Kyle and the gallery owner, Mr. McGarrett, together. Kyle came in first, looking odd.

The man that followed after him was, in a word, intense. He stepped into my puke-y kitchenette and it was like he pulled all the air out of it. I don't think I've ever met someone with so much presence. He was tall, silky brown hair a bit longer than would be tidy. He had a broad square jaw, Mediterranean coloring, and a large pointed nose. Brown-black eyes, nice mouth, a little stubble. Handsome. Probably a good ten years older than Kyle and me. I found my voice and invited them in.

Mr. McGarrett asked me to call him Hugh. His accent was obviously British, which added another level to his intensity. So, I brought Hugh to my bedroom, feeling uncomfortable for a second: him being older, successful, handsome. In my bedroom. Me trying to not look like a kid fresh out of college, which I am. He must have sensed my anxiety. He asked politely if I wouldn't mind giving him some time with the art. When he asked, he met my eyes. He was serious, and still intense.

I nodded—pretty sure I was blushing—and went back to the kitchen where Kyle was sitting. He'd put the kettle on. Seeing him there, unmoving, staring at his cup, got me really worried. Shouldn't he be in there with Hugh, shouldn't he be talking me up—or doing whatever it was he was supposed to do to earn his percentage? I whispered this to him but he seemed indifferent. I pushed, wanting to know why he was acting so strange. He just shrugged, saying he thought he made a mistake—especially bringing Hugh here. I couldn't figure him out.

Kyle acted totally weird when Hugh re-entered, he was tense and uncomfortable. I just plastered on my biggest smile. Hugh smiled back, which was reassuring. He said he liked my paintings, liked the rawness, the vitality. He loved my take on futurism and portraiture. His praise was so satisfying I can't even put it into words. His eyes were on me the whole time he spoke. I tried to engage and be cool and adult and not just pass out in a puddle. He said we'd talk soon, that he might have an opening available to give me a show, and he'd call me in the next few days. He handed me a business card. He left. Kyle stayed.

As soon as he was out the door and down a flight, I screamed, like actually jumping up and down. Kyle was still all weird, so finally I asked him what was his problem? I didn't know the gallery, sure, but it's in fucking Chelsea, and this Hugh guy seemed like just the right amount of cool and business savvy to really put me on the map. Kyle should have been jumping next to me. But he wasn't. Finally, he said again that he didn't think it was a good idea. That he got a bad feeling from Hugh, like maybe he wasn't interested in my paintings at all.

I got pissed. This was Kyle's idea in the first place! And now he was changing his mind? Just like that. Hugh came over here based on my paintings alone—that had to mean something. But I have to admit the longer he was gone, the longer we stood in the kitchen—it all seemed too good to be true. It still does. I asked Kyle if he thought Hugh was the type of guy who came around, like movie producers or theatre guys, promising young girls—wet behind the ears—that they'd make them stars. Kyle didn't answer, which was an answer.

When I talked to Gina, she had that glib look of someone who was happy that I failed. She would never say anything to my face, but I can tell. She's not that hard to read. She was jealous, and now she feels no need to be. I just don't get it. I felt something there. I think Hugh liked my paintings. I really do. I think he liked me as well. I guess I just have to wait and hope he calls, prove them wrong.

Or right?

June 28th

No call.

June 29th

No call.

June 30th

No call. I mean, it was such a long shot, anyway. Most artists spend years trying to get the contacts or get the critical reception to show at decent galleries. And most fail. I was too excited and it was stupid. What I need to do now is get back into the work. Make some great paintings, fuck everyone else.

July 3rd

Well, he called! Holy shit! I'd pretty much given up hope. I was so over it—I'd even forgotten his face from last week. Or at least, that's what I was pretending to do. Things were even getting back to normal a bit. Kyle was still showing my stuff around, and Gina was still mad about it, but she'd really started throwing herself into her work more. Let's just say the vagina trees are getting a bit out of control. But she's also working more shifts at the record store so she can try and get a studio space someplace else. Thank God. But anyway.

Hugh called. He called and he wants to do a show with me. He has a cancellation next month. Basically, the artist who was going to show wasn't finished, and the new stuff wasn't as advertised, and so different from his earlier, sellable work, that Hugh had to cut him loose. And now he has an opening in the schedule! I can't even pretend to be sad about that other artist. It's a tough business. Hugh and I are going to meet for drinks and discuss layout, themes, advertising, etc. I am on cloud nine.

I called Dad. He seemed excited. He even said he'd try and come down for it. I won't lie though, when I called home I just wished, wished, that Mom had answered. That she was still alive and she was on the other end. She would be over the moon. She really pushed me to be an artist, she was the one who arranged the after-school classes and bought me the supplies. She bragged to her bridge ladies about her daughter—the artist—in New York. She'd be shopping for a new outfit to wear to my opening, she'd be talking Dad's ear off. She'd be so proud.

Even writing it makes me want to cry.

I'm going to sign off. This is supposed to be a happy occasion. More soon.

July 5th

It's really happening! I mean really really. I just got home from measuring and deciding on the lighting for my own freaking solo show. Set date is August 10 which is unbelievable. Hugh and I spent hours and hours the other night pouring over the details, the pricing, the titles. We picked the painting to be on the mailers. It's the Red one, my baby! We both agreed on it, which was amazing. He is amazing as well, to be honest. I don't think I've had a better evening with anyone in my entire life. He's intense and smart and funny. He loves art in a way that moves me. He's not an artist, not even a little, he says, not an ounce of talent. He thinks that's maybe why he's so drawn to artists. Not envy, but appreciation. I love that. I love that he's so moved by people like me that he's devoted his career to them.

I hate to admit it, but I think I like him more than I should. It's so hard not to. But I need to button that up. This is about art, not silly crushes. And realistically, what would someone like him see in someone like me?

But then again, he is in love with my paintings.

July 8th

So this is strange and exciting and confusing—but let me back up. First off, Kyle doesn't want to participate much with the show all of the sudden, even said he'd take a smaller percentage. He claims to be too busy, but I really think that it's Hugh. He really dislikes him that much. And then when he and Gina came by the gallery space to help with the hanging order (getting Gina there in a supportive friend way was a miracle in itself), she was super weird around Hugh as well.

So, they left, and I mentioned to Hugh that they're normally so much more vibrant, both of them. And he guessed they're jealous, that seeing someone else's success was making them act strangely. The word "success" sent a chill up my spine, I won't lie. I was finishing up for the night, mainly just turning off lights, collecting measurements, when Hugh asked me out for a late dinner. It felt less like a business meal, but I agreed anyway.

He took me around the corner to a small Italian place. We had it practically to ourselves—soft candlelight, romantic. We drank wine and ate ravioli and he just seemed different. More open, less like the boss or a man ten years my senior. It felt like a date. I didn't mind that it felt like a date. He's a pretty mysterious person, and even after hours of me asking questions and him answering, I feel like I've only chipped at the surface. I guess I can blame the wine.

At the end of the night, he walked me to the corner to hail a cab. As we waited, I asked him if he was married or seeing anyone. It felt gauche, but he seemed like such a catch. Why wouldn't he be? He said no, in a sad way, like there was a story there, or maybe I'm just reading into him too much. But then he said he was a widower. What? I mean, he's not that much older than me.

I wanted to ask how she died, but that seemed rude. And he was all closed up, so I didn't pry, although my curiosity was close to bursting. Finally, he asked why I didn't have a boyfriend. I gave him the standard "all work and all art make Vivian a single girl" spiel. He said that was probably why my paintings were so good, that I was channeling all my love and passion into my art, leaving little room for anything else.

It was both the saddest and nicest thing anyone's ever said

to me. So I hugged him. Impulsive, I know, but what can you do? Blame the wine again. I said thanks for everything, for making my dreams come true, and for being so wonderful. He laughed and asked if he could kiss me.

The world slowed down then, the city vanishing, the only sound the blinker of the yellow cab that pulled up, and my heartbeat.

I already have the show, the cards are at the printers, blurbs have been published. He isn't using me. I'm not the ingénue on the sofa with the producer. I believe this. Hugh likes me, and I like him. So I said yes. And he did. And it was amazing. I didn't want to pull away it was so good. But he broke it off, and put me in the cab, handing me a twenty to get home safe.

I've been floating since I got back home, but I have no one to tell.

July 10th

The weekend was crazy busy with prep. I've decided to cram one more painting into the show. A new one. And I have exactly one month to get it and all the others completed. I have all this nervous energy I need to channel into something! I thought about doing a portrait of Hugh, but that seemed both weird and way too soon, considering. He's just in all my thoughts these last few days. After the "date" and the kiss, it was like he planted a seed in my skull. I was so on edge the next day, I just wanted to give him a call, to hear his voice. Instead, I went for broke and walked over to the gallery with a picnic basket. Figured if he was there, great, and if he wasn't, then I would go stuff myself full of cheese and wine with no one the wiser.

Luck would have it that he was there, toiling away alone in the empty gallery. The lights were all off and he sat in the gloom of the space, walls empty, air cool. He looked happy to see me, but his eyes were sunken in and he clearly was sick. He said he was just a little under the weather, but he'd love to duck out for an hour or two and get some sun and some food. I was giddy, standing there, basket obvious, knees knocking. I must have looked like such a kid—a girl with a crush. That's how I felt, but Hugh was nothing but sweet and grateful.

There's a small park down a few blocks from his gallery space. I scoped it out the other day. It was lunchtime and the park was fairly crowded, but miraculously we were able to find the perfect grassy spot, with a bit of sun and a bit of shade. I laid out the old blanket and emptied the basket, feeling a bit clumsy. Hugh just leaned back, warming himself and smiling up at me. He had sunglasses on, reflective ones that hid his eyes, but I could feel his gaze on me, and I loved it. I felt like I was a real adult, eating good brie that I could barely afford with an expensive Sancerre I bought to impress him. I wanted to show him that I have some taste, that I'm not just some college kid. I hope he sees me as cultured. I think I succeeded. His color still looked a bit yellowy and peaked under the shades, though.

Hugh told me about how he'd moved to the States when he was about my age—he's actually closer to twelve years older than me, give or take. So what? We're both adults. And twelve years isn't really that big a gap, especially considering we're both in the arts and share so much in common.

I could listen to him talk all day, with that sexy accent of his, the thoughtful way he tells his stories. He told me how his mother had also passed away. It was so nice to talk to someone who understands how hard it is to not have a mother, what an empty space it leaves. His mother died when he was a child. She was very sick, similar to my mom with her cancer. His father's still in England, but they're not close. Hugh said he was basically raised by wet nurses and nannies. His dad wasn't around much and he was something of a loner.

I told him about being an art kid in a pissant town. And I caught myself downplaying my childhood, to have more in common with him. I loved my parents and was popular, and I did win "Most Artistic" in a few yearbooks and really it wasn't that bad. But I kind of omitted all of that. Maybe not lying— just wanting him to not feel alone, wanting him to feel he can confide in me. I dug up all the isolation and awkwardness I could remember to share with him, and I may have exaggerated some of it, but I think he needed it. For all of his looks and apparent success, it seems he just wants to connect with someone.

But I needed to know about this dead wife. So I finally asked.

He told me they met in college. She was an American girl from a good family. In typical Romeo and Juliet fashion, they rushed off and got married even though her family was against it. But then she got sick (he didn't elaborate though I was super curious), and then she died. She was wealthy and he inherited a lot of money, which he used to move to New York and start his gallery——that had been their dream. He said the gallery and all his work with the arts was for her, that she'd been a brilliant artist. I have to say it was weird that he was so open, even about how his money came from a dead wife. It was clear he was still not over her, and the rest of the picnic took on a somber note. All the ghosts crowding between us.

We both lay back on the grass watching the clouds slide across the sky, and I took his hand. It was cool to the touch, but warmed quickly nestled in mine. I lifted that large hand to my mouth and kissed it. He propped himself up on one arm and looked down at me, casting a shadow over me. Even then he kept those glasses on, so I only saw myself. We kissed. It got a little adult for the park.

Hugh wanted me to come back to his place, and I wanted to go. But it was Gina's birthday dinner party. I was tempted to bail, or drag Hugh with me. But I knew Gina would be mad, and although she's been a jerk, it's still her birthday, and we were—are—best friends.

So I pulled myself away. Hugh was upset. More than I would have expected, enough to seem a bit weird, honestly, and bring back the paranoia that he was using me for sex.

So I left him and headed to the party. It was at a Tiki bar near our apartment. By the time I got there, Gina was already half in the bag, and Kyle was there, presumably back to being the boyfriend. A few people asked about my upcoming show, and it was clearly pissing Gina off. But they asked me!

Finally, Gina just freaked out on me, basically insinuating that I was fucking Hugh to get a show and that he was using me. I got angry enough that I said the thing I swore I wouldn't say, especially not at her party in front of all our mutual friends. "You're just jealous!" Gina's eyes filled with tears, her mascara running down her face. Kyle said maybe I should leave. KYLE! But whatever. I left. It was all bullshit anyway. This is a new chapter for me, one where I don't have to hang out with wannabes and never-wills.

July 12th

Hello Diary, I just read the last line I wrote the other night. Yikes.

I know I sound like a total snob, but I know I'm a better artist. I want it more. It's not a hobby, it's my career.

Gina and Kyle, they're just posers. Kyle is so hungry for the title, the fame, the success, but when he meets Hugh? When he has an actual career-creating opportunity he totally blows it, won't even return Hugh's calls. So today, I fired him as my manager. He isn't doing anything for the show, he isn't keeping up with Hugh or even working on promotional stuff. He didn't even protest, basically mumbled that I was ungrateful and took off out of the apartment.

Gina hasn't spoken to me in two days, and I know I hurt her feelings, but she must also see the truth right? Her work is inaccessible, huge, ugly. Who wants a ten-foot tree vagina? I think she likes the idea of being a New York-based artist more than the reality. If she wanted it, she should have been kissing my ass this whole time and sucking up to Hugh. But instead she gives me the silent treatment and acts like a baby. She doesn't even pretend to be excited for me. It's all about her. God, everyone is so selfish.

I shouldn't say everyone. Hugh really gets it, my work, he really loves art, and he has feelings for me. At least, I think so. I'm starting to feel like he's the only person that actually listens to me, or cares about me.

When I stormed out of the party the other night I called Hugh. It was late and I was a little tipsy, but he agreed to have a drink with me. We talked and it was nice, we made out in front of my building and it was nicer. By that time, though, Gina and Kyle were home so I didn't invite him up. Maybe another night. I'm sick of what other people think. I like him, he likes me, why can't we get together?

July 13th

Okay Diary, WE DID IT. And I think I feel okay about that. I know I'm not a gold digger, and I have no interest in sleeping my way to success. That's more Gina's thing, which is why she dates trust-fund bottom-feeder types like Kyle in the first place. But I digress.

Because what's happening with Hugh and me, it's magnetic, it's a tidal pull. Hell, it's celestial. The very the thought of him makes me feel better, happier. But it scares me; the attraction feels a bit fast, a bit dangerous.

I've been working like a maniac on the new piece. It's another self-portrait, this time I'm also using old photographs of me as a child and some of my mother to add to the time-passing effect. It's working, but I feel like something's missing.

I was tempted to ask Gina for input, since she was home, but she's still giving me the silent treatment. I had a desperate moment of wanting Hugh there. Why? I've never needed anyone to validate me in this way. About ten minutes later, the phone rang and it was Hugh! My heart somersaulted and I nearly sobbed with relief. He came over, he was in the neighborhood, calling from a pay phone, and like a knight in shining armor he arrived: handsome, but still a bit sick, and he immediately figured out what was wrong with the painting.

The portrait's eyes were staring off, he said, above and to the right. They looked too passive. They needed to confront the viewers, they needed to stare at them and not above them. It was a brilliant suggestion, and I hugged him in relief. Gina made herself scarce while he was in our apartment. She didn't even say hi to Hugh to be polite.

I'm beginning to think I need a new roommate. Or to move out.

To celebrate the breakthrough in the painting, Hugh took me to dinner at this lovely French place. I had a steak, and he had salad. We joked at the reverse stereotype, in that awkward way of first dates. We drank red wine till our lips and teeth were stained, and our eyes were glassy. We laughed, we touched hands on the table, our legs intertwined beneath.

He took me to his place: a gorgeous fancy townhouse. It has a bright blue door and Hugh explained it was a Greek thing, stands for good luck and protection. (His mother was from Greece and his father from England.) I was very, very drunk, and afraid with one misstep that I would break something priceless.

He led me upstairs to the large master bedroom, bed and curtains a crisp ivory like a fancy hotel room. I stumbled onto the bed, he crawled up beside me. In the end, I was left a puddle of sensation, slick with sweat and gasping, before passing out into a deep, coma-like sleep. Reading that back, it's a little Harlequin, but yeah, it was that good.

I woke up the next morning feeling especially hungover and if I'm being honest, I felt a little guilty, knowing what Gina would say. I dreaded doing the walk of shame into our apartment.

Maybe I should have waited until after the show, so as not to be such a cliché. But whatever, I like Hugh. Maybe I'm overthinking all of this.

What I did know that morning was that I was super hungover: queasy, shaky, and exhausted. Hugh had already poured me a huge glass of juice—thoughtful, right?

After breakfast, I went to shower. While washing up, I felt a stinging painful sensation on my inner thigh. It was a huge bite! Hugh had bitten me, hard enough to leave dental impressions. I tried to think back on when he could have done it, but couldn't. I was drunk but I wasn't so drunk I'd ignore him gnawing my leg! I don't think?

And besides, human mouths are dirty. I vaguely remembered that from science class, dirtier than a dog or cat. The bite was like a hickey on steroids and was already discolored and bruised. Everybody has something right? Some kink? Hell, I'd always fantasized about being spanked.

I won't lie though, I did feel a little weird about it. But I still like Hugh a lot. Like a real lot.

I know how this sounds, Diary, I have not entirely lost my mind. It was just one drunk night. With a particularly passionate love bite.

I went back to the apartment to grab my work clothes, and there was Gina judging me as I came in, as predicted, but this time even her nastiness bounced right off. The deadline for my show looms, and I'm just too busy to worry about Gina's feelings and opinions. Seriously, it's none of her business and I know what I'm doing.

July 18th

Hasn't been a lot of time to write the past few days. Been busy with work (trying not to get fired from the restaurant since I'm requesting so much time off for the show), not to mention I need to pay rent.

Spent another night with Hugh, and it was as amazing as the first. But sure enough, the next morning I had a nasty little reminder on the opposite thigh. I'm not psyched about this, but like the first time, I don't know when it happened! My thighs look pretty ugly, and the twin bites hurt. I planned to yell at him about it, opened my mouth to even, then he harpooned me with those swimmy eyes of his. I felt like a deer in the headlights, my anger instantly gone, leaving me feeling embarrassed. He asked what was wrong, and as much as I wanted to scream, "My fucking legs!" I clammed up. After the show, we can discuss it.

It's dumb to make it an issue, it's like one step past a hickey. A love bite.

I just need to stop obsessing over it and get my work done, focus on the good stuff.

July 22nd

Hello Diary,

Haven't been up to writing, been under the weather, and the looming gallery show and late nights with Hugh are definitely not helping. Getting sick now is just terrible timing. But in good news, I'm nearly done the new painting, working on the title now. . . . I wanted to capture time, me as child, me as teen, me as adult, and me older, all layered over each other semi-transparently on the same canvas. It's been one of the most challenging things I've ever done. But it's working and it looks great.

Hugh came by the other night and just raved over it, which made me feel good. Gina even peeped in on it and told me how much she liked it, and for her to break her silence, that must mean it's good, right?

Her compliment was the olive branch we needed. So that's a plus. I've missed her (although she pisses me off so bad sometimes). As soon as we got through the "I'm sorry I'm a bad friend" and all that, I couldn't help but start talking about Hugh. She actually listened. Gina said she would be happy for me as much as she could be (considering she still thinks Hugh has sketchy ulterior motives) and I said I would take that, on the condition that she actually give him a chance. So she and Kyle are going on a double date with us. Then she'll see that I haven't lost my mind, and that Hugh is pretty awesome.

Annoyingly, Hugh is the one acting all weird and reserved about the whole double date thing. I think it's hard for him because he is so on my side, and sees Gina and Kyle as lousy friends. Not to mention we all must look so young and immature to him. But he promised to be on best behavior and do it for me.

He's so thoughtful, and smart, and interesting. I can't wait for them to realize it.

July 24th

It's early morning. I just dragged myself home from Hugh's and wanted to write about the dinner last night while everything was fresh in my head. In short, the evening was a huge failure.

So, last night we had a reservation and Le Petit Cochon. Hugh and I headed over there after having a meeting with his art installers for the show. All that is good stuff. They helped me plan the lighting, and we even hung some things to do promo photos and get a feel for it. So that was awesome. Hugh and I got to the restaurant right on time, but of course Gina and Kyle were late. Hugh was bristly from the get-go. I tried to talk to him and he snapped at me.

They finally get there and it was weird, tense, awful, all of the above. Hugh, who is normally so charming was wooden and even shy? It was weird. Gina sat near me and talked to me, asked me questions, etc., but didn't really direct anything his way. She could barely look at him! Kyle just picked at his food and barely said anything to anyone. Gina is usually such a ball of energy and a constant stream of chatter. Kyle is the biggest schmooze around. But they sat across from us like two awkward children.

At one point, Gina excused herself to go to the bathroom, and I actually followed her, hoping maybe she would open up to me once we were alone. I cornered her and asked, assuming she was still pissed at me, or thought Hugh was using me. But she said no, insisted she was happy for me. When I pushed further, she said she just didn't like him.

Hugh? The hottest British gallery owner out there? How could you not? When I wouldn't let it go, she said he was creepy.

Creepy?

That was the worst thing she could say. It's not even that Hugh's using me, or is a sleaze, or has ulterior motives, or any of the things I expected her to say. Things that I could explain away because she was jealous. But creepy? I had nothing for that. Creepy is a visceral response. You can't argue someone out of a creepy verdict. I was upset, defensive. Gina finally, hands-up, left the bathroom in a huff, got Kyle, barely looked at Hugh, and dropped some cash on the table. And they just took off.

I was so embarrassed. Creepy?!

So that was our terrible dinner. The first part of my weird evening. Then we went back to his place, and he was all cold and aloof in cab the whole way. I only remembered I was having my period halfway through undressing. I had never let a man go down on me during my period. To be honest, I've always thought it was kind of icky. But he was into it so I let him.

I woke early this morning to him back at it again. I tried to push him off at first, groggy and feeling gross in the dawn light, but he said he loved doing it.

When he was finished, I offered to reciprocate in some way, but he turned me down and went back to sleep. I know so many women who complain about selfish lovers—it's nice not to have one! But still, the bad dinner date, the silent treatment, and then the not-totally-consensual morning wakeup all left me feeling a bit off.

So I got home, took a shower, and was happy to see no love bites anywhere. It was a relief, though I felt kind of ashamed that the first thing I did when I pulled my clothes off was to look for bites.

July 30th

God, this is hard to write, feels like I might pass out or throw up. I just got off the phone with Dad. He has cancer. How fucking unlucky.

Cancer, like Mom. The pancreatic cancer just swarmed her body and killed her barely six months after her diagnosis. He has prostate, which he told me is more common and treatable in men his age. I want to believe him, I do. But I think of him up there, sick and alone in that old house, and it kills me. I feel like the worst daughter in the world. Honestly, I wish he'd waited until after my show to tell me. And I know how messed up and selfish that sounds.

How can I stay excited for this show? Now I'll be looking for not one but two empty seats in that gallery, and it just makes me want to crawl into a hole and not come out of it. If my dad dies, when he dies, I'll be all alone. His only brother died in a car accident as a teenager, my mom was an only child. No cousins, nothing. I have no family. It's terrifying.

Dad sounded genuinely disappointed about missing my show. And I promised to head north to Hob's Valley and visit once all the craziness dies down. I even told him about Hugh a little, and he just kept chuckling and saying that he must be pretty great to have turned my head.

Anyways, enough about that, since I don't want to sit here crying my eyes out, worrying that I'll be an orphan soon.

In good news, I finished the final painting. I've decided to call it "States of Being." I'm feeling really prepared. Hugh is such a pro with stuff like this, and he's really been there for me every step of the way. I'm so grateful. I've decided once the show is over to give him the painting. I put all my excitement, all my nervous energy, all my passion for Hugh into it after all. I think it may be the best painting I've ever done.

Gina is back to the semi-silent treatment. I wanted to tell her about Dad, have a shoulder to cry on. But I'm still mad at her. I don't have the time or energy to make her like my boyfriend. That looks weird there on the page. Is he my boyfriend?! I was never much of a romantic, not really, not before this. But now? I didn't know I was incomplete until Hugh came. He's been such a constant, and he has been so sweet about my dad. I'm lucky to have someone like him looking out for me.

August 5th

Show is five days away and I'm excited, but in some ways I'll be more excited when it's over and done with. That sounds terrible. I guess I'm just scared to put myself out there. What if no one likes my work? What if it's poorly reviewed? I've always painted for myself, because I needed to. But now? It sounds pathetic and embarrassing, but, now I'm finding myself doing it for Hugh. I want him to be proud of me, I want his gamble on a nobody to pay off.

With my dad stuff, and Gina stuff, I have just wanted to be with him all the time. He makes me feel better, happier. When we're apart, even a few hours, it's like my skin breaks out in hives. When did I develop an obsessive personality? I've had boyfriends, some I genuinely thought I loved, but it's nothing compared to this yearning for Hugh. It's like I'm addicted.

I won't lie, though. I hate the bites. They hurt and they're ugly and the longer I'm away from him the more they ache, the slower they seem to heal. Everything else about our relationship is perfect, like romance-novel perfect. Being with him makes me realize that with every other guy it was just fucking. But this is different. Real. I'm head over heels in love.

I'm going to try to get some rest now. Been having a hard time sleeping, and the stress is getting to me about everything.

August 11th

I have arrived!

The gallery opening last night was a rousing success! I was so afraid no one would show up, or people would hate my work, or that Hugh would be upset with something. So many possible pitfalls! I made sure to drag every friend, colleague, and former professor in to stack the deck. Cool music, crisp champagne, wedges of cheese, the whole nine. In total, fifteen of my paintings were on display, with "States of Being" as the focus. The show was titled "Reflections in Time and Space."

At the time I came up with it, I thought it was brilliant and poetic, looking back it sounds a bit cheesy. But I digress. Even Kyle and Gina were cordial to me at the event, avoiding Hugh like the plague.

In the end, I sold nine and that totals almost five thousand bucks! I can't believe it. My bank account is trilling in anticipation. I'm going to pay down my credit card for once. If I never have another gallery show I'll be able to die happy. I did it, I succeeded!!! I had a well-received show of my own work, in an exclusive gallery in Chelsea!! I have a small stack of business cards and interested buyers. It's fucking amazing!

And through all of this, Hugh's been fantastic. The last few days I've been sleeping at his place more than my own. Granted, it's also much nicer than my place, and I don't have to deal with the roaches. Or Gina and Kyle. It's been really nice playing house with him—it's not hard for me to picture us living together down the line. I've been on cloud nine with him and the show.

But, even as I beamed and shook hands last night and received more praise than ever in my life, I was missing my folks. I don't believe in heaven, or ghosts really, but I like to think Mom was there, watching and proud. I dedicated the show to her. I'd never be the person I am now if not for her and her uncompromising belief in my talent.

And now it's done. The show will stay on view for the next month, but I won't have to be there, and if I'm lucky, more paintings will sell. What I want to do more than anything else now is just rest and sleep and regroup. I'm so tired lately, like I'm just dragging along, going through the motions.

The only thing I want to do now is snuggle up with Hugh someplace and be left alone. He understands how much this show took out of me. To celebrate, we're going away for the weekend, out of the city, to a small B & B someplace where no one can find us. It'll be perfect.

August 15th

We just got back from the weekend away. The B & B was lovely, a small old Victorian owned by a sweet elderly couple. I know I promised Dad a visit, but I knew it would be a sad visit. And I wanted to do something fun, a reward for all my hard work. The downside is that I was sick all weekend.

Hugh and I took it easy, walking the woodland trails, swimming in the local creek, picnicking. It was hard to keep my spirits up, though, feeling as lousy as I did. I thought the country air, the feeling of liberation and accomplishment, all of that would relax me, revitalize me. But that doesn't seem to be the case. I was really sick all three mornings, and weak throughout the day. Hugh was concerned, and kept giving me vitamins and trying to feed me, even when my stomach was upset.

He was very understanding, but I know he was disappointed. Hell, I was disappointed, who wants to be sick on a romantic getaway?

August 19th

Hugh had to leave town for a few days, so we've been apart. I'm feeling a little better, but still sick in the mornings, and I've been unbelievably tired. When Hugh first left I was beside myself, which is crazy considering we've been dating for such a short time. But as the days passed something else has weaseled its way into my brain. Anger about the bites. They are really gross-looking. And between the bites and the fatigue, I'm thinking about going to a doctor.

Hugh's so wonderful in every other way. But it's summer, which means tank tops, miniskirts, and shorts, and it's hot in my apartment. I don't want anyone to see my body. He's supposed to call me tonight. I'm going to try and get my courage together and confront him about it. I have to.

August 24th

I'm not getting better, vomiting in the morning, dizzy, pale. I lost a few more pounds, fast. I tried to talk to Hugh about it the other night on the phone, and he just . . . brushed it off. It made me angry, really angry, actually. I've never felt this way about him since we've been together, but the distance, his voice tinny down the line of a phone, it made me see him a bit clearer. I told him the bites need to stop and he said sure, but he thought I liked them. Thought I was into it. He accused me of being deceptive, of letting him think things were fine, while secretly feeling this way. Said it hurt his feelings. WHAT? I don't think my request was too much. I cried. He said he'd be home in a few days and he'd take care of me. He said he loved me. First time for that. I just wish it hadn't been over the phone while I was crying and angry. Much less romantic.

August 27th

Hugh dropped a bomb on me when he got back: he wants me to move in with him. It's a bit rushed, no? We've been dating for barely two months.

He's been a good nurse, forcing lots of rest and fluids. He even made me eat liver the other day, which was disgusting and I nearly threw up immediately. He's worried about my health, and I love him for it. But I can't help finding his doctor aversion strange. As soon as I'm away from him I start to question his intentions. What am I doing? I'm obviously sick. I need a doctor. Hugh keeps talking me out of going, reminding me I have no insurance, and that most medicine is bullshit anyway.

What's making me feel crazy is that he keeps insisting I'm fine, that I just need more iron, that I need more rest. He wants me to move in with him, and that way he can care for me. It feels too soon. I think I need to get better before I make any hasty decisions. I'm resting plenty. I just work at the restaurant two days a week now. Even that's wearing me out though, dragging my bones around, feeling like I creak when I move. I know he thinks I'm fine, but I know my body and I've never felt like this before.

I need time to think about all of this, and get some space. Is it weird that I find it hard to think clearly when Hugh is around? Maybe I just feel crowded because I don't feel well. Either way, I'm going to my apartment for a few days.

August 29th

Gina's taking me to the Planned Parenthood clinic. Even she's worried about me, and she doesn't care about much of anything. I must look like total shit to get on her radar.

The past few weeks have changed her attitude considerably. She didn't like Hugh initially, but now she thinks he's bad for me, that he's making me sick! I told her she's crazy, that she doesn't know him. That yes, it's a coincidence that I've gotten ill so fast but there are other reasons besides Hugh. Dad has fucking cancer after all, plus there was the stress of the big show. Deep inside I want to believe that Hugh loves me, that I love him, that he doesn't want to hurt me. So I'm going to the doctor and he doesn't need to know. I'll tell him if there's anything to tell. I'm a grown woman, I know my body, and my body is saying go to the damn doctor.

I don't want Hugh to worry over nothing.

August 30th

Fuck. I just got back from the doctor and all I can get myself to write is FUCK.

Not only do I have severe anemia, I'm also apparently pregnant. Pregnant! It hasn't sunk in yet. I'm just going to bury it a little further and focus on the other revelations of the checkup for now. The anemia is treatable, so that's something, but the doctor was suspicious of why I was suddenly so severely anemic. I thought about lying, blaming my period, blaming my diet, but as she looked at my skin, at the bites, she got more concerned.

She poked at a particularly deep bite on my inner arm. It was just about healed, the skin pink and shiny. I pulled away from her fingers, pressing my arm tight to my side. I was too embarrassed to face her, staring instead at the giant reproductive chart. It's funny how much a woman's uterus resembles a bull skull. I wonder if Georgia O'Keefe was deliberately painting women's genitals in her western paintings but not, as she vehemently asserted, in her lily paintings. Strange the things you think about when your brain is about to shut down.

I tried to change the subject, tried to direct the doctor to a different line of questioning, but she was having none of it. She asked me point blank if I was being abused. I was horrified, defensive. I explained that my boyfriend enjoyed biting but it was no big deal. She was suspicious and explained at length how germy the human mouth was, and how prone to infection those bites could be. She was doubtful that I could be losing so much blood through this practice but suggested I stop. I just nodded dumbly.

I could practically read her mind: she thought I was irresponsible, reckless, and more importantly, she thought I was in an abusive relationship.

The more I said I wasn't, the more defensive I sounded, so I gave up. Instead I just sat there, numb, my arms wrapped around my belly. I imagined my insides, past the ropes of intestines, the bags of gasses and acids, to the tiny life that was sprouting. It was horrific and euphoric at the same time. I didn't know how to feel about anything. Sure I'd thought about being a mother "someday," in that way people say things they have no concept of how to plan for. It was just something for the future. But now? I've been dating Hugh for only a few months, I'm barely employed, and I have a sick father up north and no other family. I can't have a fucking baby. Can I?

I should just get rid of it. It would be better if I put the "someday" back on the shelf—now is not the time for a baby. The doctor gave me some information on abortion, and tried again to get me to talk about the bites. I was like a fortress though, giving her nothing and trying to keep from going ballistic.

Finally, she handed over the prescription for heavy-duty iron pills and an antibiotic. I met Gina in the waiting room, but I knew if I stopped to talk I'd start crying, so I just walked out, Gina running after me. Once we were a few buildings down, I leaned against a wall, thankful for the support, and then burst into tears. I slid down to the dirty sidewalk, crying because I was fucking pregnant, crying because I was weak. Crying because I was scared. Gina wrapped her arms around me, rocking back and forth. And although I didn't want to admit it, I knew Hugh was to blame for everything.

September 1st

Today didn't go the way I planned. I have to decode this cluster-fuck my life has turned into. I feel like I'm trapped on this terrible carnival ride that I don't remember stepping onto.

After a day of crying and feeling sorry for myself, I finally resigned myself to go talk to Hugh about the pregnancy. I'd been 99.9% sure that I was going to get an abortion, unless he was so persuasive and excited to be a father that he could change my mind. So I took the train straight to Hugh's gallery. I walked right up to the door and my nerve dried up. I circled the block, bought a peppermint tea at the fancy coffee shop on the corner, and sat sipping it on someone's stoop, building my resolve.

Closing my eyes, I could feel the sun on my face, the warmth, and just breathed. I rubbed my stomach trying to think about the future. Let's say I keep the baby. In this crazy scenario, let's even say that Hugh is happy about it, or at least supportive. I move into his lovely townhouse, maybe he even proposes to make his traditional father happy, and so my sick old dad doesn't think his only daughter is irresponsible. I move in, we turn the home office into a nursery, I paint a mural for the baby on the wall. Something from A.A. Milne's Pooh stories maybe. Make the place beautiful. Hugh and I run the gallery together—I paint, he works, and we're fantastic parents. When people ask about our lives we laugh, we say it wasn't exactly how we planned it, and the baby came sooner than we were expecting, but it was okay because we loved each other. And everything worked out in the end.

But I couldn't live in my fantasy. I needed to face Hugh. I got my courage together and I went back to the gallery. I rapped on the door until he came out from the back smiling and waving. I stepped in, the space much darker and cooler than outside, the sweat on my skin drying instantly.

I had to tell him. I had to tell him everything. The fear squeezed at my chest so I was almost hyperventilating. I swayed, reached out and steadied myself against the wall. I eased into a chair at Hugh's desk and asked for water. My shaking hands were so sweaty they could barely grip the glass. I thought we'd have so much more time before life intervened in our romantic fairy tale. My mind circled back to the doctor then, how concerned she was about his bites. And suddenly, it all made sense. Everything he cooked for me was iron rich; the lentils, the vegetables, the liver. He knew. He'd always known.

And if he knew, it was because he'd done it before. I wanted to scream, to attack him, to throw up. He knew he was making me sick.

Time stretched out and my vision tunneled. Finally, I blurted out that I went to the doctor, and before I told Hugh anything more, he had the gall to actually look angry. I told him I was anemic. He was angrier than I'd ever seen. Claimed I betrayed him, seriously. He stayed on the other side of his desk, stone-faced, black eyes shining, and for the first time I understood why Gina thought he was creepy. It hurt me that the man I was so in love with could look at me this way.

I asked him why. Why did he bite me, why do it? He didn't answer, his lips a slim line. Frustrated, I told him I was pregnant. Any color in his already pale face drained and he asked if I was sure it was his. Seriously! I would laugh if it wasn't so terrible. Then he started pacing, all upset, hand over his mouth, looking at me over and over again. Like it was his life that was ruined. And then he asked how soon we could get rid of it.

Get rid of it. Get rid of it. How many women have heard those words from men who claimed to love them?

In that moment, something in me cracked. I guess it was the automatic assumption that the baby would be aborted, that we wouldn't even discuss it. I didn't even want the damn thing, but at that moment, I put my hand on my stomach, as if to muffle his voice, keep the baby from hearing. And I connected with it then. It was more than an inconvenience.

Hugh took in my body language and froze. Then he rushed toward me and I flinched, pulling away from him. There was something in his eyes, something cold and cruel and I didn't know how I could have loved this man with such mindless abandon. God, I'm an idiot.

I asked why, why was he so against having the baby? Was it his reputation? Was it about money? Was it me? He said no to all of that, tried to remind me how young I was still, how talented I was. How we were still so new as a couple. All of it, about how a baby would make it impossible to paint, of how we were still learning how to love one another. And I know that he's right, that's the crazy thing. I agree with him on all those things. I've been saying it in my head over and over for so long. And yet . . .

Then he pulled out the big guns—he thought I wasn't responsible enough to be a mother, that I wasn't mature enough. I stood up. I know this sounds weird but I could almost feel him in my head trying to manipulate me. And weirder still, I felt like he's been doing it to me all along.

His touch, his voice, all turned my stomach in a way they never had before. I could see he was lying, that none of his reasons were the real reason. I demanded the truth. He wouldn't answer, so I turned to leave.

A few steps from the door he grabbed my arm. Hard. He slammed me against the wall. I have never in my life been so scared as at that moment. He was nearly nose to nose with me, eyes wild. I begged him to let me go and he said no. I started to cry. He wants to kill me. There was malicious violence in his eyes, in the set of his jaw, in the crushing grip of his hand on mine.

My tears must have gotten to him, though, because he abruptly let go and stepped back. I just stood there crying and scared. After a long pause, he told me that this baby would kill me. That if I survived the pregnancy, which itself would be a miracle, then the baby would be my undoing. That was the weird word he used—undoing. He said if I had the baby, it would be my problem and mine alone. That he wasn't responsible for what happened.

And then Hugh begged me one last time to just have the abortion so that everything could go back to normal.

To normal? How could we ever possibly do that?

I left.

September 3rd

I just reread my last entry and it got me crying all over again. I haven't been back to see Hugh and I won't return his calls. He came by the apartment a few times with flowers as if that would mean anything and Gina threatened to call the cops on him. I've barely been able to get out of bed, but I've made my decision.

I called Hugh and left a message on his machine that I'd had the abortion, and that everything would be fine. He called back but I let it go to messages. His relief chilled me. He told me I wouldn't regret this choice, and that it just wasn't the right time. He apologized for overreacting. He wanted to take me to dinner, to apologize, and to give me the money to cover the procedure. . . . Quite the gentleman. I didn't return the call.

Then I called Dad, told him I was coming up to stay with him for a while. That I wanted to make sure he was doing okay and I wanted to help him through the chemotherapy. He sounded so old and frail on the phone that I couldn't bear to tell him about the baby.

I'm so scared right now. I remember Mom, bald and thin, the wounds that wouldn't heal, the stomach that could barely keep water down. I don't know if I can stand to watch another parent die of cancer.

How could everything be so good and then suddenly be so bad? I just don't know how to feel anymore. Gina thinks I've gone insane. She doesn't want me to go to Dad's. She thinks it's the worst idea. I tried to explain to her: Dad's sick, I'm pregnant, I'm broke, and I lied to Hugh so I can't be in the city. She just doesn't understand why I need to have this baby. I guess I don't either. It's like my body is on autopilot, and this baby has already taken the wheel. Maybe that's just biology, and how all pregnancies are. It's all very irrational. I mean, my life's just fallen into place, the stepping stones all laid out, the opportunities, the (not so) great relationship, everything. But, and I can only admit this here in my diary, I can't give up this baby. I try to picture getting up on that table, spreading my legs, letting them cut it out and I can't. It's like it, the fetus, won't let me. Now isn't that crazy? How could everything I ever wanted turn to straw in a matter of weeks?

Doesn't matter. I'm going. To be with Dad, to give this kid inside me a fighting chance.

X.

It was almost dawn. I stared at my mother's words for a long time. I wanted to read on, but my eyes ached, and my stomach was squeezed into a fist of nerves. I understood how she felt at the moment she wrote that last entry. I too had a monkey's paw wish that had gone sour. I wanted the diary to fill in the spaces, but more than anything it opened gaps wider.

I stood and stretched, my back popping. So, my mother had been in a relationship with a man who was biting her and drinking her blood. That explained the scars everywhere for sure. He'd also been terrified of her having a child, namely me. He'd warned her that having me would be her undoing, a flowery and strange warning. And now she was downstairs dying. He was right. His predictions had come true, and I looked to be following in his footsteps without knowing he existed. A silent fear that I didn't dare give voice to rose up, an image of Sabrina beneath me, my mouth to her throat. I weighted it down with a mound of stones and left my room. Tommy slunk from one of the smaller middle bedrooms, meowing loudly for breakfast, startling me. I patted his head and picked him up as I passed my mother's bedroom.

My mother was where I'd left her, but I couldn't go in just yet. My emotions were swirling. There was a temptation to erase it all, to pretend the last three days had never happened and just go on from where I'd left off. I watched her from a crack in the door, the bedroom dimly lit by a seam of light between the curtains. She was bundled in her blankets, her pale skin deeply lined and shadowed. Her hair a thin puff of cotton candy, her rheumy eyes shiny in the scant light. Forty years old . . .

If she'd never met Hugh, if she'd never had me, what would her life have been like? She was a talented painter, she had friends and a life. Happy. She'd have been happy. I closed my mother's door and went to the kitchen to start a very early breakfast since I was too wired to sleep.

Once the water for oatmeal was heating and the coffee was burbling, I plopped down into a chair, fists pressed to my eyes. I wanted desperately to not feel bad for myself, but I'd never been more conflicted, never felt more unwanted. Obviously, my mother had had me, since here I was, and it was as horrific as Hugh had implied. But how much of that was self-fulfilling prophecy? How much of that was an isolated, unbalanced artist trying to raise a child on her own? And if illness ran in the family, it wasn't too out-there to think that there would be a combination of postpartum depression and complicated health issues. I'd believe my mother went mad and was riddled with cancer more than that she'd had an affair with a vampire. . . .

And there it was. The word I'd been hiding from all this time. It came with a slippery, nauseous feeling. Vampire. Vampire.

Vampire. Vampires weren't real. They were fairy-tale monsters.

But there was no question that I had bitten Sabrina. That Hugh had bitten my mother, over and over.

While the oatmeal cooked, I washed the dishes, wiped the counters and table. It did little good. This poor old house needed a bulldozer more than a mop. The floor sagged, the sink leaked, the drafts caused wind to scream through. I stared out the window at the woods, desperately wanting out of my head. I focused on the barren, gnarled trees and angry churning sky. Anytime now it would be winter. And the fields would be covered with white.

I gathered my mother up, changed her, and brought her down to the parlor. Once seated and blanketed I brought out her breakfast. Instead of fleeing back to the kitchen, I sat with her by the stove. The moments ticked on, the scrape of spoon against bowl the only sound between us. It yawned wide, the oceans of unsaid things, repressed anger, and a lifetime of disappointments. Mine, hers, it was hard to find where one began and the other ended, our lives braided tightly in a sad, silent symbiosis. Deciding to go for broke I cleared my throat. Her eyebrows squeezed together, just once, so I knew I had her attention. I turned to her.

"I went up into your studio yesterday."

I waited and watched her face. No response. She watched the firelight in the stove, I watched her. The clock ticked in the corner. Why lie? Even having the evidence of the paintings and journal, I was a coward. I scrutinized her ancient-looking, empty face, tried to reconcile it with the girl in the photos and journal. Tried to understand her choice to move up her to her father's house and have me, giving up everything she cared for. I stared at my hands, nails blunt, fingers long. Not my mother's hands. Hugh's apparently. I steeled myself and pressed on:

"The paintings in the attic, of me as a monster . . . hurt."

Still nothing.

"And I found your hidden journal. I hoped it would give me some context. Help me understand who you are, why we live the way we do."

This got a reaction. When I said journal her face contorted, the sides of her mouth pulled down like they were fish-hooked. She nodded solemnly, and with one shaky hand she pushed up her sleeve revealing her forearm, mottled with scars and ropey veins. She slowly lifted it to me. When I didn't take her arm, she frowned, easing her hand back into her lap, her gaze back to the fire in the stove.

"Why did you let him do this to you?"

My mother swallowed audibly and looked distressed. The emotion surprised me. I had the fleeting urge to take her hand, offer comfort. One tear glinted on her face, hovering on her waxy cheek. Time stretched, her silently crying, while I tried not to fidget and demand answers. She cleared her throat. It was loud and phlegmy, no doubt a challenge since it'd been two years since she'd truly spoken. I waited expectantly. She swallowed again, looked up at me. Her eyes intense, focused on mine, and unnervingly clear.

"If you still don't know, you're blind," she rasped.

I nearly fell to the floor. It had been years, actual years, since this woman had said that many words. Her voice sounded like storm winds cutting through drafty houses. Her fetid breath still hovered in the air between us long after she spoke. And this was what I got? I wanted to probe, to ask more questions, to actually have a conversation. But her eyes were clouding over, her head slowly turning back toward the fire. Dismissed.

I jumped up fast, the urge to shake her, or slap her overwhelming.

"If you still don't know, you're blind? What the hell does that mean?"

Nothing. Not even a blink. My mother had retreated into her head again, to wherever she spent her days, escaping this life she'd built. I waited a few beats. Finally, after asking, shouting, begging with no response, I stormed out of the room. I was honestly scared of what I might do if I stayed.

My hands trembled. Two years of total silence, and now this. My mother was as inscrutable as a sphinx. There was no questioning the blatant hatred that filled her eyes when she'd said those words. I had been a fool all these years, cleaning, cooking and slaving. Enduring the quiet loathing, the loneliness. All of it for nothing.

If I didn't know why I should not have been born, then I was blind? Bitch. Nasty, evil old bitch. Was it my fault she got involved with a fucked-up man, a wannabe vampire, who didn't even want his baby? Was it my fault that my mother decided to have that baby on her own, isolated, and poor, without a support system? Was it my fault her parents were dead, that she had no friends, that she was sick?

I paced like a caged animal. No, it wasn't my fault, but that was the universe for you. It was intrinsically unfair. I would never get an apology, and I would never get the answers I needed from my mother. There was no justice. I was a child of spite. Hugh had controlled my mother, and she'd had me to prove she could. My mother had molded all of her anger and disappointment into a daughter-sized shape.

I was in the kitchen breathing heavily, my anger looking for an outlet. I glanced at the stove, the temptation to turn on the gas and just fucking leave this place beckoning. The black thing in me, the snake beneath my skin, demanded restitution and violence. Destruction. Pain.

But it was futile, and a cold truth burrowed out from deep inside me: I had no one else. My mother hadn't ever wanted me, not really. I now knew my father wasn't some Prince Charming, but instead something much darker.

If I weren't terrified of what would happen to me, I'd put my mother in a nursing home, let the state take her right then. Or if I found her dead tomorrow morning, fetal and stiff, cold in the dawn light, I wouldn't even feel sad, I would feel free.

"If you still don't know, you're blind." I repeated this to myself, looking out the window at the backyard. The rusty swing set was moving in the breeze. I could picture myself a young girl sitting on it, alone, whiling away the hours.

But my mother assumed I knew something from that damn journal, something that would explain why she hated me so. So the only answer I would get would be to finish it.

I was so tired.

In my room, the ghost of Sabrina was everywhere. I could picture her spinning in my desk chair, dancing, sitting with me on the bed. My breath hitched. I wanted her back. I wanted a life where I wasn't on the outside looking in. And if I couldn't have Sabrina, or any sort of normal life, then I needed to face that. I needed to know why, even if it hurt.

I pulled out the journal in a vain attempt to solve the sphinx's riddles.

XI.

November 3rd

Hello, old friend. Sorry it's been a while since I've written. I guess I just haven't had the energy. It's funny, since I've never been one to keep a journal, and always thought there was something kind of sad about dumping all your secrets into a book. Something egotistical at its core. But I've come to understand something over these past few months. Mainly that I literally have no one else to talk to. I can't go to a therapist. They'll think I'm crazy, delusional. I can't tell my father, he's too fragile. It's only me, alone.

It's amazing how quickly you become alone. I had a life, and now it's all gone. I can't even tell you exactly when it went, really, but I need to vent. I need to write, or I'm afraid of what I'll do.

I don't want to do this alone. But that's the choice I made, and I'm stuck with it now, I guess. And I don't want this child. A part of me, a big part, doesn't understand why I don't just go and do it. Get rid of it. It all sounds so simple. But, and here's the strange thing, even though I want to make the appointment, I can't. It's as if this baby already has some control of my feelings and my choices. Crazy-sounding, huh?

But I'm starting to think things weren't as good with Hugh as I've been telling myself. When I left the gallery, my arm still stinging where Hugh squeezed it, it was like the tether between us snapped. I think about his face, his voice, and his touch and it repulses me now. Psychologically, even physically.

A man who doesn't stand in solidarity with the woman he knocked up is a coward. A man who is cagey about something potentially life-threatening to me, or whatever bullshit he's peddling, is a coward. The man who scars my body for his own pleasure without my consent is a coward. My desire for him and for the life he could give me really messed with my judgement, but it's finally leaving my system. It feels good to write this, cathartic, therapeutic. The man is obviously disturbed. Eccentric is one thing, kinky is another.

I have to take supplements now to improve my blood volume and deal with my iron deficiency. The bites Hugh left won't heal. It's like they don't want to scab over, and when they finally do, they scar. It's strange how the longer I'm away from him, the more I can see him for who he really was. The revulsion isn't just morning sickness, I know it. He may be handsome, and funny, and wealthy, and intelligent, and a million other things, but that's not enough. Maybe it's the pregnancy or the hormones, but it's like a lightbulb over my head. A wake-up call that I was in an abusive relationship with a sick person.

It's insane that I'm going to keep this child. And I worry I won't be able to love it properly. And besides, I have no job and my painting money will last us maybe a few more months—if

I'm super careful. I love NYC—hell it was always my dream to make it here—but I can't survive here as a single mom. God, I'm going to miss the city, miss my friends and my life. But I have to have this baby. I have to, like some sort of compulsion. Maybe all the love I had for Hugh has transferred to this life inside me?

Hugh is obviously unwell, and maybe even psychotic.

But I can be a good mother to this child. I can give it a chance.

It's all nuts. And I'm terrified. I've stayed in the city as long as I could, but it's becoming obvious that I'm pregnant. I'm packing up and will be out of here by the end of the month. My dad is excited for the company—his last surgery had complications and now he has home nurses visiting. So it's good that I'll be there. We'll be a good family, the three of us, I really think so. Maybe I'm delusional, but I need to believe that Dad will get better, he just has to. And who knows, maybe he'll be well enough to watch the baby while I work in the daytime? Or maybe I'm crazy. But there are no other choices. Dad has to get better and I have to have this baby. It'll all be okay, it has to be. Hugh is too connected in NYC. This is a small city when you're trying to hide. So, Fresh Start—here I come!

November 10th

My father's recent surgery didn't go as planned, and he may need to go back into the hospital. I have to leave sooner than planned to be with him.

I work, I sleep, and I lie. I feel this is all I do in a day. I haven't had time to paint, and the doctor has frowned upon me being near all the turpentine and fumes anyway. Carcinogens, apparently. I thought I'd go nuts without being able to paint, but I've been so dead tired that my free time is reserved for sleep anyways.

The doctor's noticed something problematic with the pregnancy already, mainly that I can't shake the anemia. How am I still anemic? I take so many supplements and shit I'm practically an exclusive carnivore. I only went to the appointment because there was blood in my urine. Apparently, anemia while pregnant is not uncommon, but it's worrying that nothing seems to be getting my iron count up. I'll work on it with whatever doctor I go to up north. I can't hide my pregnancy much longer. I've gained very little weight though. I think I've lost more than I've gained. But my stomach grows. I look like a starving child from those fundraising commercials, all distended bellies and skeletal limbs.

Whenever I start to lose my nerve about all of this, I think of Hugh's face nearly nose to nose with mine, the vise grip on my arm, that wave of fear. The knowledge that he'd truly hurt me and the baby. It gives me the resolve I need to keep going. It's survival. Soon, I'll be out of the city and starting a new life. A new family.

November 15th

Dad slipped into a coma last night. I'm writing this in the waiting room of the hospital. Visiting hours aren't for another hour.

I can't stop crying, nearly crashing my rental van driving up here. I packed up everything, filled the U-Haul with my paintings and hit the road. I basically just drove off the face of the earth, didn't even leave Gina my dad's address. Have I lost my mind??

I got home to Hob's Valley late at night and it was such a relief to be back in the house. It's still the home of my childhood. Mom's presence is everywhere, and though it's gut-wrenching, it's also comforting. The house is looking rough, though. Even at night I can see the peeling paint, and the porch is lopsided, but it's home and I don't care.

My dad's been living on the first floor only, sleeping on a cot in the front parlor, so the upstairs is quite cold. It was a relief to see my room's still like I left it. I haven't been to visit in almost two years, but it's all the same, just a bit dustier. I curled up in my old bed and I was asleep before I even peeled off my coat.

This morning I headed straight over to the hospital. Dad was asleep, looking small and fragile, wires and tubes covering him, sustaining him.

No one's here besides me. I'm in a dingy waiting room, news blaring, yellowed magazines in front of me, alone, writing. The longer I sit here, the more I fight the pull to flip through ancient parenting magazines.

November 28th

He died. He fucking died. Never regained consciousness, and then died in the night. I dropped the phone when the call came through, crumpled to the floor in my kitchen like a stringless puppet. Just hugging my ever-growing belly, not sure if I wanted to scream, puke, or cry. Or maybe all three.

My poor dad. He was the sweetest man alive, and I really wanted him to be a grandparent to this little girl. It's a girl. Dr. Blake, my old pediatrician and the only doctor in town, confirmed it at the ultrasound I went to three days ago.

I can't believe Dad is dead. I rubbed my belly for support the whole ride to the hospital, where I got to say my goodbyes to a corpse. Dad was so tiny, face all hollowed out. When I think of him, my childhood memory of him, it's as a big jovial man. Big bear hugs, a place of comfort. Having Dad to help me, to love us both, I don't think I realized how much I'd banked on that. How through force alone I thought he could kick the cancer and we'd all be all right. And now there's no one. I was a fool, again. And now he's dead and I need to survive, somehow. I have a funeral to arrange, and a house to take ownership of. Good thing Dad had some savings and a life insurance policy. It'll keep me in paints and electricity for a while, at least.

Turns out Dad also prepaid his funeral arrangements—thank God!—and he's going to be interred beside Mom in the town cemetery. That's a relief since it's shockingly expensive to dig a hole and put someone in it. That said, I would've much preferred Dad alive to the damned money.

I finally emptied and returned the U-Haul. I just dumped all my stuff in the old guest room for now. I don't really need party dresses or old prom photos right now. I don't know why I didn't just toss everything before leaving the city. It all means nothing to me now, here. Earrings? Who cares? I'm alone, totally and utterly alone. God, I wish Mom was here, that someone was here to tell me everything is for a reason, everything will work out, when a door closes a fucking window opens, all those useless platitudes that might help me at this moment. I can't believe I never even got to say goodbye.

I whisper to the baby that we'll be a team. That everything is going to work out fine. I hope she believes me. I don't.

December 2nd

The funeral was small, cheap, and sad. Dad wasn't a very social guy, and a lot of his friends are gone, or old, or dead. A sprinkling of Mom's friends came, left over from her Rotary Club days, and the few old timers that still lived in town. My pregnancy was a definite topic of conversation—the unwed mother who came back from the amoral city to bury her father. An orphan now in a big old house. I'm going to be the cautionary tale to scare the high school kids into marrying early and staying in town where they're safe from horror and temptation—I just know it.

I cried openly and dramatically in church. I've never cared what this town thought of me, why start now? I could barely bring myself to look at the photo of my parents on the casket. Their wedding photo. They were so happy, so young. I see so much of my own face in both of them. Mom's ginger hair, Dad's nose. I think about the baby. I wonder if she'll look like us as well. Of course, it makes me think of Hugh.

Dr. Blake was kind enough to prop me up at the gravesite and even drive me home. I remember getting lollipops from him after a shot, and stitches from a fall off a bike in junior high. I think he went to the funeral because he pities me. But I'll take what I can get. And whatever his reasons, he's been really kind to me, going above and beyond for me and my baby.

December 10th

A few days after the funeral, I went to my monthly checkup, and Dr. Blake's brows were knitted together in a frown the entire time. He was very concerned about my iron levels and blood pressure. My heart is being stressed by the lack of oxygen in my blood he said. He prescribed some medication and gave me a transfusion. I debated telling him about Hugh's warning. That the baby was a monster, that it would be my undoing. But I didn't, and besides, the baby is fine, he says, in fact it's surprising how good the baby is doing considering how ill I am. It's such a relief. I tried not to think about Hugh. I tried not to think about anything. I dug out my old bassinet and playpen. Luckily my mother was a hoarder who really wanted grandkids, so there were bags of ancient baby clothes, high chairs, and toys.

December 20th

I'm chugging on, sad but surviving. The days are long and snowy and boring. I'm realizing more and more why I left and went to the city. It's just so lonely here. We live on Main St. which you would think would have a little more life. But it doesn't.

I go to the general store and get the hairy eyeball for being a fallen woman. The library's the same, me and a dusty, judge-y librarian. I think being alone, cooped up and pregnant is making me crazy. It's embarrassing to write, but here it is: I've been eating things I shouldn't. It's like an obsessive desire, but not for food. Chalk, buttons, pencil erases. My regular appetite is non-existent, but every time I find one of those items in a junk drawer or on the floor, my mouth starts salivating. I need to talk to Dr. Blake about that at my next appointment, but I'm afraid. I just can't take much more.

The complications in this pregnancy are making it impossible to not think about Hugh's warning. What could run in his family that would be so dangerous to mother and child? My "undoing."

I can't think. I need to rest.

January 10th

Dr. Blake was kind enough to start making house calls. It's uncommon, but everything about my pregnancy is a little off. I'm pushing that to the side. I can't think about that; I can't think about what will happen when She arrives. I just have to eat, sleep, and take my vitamins. I finally confessed my peculiar cravings, and after some tests it looks like I am suffering from pica. Which is a crazy disease I have never heard of that can sometimes be triggered by extreme anemia.

The doc told me as soon as he can get my iron levels evened out, the cravings should go away and I'll just want pickles and ice cream like most pregnant ladies.

I want to believe him. I feel like a lunatic frantically stuffing buttons and chalk in my mouth all the time. I need to get healthy for this baby. I'm looking forward to meeting her. Just to have the company will be nice. I'm so alone here in this big old house. I only have pictures of myself on the walls to keep me company. I try to sketch to pass the time, but the exhaustion's made everything a challenge. Even writing is hard. My thoughts are too boggled.

February 14th

Well, it's Valentine's Day. I'm celebrating it by sitting alone in a freezing giant old house in the middle of nowhere. Dr. Blake was sweet enough to call and check in on me today. He insists it was a coincidence that it was Valentine's Day. I don't believe him, and that makes him all the sweeter. I keep wanting to call Gina, or some of the old gang, but I'm scared to. I picture Hugh's face, the cold, crazy, threat in his eyes. I don't want him to find me. And worse, in a way, I don't want Gina and them to know where I am, and what a charity case I've become. Would they think I got what I deserved? Sleeping with a gallery owner, being charmed like a naïve child by his wealth and influence. And what would I to say? They were right. I was such a fool falling for Hugh the way I did. I can't stomach Gina's glib judgement—better to just keep on alone. Besides, I've made my choice, probably the worst choice in the world. But She will be here in April whether I like it or not. So I better prepare.

April 16th

Two nights ago, I went into labor, when a piercing pain woke me up. I got myself up, more scared than I have ever been and waddled to the bathroom. I felt wet and was surprised to see my water had broken, soaking my nightgown. I called Dr. Blake in a panic, and he called me an ambulance. I changed, cleaning myself up as much as I could before the main event. I've never felt such choking terror, such a need to go back in time and put the genie back in the bottle.

The whole time in the ambulance, I just kept wishing all of this had been a terrible dream. I'd wake up to find I was in my apartment in NYC, Hugh with his arm over me, his body pressed to my back. In the next room over Gina would be sound asleep—even Kyle would be there, snoring softly. We'd have stayed out too late having cocktails and discussing a museum opening we'd just attended. It would have been a fantastic night.

Reality intruded when I felt more wetness spilling from between my legs and it was red, everywhere red. I was screaming until I lost consciousness from blood loss.

I feel like my world is centered on blood. My blood. My relationship with Hugh, my pregnancy, and my hospital visits, all sanguine. Apparently, I had a hemorrhage, my chronic anemia making it even worse, and I was bleeding like a stuck pig.

I went into shock and almost died. After copious transfusions, they saved the baby and me. I named her Jane, after Mom, who'd wanted a granddaughter so badly, but never would get to meet her. It was scary and exhausting, all the more surreal blinking in and out of consciousness. And at the end of the tunnel someone drops a baby on your chest. A small thing you made, grown inside you, and fed by you.

When I came out of surgery and was lucid enough to see the baby, I nearly recoiled. She wasn't a redhead like me and Mom, and she didn't look like Dad. She was dark, Mediterranean, olive skin and black hair. She looked like her father. I felt so guilty looking at her, as if she was a completely foreign thing. I wished my heart overflowed seeing her. But more than anything, and guiltier still for admitting it, my heart was cold and I felt nothing. I yearned for a scenario where Hugh leaned over, wearing scrubs and a hairnet and looked at our baby, overflowing with parental joy. It's sick, but true. Whether he knew it or not, Hugh had a daughter.

I look at her, and I see Hugh. So far, Jane is perfect, appropriate numbers of fingers and toes, cute even. But in the place where transcendental euphoric love is supposed to be, I feel coldness. As if I hadn't been hauling her around in me, as if I hadn't given up my life to have her. I'm sure a lot of it is postpartum, and just the recovery process from nearly dying, plus grief over Dad. But the love I thought I'd feel when I truly met my daughter, it wasn't there. The feeling of rightness, that I made the correct life decision, that it was all worthwhile—I didn't feel it. I felt nothing. For the first time in months my first instinct wasn't to cry, but feel regret. Were all new moms like this?

May 5th

Jane and I stayed in the hospital for two weeks. My recovery was slow, and painful, but I got better. Once my blood count was up, I began to lactate and started breastfeeding. I found the whole thing exhausting. Plus, I was starving all the time because so many of my hard-earned calories were stolen by this tiny baby, like it was sucking the life out of me. One morning, I noticed the milk that came out of me was pinkish or streaked with blood and began to panic. I confided in an older nurse who'd been looking after Jane and me all these weeks. She chuckled at my concern and patted me on the shoulder.

"It's scary dear, but totally common. In the old days we used to call it 'Rusty Pipe Syndrome.' Not the best name for it, certainly. But it's totally normal, especially for first time mommies. It'll clear up in a week or so. And the blood consumption is harmless to the babies." She gave my shoulder a squeeze and continued on her rounds. I stared at the pigmented blood that had stained my hospital gown and frowned. Seems I can't escape my blood.

It was indescribable—the loneliness I felt—when I realized there was no one to sign me out and drive us home from the hospital. Dr. Blake, my guardian angel, offered to take us home. I held Jane, although it was technically illegal since I didn't have a car seat with me. I buckled us both in and held her tight, watching the road fearfully.

Turns out, Dr. Blake had an ulterior motive for driving me home. Things he was struggling to say and didn't want to say with an audience. We went a few miles before he cleared his throat. Dr. Blake is a good person, he has a careful voice, and kind eyes. His sparse hair the color of crisp snow. He wears grandfatherly cologne, Old Spice, or something like it. He's someone I've grown to feel safe around over the past few months.

Finally, he confessed that he found my pregnancy perplexing. There was something off about it from the beginning, mainly the extreme chronic anemia. Turns out anemia's common in pregnancy, since the body has to produce more than fifty percent more blood to support the baby. But, with vitamins and a good diet, it should level off. But my body would not, could not, level off no matter how many supplements and transfusions I got. He said my body was literally killing itself making so much blood. I finally asked why I needed to make so much blood. Where the hell was it going?

Dr. Blake was silent for a long time as he drove, weighing the words before he said them. Finally, he glanced at Jane. I squeezed her tighter. He told me Jane started to exhibit a similar anemia when I was in ICU and unable to nurse her. He had to give her transfusions as well, surprisingly large transfusions considering her size and no place for all the blood to go. I felt like I was going deaf, or about to pass out. It was Jane. Jane was taking my blood. When she was separated from my blood, she needed transfusions. The pounding in my temples felt like a migraine. Images of Hugh filled my head, old ghost stories and B-movie monsters haunted me.

Dr. Blake said Jane didn't make enough of her own blood. Like she has a hole someplace where it all drains out that they couldn't find. But what he really thinks is that she's digesting it and passing it through her urine which is, biologically . . . impossible. I squeezed my eyes shut and let out a sob before I could clamp it down.

This couldn't be real. Vampires, and I hate to write the word, believe me, are made-up magical creatures, right? But Jane was like Hugh: she needed blood to survive. This was what Dr. Blake didn't want to tell me even though it had been in my face the whole time. Jane had been living off of me from the inside, stealing my nutrients like a tapeworm.

We pulled into my driveway, and the idea of being in this big empty house, alone, chilled me. Dr. Blake was kind enough to come in with me. I set Jane carefully in her bassinet where she kept sleeping peacefully. I traced her soft baby face with my fingertips.

Dr. Blake seemed to realize how upset all of this was making me and said we could talk about it another time. He left me and the baby to get some sleep. When I woke up hours later, Jane was still tucked up in her bassinet. Downstairs was a simple meal for he'd left for me on the table. I've never wept more for a sandwich than I did that day.

May 10th

I told Dr. Blake about Hugh. I had to, and I left nothing out. He thought for a while before saying that Hugh might in fact be someone who drinks blood, because he doesn't make enough of his own, or he lacks something in his own chemistry. There's a rare disease, porphyria, that a lot of vampire mythology was based on, it turns out. A painful disease that blood consumption has had success in treating. Dr. Blake theorized this could be something like that. But none of the other symptoms are there, the photophobia, the purple urine, the gum recession . . . but he thinks that something like it, something even rarer could be what both father and daughter suffer from.

He asked if I'd be interested in sending Jane to specialists, and a part of me, maybe my newfound mother's instinct, flatly refused. I want her to have a normal life. We can manage Jane's condition together, without a lot of attention. I don't want a life of hospitals for her.

Dr. Blake stared at me a long time. I finished my tea and rinsed the cups out. By that time, Jane was fussing to be fed. He agreed to do her checkups here at home, pro bono. And to "lose" any of the paperwork that could be damning to Jane's future. He would respect my wish to give her a normal life. As I watched her nursing, it was hard not to think of her as just a normal baby, suckling on her mother, and not some sort of monster. I promised her then I'd protect her, keep her safe, keep her secrets, and keep her healthy.

July 5th

I've not been writing much these past few months, not much to report. Jane grows and changes more each day. She's a serious child though, hard to make laugh, hard to play with. But she does respond to physical affection. I'm beginning to wonder if it's more because she gets to be close to her food. And then I feel guilty for thinking that. It's all so messed up. The "Rusty Pipes" have never cleared up and my breast milk is primarily blood. It wipes me out. I take my weight in vitamins, and eat enough iron and protein to kill a healthy person. But it's never enough.

Dr. Blake has started giving Jane transfusions every other week, to give me a break. She responds well. The day after the transfusion she's almost always a bundle of energy. Dr. Blake makes notes, does tests on us both. We've become something of his hobby. His wife died years ago, and his grown children have moved away. So we fill the empty spaces in each other's lives, I guess. He gives me sanity, and as sad as it is to write, he's a stand-in for Dad. And I think he sees Jane and me as something like family. He's affectionate with her, which I'm grateful for. I try to be like him with Jane, I really do, but more often than not, when I put her to my breast and she hungrily slurps up my blood, it takes all I have to not drop her to the ground on purpose.

In darker moments, late at night, when I'm lonely and sleep deprived, I look at Jane sleeping and think of doing something. Something terrible: a pillow over her face, drowning her in the tub. It's so, so awful. And I do love her, I'm pretty sure I love her, because it's my job to love her, it's my obligation. It's also my fault she exists.

Because Jane is also a thing. A monster that wears a human face. And it's convincing from afar. But when we go to the store, or the park, and people peek into her stroller, they recoil. She puts them off, as if they have natural radar warning them to fear her, to avoid her. She's a beautiful child. Her thick dark hair, olive complexion, and big brown eyes. All so like her father. She does seem to have my dimples, at least, and my chin. Hugh had a large square chin. My face is more heart-shaped. So, I'm in Jane, somewhere. Which makes it hurt all the more that deep down I loathe my own child.

XII.

I stared at the last page of my mother's journal for some time. The word "loathe" appeared bolder on the page the longer I stared. I pinched the bridge of my nose, sending stars skittering across my vision. I yearned for this to simply be the ravings of a seriously disturbed woman. A woman who shouldn't have been a parent, who probably would've done the world a favor by dropping that baby in a hospital bin. But the bites were real, and me hurting Sabrina the other night was real. I scrubbed at my eyes, fighting the tears.

This couldn't be true, none of it could be true. It was sick and delusional. It was fiction. I looked at the journal, tempted to throw it in the trash. I turned the worn leather in my hands, trying to summon an image of my mother, young and isolated, frantically scribbling on the pages.

I thought I'd read the last entry, but as I shakily fanned through the blank pages, I found another page of writing. It was undated and the script had lost a lot of legibility. The scrawl was shaky and unsteady on the page. My heart was in my throat, but my own curiosity made me read on. I'd said I wanted the truth—and I did.

XIII.

I'd nearly forgotten about this old journal, hiding away up here. It's like meeting an old war buddy again after many years. Makes me want to root around and find my old sketchbooks, from when I was a teenager, a carefree girl who just wanted to get out of her redneck town and paint. God, I miss her. I miss city lights, and espresso, I miss handsome boys buying you a drink from down the bar. I miss my youth, my beauty. I didn't treasure it, and had no idea of how fleeting it would be. I think I miss my humanity most of all. I need to write this out, because I need to confess some things. I can't kill myself without laying it out somewhere and I'm too much a coward to tell someone. I want to turn the gas on while we're sleeping or burn the house down. Kill us both. She's guilty, but I'm guiltier. I'm the enabler, I'm the adult, hell, I'm the fucking Renfield.

Let me go back a bit, since last time I wrote anything, Jane was still a baby. And when Dr. Blake got sick a few months before Jane's sixth birthday . . . things took a turn. He was our angel, he gave the transfusions so that I could get a break, but then he had a stroke while driving on another of his house visits. Not totally unexpected, he was in his eighties. The stroke damaged his speech center, and the accident took his mobility. Poor Dr. Blake ended up in a nursing home. We went to visit him a few times, and seeing him so frail was almost too much to bear. And then he died. I wept as loudly and pitifully at his funeral as I did at Dad's.

Without Dr. Blake's transfusions, I became Jane's sole donor. I've become an excellent phlebotomist over time, and I give her my blood in glasses instead of from the vein. That way, I can do portion control as she gets older and smarter. If I want her to grow up normal, she has to eat and drink like a regular person. But she needs too much.

Thank God she does eat food, so I give her a meat-heavy diet and lots of supplements. It helps. But I'm so tired and so delirious, my body a blood factory, and it's really taking its toll. I've reached a point where I can't give her anymore of the "red juice"—yes, that's what we call it. Sooo fucked up. I'm so fucked up for normalizing this. But Jane asks for red juice constantly, and as she grows, she needs even more.

I've tried animal blood. Dr. Blake and I experimented with a bunch of different animals, and they did nothing for her. It has to be human.

I'm going nuts. Without Dr. Blake, I'm entirely alone. He made our secret bearable, we were a team, he was my support. But alone, I have no place to go, no one to turn to. I paint, and Jane keeps to herself enough that I can stay up here all day. She's not sociable, but she doesn't seem a danger to other children. So, I send her to school. She needs to be part of the world and around other people. And I need to be away from her. People give her a wide berth, children and adults alike, like they know with some predator-sensing animal part of their brain that she's not really human. But Jane needs to learn to live in the world, like Hugh did. I'm trying to raise a vampire and shield her from the horror of it. But to do it, I've become more monstrous.

Right, moving on, the confession. That's why I'm writing in this moth-eaten book of tragedy in the first place.

One night, I got in my car to go to the store and to get gas in the neighboring town. I hate going to the small general store down the street where they all stare at me like I'm the town witch—though they're not that far off. We pass by and they all move closer to their loved ones, practically cross themselves like villagers in an old Hammer movie.

Jane's a pretty child, with her big fathomless eyes. She's always trailing around me, silent as a shadow. She's so hungry for hugs, for contact, and it's draining. It's crazy to think it, but I know it's true, she's feeding on me all the time. It's not just the blood, it's skin to skin, it's body heat, it's fucking lifeforce. So I avoid touching her if I can. I've given her too much. There's nothing left. The only thing I have is my art. When they find my bone-dry corpse up here, like a hollowed-out caterpillar casing, at least my paintings will be my legacy.

Anyways, I was driving, and I was so tired. Jane was in the backseat, silent as always. When I met her eyes in the mirror she smiled, small, timid, starved for attention. I sighed and returned to the road. It's not in me. You can't have it all. You just can't.

There was a young guy walking along the road, small and rangy, thumb out. My brain was whirring with ideas suddenly, misfiring, as I hit the blinker and pulled to the side of the road. I officially descended into madness, a little voice whispered as I sat idling, watching the guy in my rearview. Like a spider in a web. Even writing it out makes me shake and want to vomit. My memories of that night are a blur. I remember calling out to him, I remember offering him a ride. I was driving Dad's giant old Cadillac and I had to manually unlock the trunk. Told him I'd give him a ride if he could change my tire. As he leaned into the trunk to pull out the spare, I reached in for the tire iron. I hit him hard, in the back of the head. There was a small explosion of blood and he dropped to his knees, hanging half in the trunk. Heart racing, running on mania and endorphins, I hit him again for good measure. It wasn't like the movies—it was hard to knock him unconscious. My adrenaline was pumping and I managed to get his legs into the trunk. While he was still unconscious, I tied up his wrists using some old rope my dad always kept in the trunk for emergencies.

Instead of going to the store, I pulled a sharp U-turn and headed home, fast, but not fast enough to get pulled over. By the time we got there, I was all sweaty and dizzy from nerves. Jane watched me in the back seat, eyes large and curious. She's a polite child, almost unnervingly considerate, so she didn't even question why we came home without going to the store. Or what happened to the man.

I sent her in to watch television. She went, though it was obvious she thought I was acting weird. My heart felt like it was being torn out. WHAT ARE YOU DOING? I sat in the car, making myself breathe as I watched the lights turn on inside. I just kept repeating to myself: I made a promise to her. No matter what ring of hell it forces me into, I'll do what I need to.

So I dragged the hitchhiker out of the trunk. He was still unconscious, the wound deeper than I initially thought and bleeding quite badly. I was weak and he was heavy. It took a long time to drag him around to the back of the house, but I finally managed it. I opened the bulkhead to the basement and then very ungently dragged him down, cringing as his bloodied head bumped along every dusty step leaving a spot. It took all my strength. Dad had started to build a rec room in the basement when I was young. He didn't get past enclosing the room in sheetrock and rough-plumbing the half bath, and that's where I took the unconscious guy. There was a sofa and a dartboard. There was a door and a dingy wire-covered window that was sealed and faced the side yard.

I dragged him into the room. I got him onto the sofa. He was still unconscious, and a dead weight, so none of this was easy. I retied his wrists and ankles, and once he was secure, I dealt with his head wound. The guy was woozy, but came around as the hydrogen peroxide touched his skin. He bucked and screamed, so I gagged him.

His eyes rolled wildly, the gag soaking with his drool as he pled and moaned. I explained that it would be as painless as possible. I even thanked him for his contribution! I looked like a scarred-up old junkie more and more each day, and I was so glad to get a break from the constant bloodletting. Once I'd filled two mason jars and he was weak and gray from blood loss, I undid his wrist restraints, and he immediately lunged at me. He got in one good punch, splitting my lip, but was too weak to do much else. I retied him, watching him the whole time. I learned I'd need to be much more careful.

He woke up later night and started to scream, scaring Jane. He'd managed to loosen his gag. I gave him options: duct tape over his mouth or sleeping pills. I'd gotten a prescription a few years back in a moment of weakness when I'd gone to the doctor. I'd never liked to take them though, too scared of Jane being up and around without me to watch her. I snuck the pills crushed up into his food. When he was more lucid, he begged. But I learned to ignore it, I needed his blood. I know what I've done is wrong. I understood he had dreams and a name. Though I never asked him what it was.

I'm not a monster. I'm a mother. I tell myself over and over, to try to make what I've done okay.

It's not our fault. It was nature that created Jane. But it wore on me. Terribly. I'd come up and see Jane, working on a puzzle, or a book. Slurping away at her "red drink," a blood mustache on her young mouth. I'd sit in the bathroom for hours staring at my reflection.

I have Dad's old straight razor. I've sharpened it. I push it against my scarred wrists. Trace the blade along my throat, whisper coward at myself when I can't push it in. Because I am a coward.

Jane grows older every day. She was in third grade, then, able to read. How could I continue this way? How old would she be before she realizes what I'm doing? How long could the hitchhiker survive? These questions weighed on me every day.

And worse still, I got good at being a jailer. I bought feet of chain and wrapped them around the pillar in the basement, secured him with padlocks. I made caring for him my routine, changing his toilet bucket, bringing his food on trays, filling my jars. Day in, day motherfucking out.

Miraculously, he lasted for six months. By the end, he was a shell. He tried to go on hunger strikes, he tried to kill himself by wrapping the chain around his neck. I found him just in time. In the end, he died of exsanguination, a fancy word that I wouldn't know in another life. I'm no doctor, but I think it's a fair guess. The idea that I'm a murderer is . . . surreal.

But I learned, and I got better at keeping them after the first. Silent, cleaner, less blood. But then you reach a point where you can't do this any longer . . . at least, I can't.

There are three bodies in my garden.

I can't even look at Jane anymore. I hate what she's turned me into. She's a clever girl in most things, but in this she's oblivious. She has her red drink, never questions it. I watch her drink it. And it's almost mechanical, almost like she slips into a trance.

God, she's a frightful thing now. She's tall, her brown hair long, nearly to her bottom, and the spitting image of her goddamn father. She's starting to develop, and she'll be beautiful. A terrible beauty.

I decided to stop feeding her. No more red drink, no more basement feedbags. I bleached the floors, cleaned out the space. I pushed a workbench over the door and plan to never go in there again. We'll do something else, find another way to survive. That's what I told myself, anyway.

Soon after, Jane got sick. Thirteen years old and she was dying. Her body was skeletal. It was summer vacation and I told myself: if she dies, I'll bury her out back with our victims, and we'll all be free.

But then one day, things changed. Jane seemed alert, her cheeks fuller, her eyes sharper. And later, in the bath, to my dawning horror, I found it. A bite, discreetly behind my knee. It didn't hurt until I noticed it, like the old days, like Hugh. It filled me with such rage and horror that I nearly passed out.

It took everything I had to not get a knife out of the drawer and stab her while she sat in her room, reading. I stormed in and asked her if she came in my room that night? She seemed confused. I know my kid: I would know if she's lying. And she wasn't. She just got better, she doesn't know why. But I do. The monster in her wants to survive, and in my sheltering her, I've cut her in two. A day Jane, and a night Jane. I've been trying not to sleep, trying to barricade the door at night, but at some point between dusk and dawn she gets in, and a new bite appears.

I finally figured out why I never felt the bite, hers or Hugh's. It's in their saliva, like a mosquito, or a tick, or a fucking bedbug. Any of the filthy creatures that steal blood while the victim slumbers away. It anesthetizes the skin, numbs it.

I woke the other night to a suckling sound, pulling back the covers, found Jane sucking at my wrist. Asleep. Her eyes shut, her throat swallowing robotically. I screamed in horror, weak from the blood loss. She woke up suddenly, confused. I slapped her hard across the face. I hit her again, this time with a closed fist. She fell back cupping her cheek, her strange sleep state dissolving as she stared at me. Her eyes filled with tears.

Oh God, she had no idea! She's still so young and innocent, this horrible creature. Hugh was right. She'll be my undoing. I can't starve her to death, and I'm too much of a coward to just kill her. And after all, I made her a promise, a life—that I would give her a life. I had no idea that life would be mine. Oh Hugh, I wish I'd believed you all those years ago.

PART II : Imago

Or words she murmured while she leaned!
Witch-words, she holds me softly by,—
The spell that binds me to a fiend
Until I die.

—Madison Julius Cawein, "The Vampire"

XIV.

$\mathcal{I}$ dropped the journal in breathless terror. My mind raced. How could this terrible retelling of my childhood be real? I was there. Surely, I'd remember if this was true.

But you know it is, a voice whispered at the back of my mind.

No. It was impossible. I was dizzy when I stood, moving just to move, no place to go. Nothing seemed solid. This was all one long terrible dream. An addled fantasy world created by a half-mad shut-in. Surely, I'd remember my mother feeding me glasses of blood. I'd remember men screaming in the fucking basement! I vaguely remembered an elderly doctor when I was a kid . . . but he wasn't some terrible accomplice. This was her version of the story, nothing more.

But as much as I desperately wanted to believe it was all a lie, I knew, deep down, that something in there was true. I wasn't right—something in me wasn't like other people.

And I'd made my mother into that thing in the other room. Her dogged maternal instinct to care for me, this horrible bloodsucking thing, had cost her life, her sanity, her body, and her identity. I bit into my knuckle, trying to keep myself from screaming. It all made horrible sense. She was dying, the nightly feedings depleting her to nothing.

And then Sabrina, I lured her to me, to my home, to my bed. Who the hell was I? I felt like someone was sharing my body with me, possessing me.

I yanked the door to my room open, running down the hallway, down the stairs, stumbling through the kitchen as if drunk, down, down, down, the rickety basement stairs. I spun in a circle, finding the washer in the corner, the water heater and a tool bench, all where I'd left them, all familiar. I was in the basement daily; I knew every inch . . . didn't I? I couldn't have overlooked a fucking torture chamber down here after all these years. I followed the corners of the room to the tool bench and the small door behind it. Fear sweat dripped into my eyes and gathered on my upper lip.

I frantically pulled everything off the table: the calendars from many years past, the stacks of boxes I could now see were all very carefully placed to hide the door. I found a crowbar and forced the heavy bench away, the floor beneath covered in mildewed dust. At eye level, the door had a deadbolt. And the doorknob had a lock on the outside. With shaking fingers, I unlocked the deadbolt and turned the knob.

The smell, although ancient, was there. Urine, human urine. The room had a dingy, disgusting couch. And true to my mother's word, the walls were covered in a rushed, clumsy whitewash. The space felt haunted, terrible. I didn't need to see the chain wrapped around the post, or the stains, to sense that something awful had happened here. Even someone who was a complete skeptic, a psychic null, would walk into this space and feel it. This room was clearly a place where wretched, evil things had gone down. Where my mother had killed people on my behalf. I could barely breathe.

How was I supposed to deal with this? How had I convinced myself for seventeen years that I was the victim of the story? That I was in need of rescuing? My fairy tale was wrong. Sleeping Beauty should never be woken up, but locked away. Rapunzel was put in that tower for a reason. I staggered up the stairs, weaving my way to the parlor and to my mother's seated form.

She watched me as I barreled in and sat heavily on the chair beside her. I slumped forward, head in my hands. I couldn't stop shaking. I wanted to strangle her for lying to me, for hating me, for allowing me to exist. My shoulders trembled as I fought the hysterical tears that wanted to explode out of me. I repressed the scream that had been building since I saw that room. I remembered my face in the mirror, crusted with Sabrina's blood.

The spell was broken. I knew the secret in the attic, and it was me.

"Why didn't you just kill me?"

It took a while before I got control over my voice. I wasn't expecting an answer as I stared at the dingy floor, at my dirty socks, at nothing.

"Because you're my child."

I was surprised when she rasped out the reply, but my surprise was quickly replaced by anger.

"So? You hated me! I read the journal, I know how you feel about me. How everyone feels about me. You fantasized about killing me and being free. Maybe it would've been better. Maybe I should just do it. I mean why not, right? Why go on as this thing?" I turned away, arms crossing tight around my torso to keep from exploding. "You became a murderer for me! How can I live with that?"

My mother didn't answer, nor did I think she would. What was there to say? She did what she had to do. She gave me seventeen blissful years of not knowing I was a fucking monster. That was her gift to me.

I got up and walked out of the room, heading to the kitchen. Everything felt unreal, the small pitiful life we shared here, my lonely place as the weirdo in school, the brief moment of joy with Sabrina (which also was a lie). I stared out the window at the back garden, it was all dead grasses and brown leaves now, but there were bodies out there. Fuck. I entertained a fantasy of opening the door and running out into the woods, just being swallowed by it, and never coming out again. But I abandoned it as soon as I thought it.

Who knows how long I stood in that kitchen. Eventually the sky darkened and I put the pan on the stove and dragged out the liver. It was as if my free-falling mind put me on autopilot, relying on the muscle memory of a regular day. While frying it up, I got my mother's vitamins. I brought all of this on a tray and set it out for her. As I turned to go, she reached out and touched my hand tenderly. Staring down at her old claw on mine, I felt fresh tears trailing down my face.

"It's too late, Mom. You know, most of my life, I would have given my right arm for that touch."

I clicked on the television and left the parlor, almost as an afterthought I turned to her.

"I won't come into your room tonight, even if I have to tie myself down."

She nodded, and I walked away. I went into my bedroom and found my school bag. I put the journal in it. I changed into clothes not covered with basement grime and washed my face. I looked less like a hysterical monster and more like a person. But barely, since apparently I wasn't a person. My skin seemed too tight for my skull, a vein throbbing on my forehead. Taking a few deep breaths, I put on my winter coat and some shoes. I wrapped the scarf around my neck, slung my bag on my shoulder, and set out.

XV.

Though it was only dusk, it was already dark and frigid, so cold my eyes burned and my nostrils ached. My gloved hands in my pockets, face burrowed into my scarf, I set out down the driveway. The street was ill-lit and barren; even the animals were curled up in their dens, no doubt. The air tasted like snow. The rawness chilled me to the bone, so I picked up my pace to get the blood flowing. The stolen blood.

I swam through an ocean of guilt. So I just kept walking, pushing a jog. I focused on the air rushing into and out of my lungs, on my legs moving fast and strong along the ditch. I ran. I followed the tar road until it forked. One side stayed Main St., the other turning to dirt with a hand-painted sign saying Elmgrove.

I wracked my brain to remember Sabrina's address. It felt like a hundred years had passed instead of a weekend.

I slowed back to a walk, not wanting to rush to her. Since I wasn't entirely certain I could muster the courage to talk to her. How was I the bad guy in the story? But I was, and I had preyed on her. I might not have meant to, but I had.

Heart heavy, I slowed and trudged along the empty road, crunching over the frosted dirt and leaves on the shoulder.

Finally, a house cropped up, then a few others. Sabrina was definitely farther than two miles away. By the time I found number 55, my teeth were chattering and the sweat had cooled. It was a McMansion house, which looked nearly identical to all the others I'd passed. It glowed like a beacon in the woods, the winding driveway's smooth new blacktop under my feet. The house was a combination of stone and siding. The front jutted out, rounded like a castle turret.

I stepped up to a giant set of ornate French doors, above which tall windows let me see a twinkling chandelier and the grand staircase in the foyer. I suddenly felt more afraid than ever before in my life. The urge to turn away and run home was overwhelming. Yes, little monster, flee back into the shadows. I pivoted on my heels, ready to leave, and stopped. Sabrina was the first real friend I'd ever made. I owed her this. I might be . . . a parasite, but I could still do the right thing.

Steeling myself, I pressed the decorative doorbell and listened to its chime echo through the house. I heard clomping on the stairs before the door was yanked open and a flushed young boy stared up at me. He looked like Sabrina, a little chubby, same round face. He had the same twinkling, rascally eyes as his sister. They were hooded when he looked at me.

"Yeah?" he asked in the indifferently rude way of preteens.

"Is Sabrina here? I'm a friend from school."

He looked me up and down and shrugged, walking away from the door, leaving it ajar. I took that as my invitation and stepped inside. Looking around the house, it was remarkable how different it was from my own. It smelled of dinner and it was noontime bright, lights on everywhere I looked. Photos of the family were on the side table. There was Sabrina, not smiling per se, but it was obvious she was having a good time with them. I stood in the foyer, confused as to where the boy went.

"Hello?"

A feminine voice made me turn, startled. This was obviously Sabrina's mother. She grinned warmly, which surprised me. She came closer, wiping her hands on a dishrag.

"Hi. Um, I'm Sabrina's friend from school. Is she home?"

"Oh! Are you Jane?"

I nodded stiffly, feeling the urge to run.

"I'm so glad she made a friend so fast. You know, it was a hard move for her. I'm sure she'll be happy to see you. She's been in a nasty mood all weekend. Just head right up the stairs. Her room is the second door on the right, past the bathroom."

I nodded again and went up the stairs. From this height, I could see into the recessed living room where Sabrina's brother was playing video games intensely. To the left, there was a formal dining room, and what I assumed was the kitchen beyond that.

Once at the top, I fought the urge to flee back into the cold. I didn't belong in this nice warm house, with bright lights and new appliances. I shouldn't be allowed to pass the threshold. But I fought it, I owed it to Sabrina. I'd wronged her, and I knew that now. So I marched past the bathroom to the closed door with a Barbie head on a ribbon dangling from the knob. For some reason, this made me smile, but even smiling skewered me with guilt. I had no right to be find anything amusing, I needed to be suffering, forever if need be. Finally I got the nerve and I knocked on the door.

"It's open."

The voice was distracted. I slowly opened the door. Music blared loudly. The room was covered in band posters. There were velvet curtains and the smell of incense and cigarettes was thick in the room. I noted the towel on the floor that she must jam under the door to keep it in. There was a full-sized bed, a desk, and a worn-out plaid chair and ottoman. The closet door was open and the light was on, and as I stepped fully into the room and closed the door, Sabrina emerged from it, stopping short. Her face suddenly fearful and wary, the urge to call out obvious. For the first time in my life, I tried to talk as fast as I could, hands up palms out.

"I know I'm the last person you want to see. And I know things got out of control and I really want to apologize. After you left, I . . . found out some things. Some pretty horrible things, honestly. I'm not trying to be vague, I just have no idea how to begin to explain things to you. I understand that you're pissed at me, and afraid of me, and you should be. I brought you my mom's journal. It really . . . illuminated some things for me. And I really need to talk to someone about it, and you're the only person who has ever, ever been a friend to me."

I realized my voice was shaking, Sabrina still glared at me, arms crossed, and I couldn't help but notice the bandage peeking out from her cowl-neck sweater. I wiped at my eyes and continued before my nerve dried up.

"I'm going to leave it with you to read. Honestly, I'm terrified to give this to you. I'm terrified of what you'll say, or not say to me. If you don't want to read it, then bring it to me at school tomorrow and I'll never talk to you again. I'm good at that, I promise. And if you do read it and don't want to share the same state with me, I also understand. Hell you may read it and call the cops. And maybe that would be for the best. I just . . . everything in my life is a lie. Everyone in my life is lie. I don't want to be like that. You were kind to me. I'm so sorry I hurt you."

With that, I took the book out of my bag and set it on the chair closest to me. I couldn't bear to look at her. So I opened the door and stepped out, praying I did the right thing. At the bottom of the stairs I looked back up, and noticed Sabrina was standing at the banister, watching me go.

Outside, I welcomed the punishing cold. It cleared the cobwebs and froze the tears.

I was unsure where to go; the urge to just walk forever, just wander into the woods, never to return came back again. You can relax, villagers, the monster has gone away.

Instead, I went home. I ate a small dinner of the liver leftovers, since I'd barely had any food that day and I needed to keep my strength up. I didn't know what my relationship with food and blood was, if I needed more of one if I didn't get enough of the other. To be safe, I decided to make sure I was eating, especially iron-rich, blood-healthy foods.

Eventually, after putting my mother to bed, I took my schoolbooks into the bedroom with me. It seemed absurd to worry about homework knowing what I now knew. But I drowned out my sorrows in algebra anyway.

I couldn't stop looking at the closed and locked door to my bedroom. I couldn't stop picturing myself getting up in the night and wandering in there, into my mother's room, crawling up under the blankets and biting down on her someplace. I shuddered.

Once I had my fill, did I just wander back in here and go to sleep? It was terrifying to think my body had that type of uncontrolled locomotion, or desire, completely closed to my conscious brain. Even if I jammed a chair under the door, would I just move everything out of my way to get to her? If Sabrina had just slept over, and nothing alcohol-related or sexual had happened, would I still have fed off of her while she slept? Was it better now that I knew?

I finally gave up and tossed my textbook to the floor, enjoying the satisfying clunk. Kicking my blankets off, I prepared my room. First, I tied a scarf to the doorknob and knotted it with tights, attaching the makeshift rope to my bedpost. It was so taut that I'd probably need to cut it off the next day. Next, I jammed a chair under the doorknob and littered the floor with debris that would hurt on bare feet or make a ruckus. My hope would be if I did get up and start moving, that the noise or pain would wake me.

Then I crawled into bed, exhausted. Even as I dozed, the fear prickled, the fear of what my sleeping self would be up to. I begged her to behave, and eventually slept.

XVI.

When my alarm went off at seven, I rose like a shot and looked around. My door barricades looked to have held, which filled me with immense relief. Slowly, I cleaned up the obstacles I'd set out, finally cutting the tights to free myself from the room. I went to my mother in her bed.

After two consecutive days of not being a human feed bag, and eating all that liver, she definitely seemed a little more vibrant. Some color in her face, a bit more focus in her eyes. I couldn't help but smile when I came in, proud of myself. The pride didn't distract from my physical exhaustion, though. But I wasn't as tired and weak as before. Apparently, Sabrina's young, healthy blood was keeping me running much more efficiently than my mother's, but for how long? I could sense the familiar fatigue at the margins, and a hunger waited there as well.

Now that it had a name, I couldn't deny the hunger inside me. I noticed how it flared to life as I neared my mother. My body urged me toward her, toward what it needed. No wonder people felt uncomfortable around me. I was probably eyeing them all like potential meals. If I was going to live with this,

I would need to learn to control myself. I took a deep breath and shook it off.

I walked my mother downstairs and settled her in the parlor in front of a roaring fire and the news, her breakfast on the TV tray beside her. I pulled back the shades, letting the pale light in. Winter was near, the trees black outlines, the sky a swirling pea soup.

"I think it's going to snow today," I said to her. I needed to hear my voice.

It was a regular morning, so she said nothing, and I didn't prod. Instead, I got ready for school and tried to ignore the ball of stress surrounding school and seeing Sabrina. Outside, the air was cold and clean. I sucked it in greedily, liberally, enjoying the burn in my lungs. I headed to school, trying not to think of Sabrina, or the journal. Or what I was. And failing at all three. The combination of desire and shame was almost overwhelming. But I couldn't hide from myself anymore. I lifted my chin, picking up the pace and crossing through the doors a second before homeroom rang.

When I got to the classroom, it was as if I was seeing the world with new eyes. I was a wolf among sheep, a fox in the hen house. A predator slinking along in my classmates' unsuspecting midst. They couldn't pinpoint why I made them uncomfortable, just that I did. I thought back to my mother's journal, how she would lament my desire for affection, to be touched. It was no wonder now that I had pounced on Sabrina, I was starving for touch, for love, for food. When the bell rang, I walked to my first period as if my feet were encased in cement. If Sabrina was there, if she turned away from me . . . better not to dwell.

I entered the class, getting the familiar eye aversion and icy reception. My empty desk and the surrounding buffer of vacant desks was unchanged, an element of normalcy in the chaos. Sliding in, I noticed Sabrina wasn't there. My heart fell. Maybe she was skipping school, maybe she was transferring classes, maybe she confessed to her parents what happened and they were taking police action right now. For all I know, the cops were exhuming bloodless hitchhikers from my backyard as I was sitting in class. Medical experts were preparing a special prison to study my unique physiology. All those thoughts swirled through my head as the teacher wrote on the board and the rest of my classmates scribbled notes. What I wouldn't give to think this vocab test meant something. Even as I was thinking all this, the door opened, my heart did a flip, and Sabrina came in.

She looked exhausted, dark circles under dark makeup. Her hair was dirty, her bangs hanging lank in her face. She entered without looking at anyone, including me, but she did sit directly next to me. I felt anxious. I wanted to talk to her. She didn't look at me, and instead just pulled out her notebook and opened the text up to the correct page, and began taking notes.

I was thrumming, but I kept composed. Sabrina ignored me through the entire class. I stared at the side of her face, willing her to look my way. At the bell, she jumped up and quickly headed toward gym class, not waiting for me. I stood too, crestfallen, and trailed behind her.

In gym class, she changed quickly and avoided me. I resolved to respect her wishes. I couldn't help looking at the bandage at her throat, visible above her T-shirt, even with her shoulder-length black hair down. Seeing it filled with me with shame, and hunger. The memory of her skin against my lips, her blood in my mouth, unavoidable as I watched her. I pushed it all away, trying to see her as just another face in the crowd. Another person who wanted nothing to do with me.

After a gym class spent standing at a volleyball net and never raising my arms, I cleaned up and returned to my gym locker. Inside, my mother's journal was placed on top of my clothes. Sabrina was nowhere in sight. So that was that. She had made her decision to return the book to me, and not continue our friendship. It was the ultimatum that I'd offered, so I had to respect it. But I still felt like a horse had kicked in my chest. I wanted to cry, or punch the locker, all too aware of the girls around me, both watching and ignoring me at all times.

The rest of the day was a blur, the walk home just as fuzzy, and by the time I got there I felt weak, the familiar headache creeping in behind my temples. But as if these last few days had never happened, I cleaned my mother up, ate a Spartan meal, and crawled into bed before it was full dark. I woke with a start in the early morning, noting that I was standing in the hall. Swallowing and looking around, I realized I had been heading to my mother's room. Disoriented, I went back to my bedroom, the horror of what I had been going to do dawning fully. I'd been so tired and upset I'd forgotten to barricade myself into my room like I had the night before. The hunger raged, it throbbed in my temples and squeezed my stomach. I clenched my jaw and barricaded the door.

I felt terrible later in the morning when I got up again. My joints burned, my head pounded, and I couldn't stop shivering. I took a hot shower to knock the chill out of my bones, but to no avail. I couldn't get warm. At school, I sat in English class, hunched over my desk, hair a brown curtain around me. Sabrina sat beside me again, glancing my way periodically with a frown, in between taking ambitious notes and even raising her hand. In gym, I stuck to the corners, stiff. When finally forced to join into a game of basketball by the teacher, I just stood there. Balls whizzed by my head as I tried to stay on my feet. I could feel Sabrina's eyes on me, but didn't bother to look up. I'd given her the out to leave me alone and she'd taken it. It was the smart choice.

After showering and dressing, I debated going home. Something hungry and predatory had woken in me, and now I could not turn it down. I was so aware of the blood-filled bodies moving around me, hearts chugging, glands sweating. And I was starving to death in their midst. I didn't know if it was the knowledge of what I was that had suddenly made me aware, or perhaps Sabrina's young healthy blood after years of barely subsisting. But I was cruelly aware of every person passing me by. Did they know how lucky they were? Now that I knew it was their blood I wanted, I couldn't stop thinking about it, I could almost smell it, imagine what it would be like tasting their salty skin, biting into them. I stared at a husky, brown-haired boy in the lunchroom. Sabrina was nearby. I could feel her as if an invisible rope bound us.

I can't do this, I'm giving up. I can't torture myself this way anymore. I took a few steps before the world tipped quickly and violently sideways. I felt myself falling, almost floating, then hit the ground.

XVII.

I could hear voices, sense movement near me. My skin tingled all over, my knee ached. What had happened? I must have passed out. I tried to sit up but as soon as I did, my vision swam and I had to drop my head down. I was in the nurse's office. A middle-aged woman with a severe haircut rounded the curtain and did her best to smile at me, though I could sense her reluctance.

"Welcome back, Ms. DeVry, I'm Nurse Hopkins. How are you feeling?"

I stared blearily up at her, confused. I must've been carried in here. My head was splitting, and my limbs were weak. I glanced around warily and cleared my throat.

"Did you eat breakfast?"

I nodded, and she frowned while taking notes. She asked about medicine, drugs, even if I might be pregnant.

"Well, I've been trying to call your house for a while. I have your mother here as the emergency contact. Is she home? Or do you have a work number for her? I'd love to have her come get you."

I quickly looked away, too tired to lie.

"My mother's very ill, and doesn't drive. I don't live far, I can walk . . ."

"Nonsense. Is there anyone else?"

"I could give her a ride."

My head shot up to see Sabrina standing halfway behind the curtains. She stared at the nurse, avoiding me at all costs. I rolled over to face the wall, biting my lip.

The nurse hesitated. "That isn't policy I'm afraid . . ."

Sabrina gestured for Nurse Hopkins to talk to her privately. She spoke softly but I could hear her. The room was small, and the wall dividing us was a sheet.

"Her mother's practically an invalid, and she has no other family. I've been to her house. No one can come get her. I know it's not standard, but I'd be happy to drive her home and keep an eye on her. You can call my mom, I'm sure she'd allow it. She's met Jane before, and she's familiar with her situation."

Nurse Hopkins whispered back and eventually called Sabrina's mother, getting permission. The nurse rounded the corner back to me. By this point I'd managed to sit up. She crossed to me, shining a light in my eyes, listening to my pulse again.

"You're lucky to have a good friend like Ms. Karnstein here. She's willing to take you home and get you to bed. But if you feel faint again, or any of these symptoms continue, I want you to go to the hospital."

I nodded and rose. As soon as she didn't need to be next to me, she wasn't. Sabrina stood with my things. I raised an eyebrow.

"When you passed out, I grabbed your stuff. Hope that's okay."

I could see the journal peeking out, relieved that it wasn't on the floor in the cafeteria. I was stupid to not take it out of my bag last night, but I had been so tired. Sabrina followed my eyes to the diary, then handed the bag to me. I crossed my arms over it possessively and meekly followed her out, down the institutional yellow hallway, over the gleaming buffed floors, and out the side entrance toward the student parking.

The winter air helped clear my head a bit. I still felt like road kill, but at least I wasn't unconscious. Once out of the school's sightlines I stopped, Sabrina continuing a few paces before noticing I wasn't behind her. She stopped, confused.

"Thank you, for doing that in there. And for getting my things. It means a lot. But you don't have to take me home. You made it clear yesterday that you want nothing to do with me and I totally respect that. I can get home on my own."

I walked past her, planning on cutting through the sports field. She didn't call out, or try to stop me, reinforcing that she was just being a nice person, but we were still not friends. It was better for her to stay away better for everyone to keep their distance. I'd reached the other side of the field and was just about at the end of school property when Sabina, in her mother's car, pulled up beside me, rolling the passenger window down.

"Just get in the car, Jane. It's cold and you look like shit. I don't think you'll make it."

I wanted to fight her. But, she was right. Even my hair ached. Resigned, I got in, grateful for the heaters on full blast and the kindness. I was so conflicted. I rested my forehead against the glass, eyes shut.

"Thanks," I whispered. She just grunted in reply. The silence in the car had mass. We drove along for a bit before I noticed we had passed my house.

"You just missed . . ."

"I know. I figured we should talk." She lit a cigarette and rolled the window down a scant inch, blowing the smoke out through her nose.

"You don't have to—"

"Yes, we do."

"Really Sabrina, it's fine. I understand—"

"I read the journal," she cut in.

I didn't know what to say. My breath stopped for a second.

"I stayed up all night after you dropped it off, reading it. I was so angry with you, and freaked out. I couldn't imagine what your crazy mother's diary would do to change that. At first, I thought it was the most fucked up thing I'd ever read. Then I thought, maybe I should call DCYF because she's obviously neglectful and insane. And she was obviously abusing you back then. But then I thought about the other night, how you acted, and then how you seemed totally unaware of biting me, and looking at you now . . ."

I exhaled, "It's true. What my mother says, it's all true. But I don't want to hurt her anymore. I've been barricading myself into my room at night so I can't get at her."

"But that'll just make you sicker, won't it?"

"It's better than killing my own mother, don't you think?" I glared at her. She winced and I could see her fear. She believed.

Sabrina steadied herself and put on her turn signal, dragging the car along a remote logging trail. Once all we could see was woods, she killed the engine, and turned to me.

"I feel bad for you."

I covered my face with both hands. Being pitied felt worse than being hated.

"None of this is your fault, Jane. You didn't ask to be a vampire."

I cringed as the V-word passed her lips.

"I made a choice last night. Or, well, I guess early this morning, and it took me seeing you so sick today, and realizing what that meant, and if you promise not to take too much . . ."

She rolled up her sleeve and jutted her arm out to me.

"Sabrina!" I knocked it away horrified and wrenched the car door open. She grabbed my coat sleeve.

"What else can you do? Are you just going to starve yourself to death, locked up in your room? Or what if it's like when you were a kid? What if you just go into one of your weird 'states' and crawl out your window and go after someone?"

I closed the car door, but wouldn't look at her.

"Oh my God, that's your plan? Hope for the best and starve to death?"

"There's nothing else I can do. I don't want to hurt anyone . . . I don't want to kill my mother. And I don't want to go be a freak in a hospital either. There are no other options."

Sabrina shook her head, offered her arm again.

"This is an option." Her wrist was inches from my face.

"Why would you do this? I don't even know if I can. I never have, you know . . . consciously done this before." I was mortified by how badly I wanted to.

"I trust you not to hurt me."

The headache roared in my ears, my mouth filling with saliva.

"Why do you trust me? You have no reason to."

"Someone needs to believe in you."

Her arm was warm in my cold, trembling fingers. I stared at the smooth pale skin, the tracery of blue veins. I released something of a sob.

"I have no idea what I'm doing. This is totally weird."

Sabrina laughed nervously. "It does feel crazy, right?"

We watched each other. Her soft hazel eyes trusting. I held onto that feeling and followed it deeper. The heat from her arm warmed my hands, but it was more than that. The electricity ran from her to me like a conduit. My mother was right; I was absorbing something of Sabrina through her touch. Engrossed in the sensation, I leaned my head down, running my face along the silken skin of her forearm, breathing in the perfume at the pulse point. My tongue snaked out, running along that vein from the wrist to the crook of her elbow. She gasped at the feel of my mouth on her, a combination of fear and surprise. I began sucking, pulling the tender flesh into my mouth, and, as if I had done this a thousand times before, I bit down.

The blood eased out slowly at first. I bit down a little harder, trying to nick the vein without chewing her up, to tease more out. My teeth parted her flesh as if through butter and with one more good tug, my mouth filled to the brim. I moaned, swallowing greedily. The energy raced through me from the tips of my toes to the top of my head. I could feel the healthy, hearty thump of her heart on my tongue.

As if from another world, from hundreds of miles away, I heard a voice, calling my name over and over. I felt a pressure on my shoulder, a pinching. Finally, a wrenching on my scalp that knocked me back into reality. It was daytime, I was in Sabrina's mother's Buick, and she was letting me drink her blood. I sat up too fast, pushing myself as far from her as possible, looking frantically for the door handle. I felt scared, disoriented, trapped in the car.

"—Jane? Can you hear me? Are you okay?"

Sabrina was staring at me, eyes concerned, face pale as parchment. I felt like an animal in a cage, but slowly the instinct to flee abated. I breathed, letting myself remember. And with the memories came the disturbing reality that my mother was not insane, and that I needed to drink blood to survive.

"How do you feel?"

I blinked a few times, pushing down the rush and the adrenaline. I scrubbed my hand over my face and tried to stamp down the rush of giddiness and adrenaline surging through me.

"Good. Weirded out, but really good. Really, uh, hyper-energized, I guess . . ."

I pulled down the visor mirror, recoiling at the bloody face staring back at me.

"Jesus." I found a tissue in my pocket and proceeded to wipe up. Sabrina sat crumpled in her seat: too pale and sick.

"Are you okay?" I asked her. She nodded, trying to smile, but it didn't reach her eyes.

"Yeah, it was, um, intense. You were you, and then you . . . weren't, like you went into a trance, and when you bit in it didn't hurt. It felt more like pressure. I think that's how you could bite your mom without her knowing, or me the other night. It kind of felt good, actually, I mean it was kind of . . . hot."

I blushed, now that I had enough blood in me to do so. I could feel it flushing my cheeks.

"It just got a little scary when I started to get dizzy, and then I felt queasy. I kept calling you and I tried shaking you. But you were in the zone or whatever. But I got you off eventually, so it's okay."

"I'm sorry. It was hard for me to stop."

Sabrina nodded, pressing a tissue to the wound. "Well, you were starving, and it's not like there's a manual for this fucked-up shit."

"Thank you for not being afraid of me." My voice cracked, but I didn't care.

She lifted the tissue to look at the wound. "You don't have fangs. But you bit through my skin like it was nothing. I've been bit plenty—I have a little brother after all—and regular teeth are too blunt."

I ran my tongue along my teeth, and had to admit that they were all quite sharp. "No fangs," I replied.

After a long bout of pregnant, strange silence, Sabrina finally blurted, "I'm still a little scared, Jane. It did take me two days to come to that conclusion, and I won't lie to you. I did just have to pull your hair to get you off of me."

"Sorry for that." And I was. But more than anything I was enjoying the feeling of Sabrina's life inside of me, reviving me. I stared out at the forest, the trees barren and gray. Her blood was virile and healthy, not like my mother's. I felt like a new person, my senses sharp, my muscles strong. I'd never felt so full. Sabrina had been watching me out of the corner of her eye.

"Thank you for helping me."

She turned away, a blush now warming her neck and cheeks.

XVIII.

We talked for a while longer, sitting in Sabrina's car. Night came swiftly in the winter country, and by five o'clock we were shrouded in darkness. She slowly, gingerly, backed up along the rough logging trail and onto the main road, driving me home. I had her leave me at the gate. No point in further abusing her mother's car by driving up it. Stepping out, I waved at the red taillights and made my way to the house with a lightness I'd never felt.

Inside, the answering machine flashed with missed calls. I didn't bother listening to them before erasing, knowing they were the nurse from school. I stared at the nearly dead creature in the chair, my sleeping mother. She'd no doubt heard each of those messages. Was she concerned for me? Did it matter anymore? I made extra noise when I came in, which woke her. She stared around blearily. I spoke to her as I refueled the small stove,

"I had a close call today. Passed out at school, was so weak I could barely walk. Nurse called a bunch." I paused.

"You look all right now." She whispered suspiciously, blankets up to her chin, barely visible besides the dryer lint fluff of hair and two intense, bloodshot eyes. She knew I was full of blood, and she knew it wasn't hers. I was tempted to tell her about Sabrina. A fucked up part of me wanted her to be jealous. As soon as the feeling rose up I couldn't push it down. She'd been using me as her long-term suicide attempt, and now I was disturbing the plan. If I stopped feeding on her, she'd eventually recover, she'd eventually have to face her actions. She wouldn't get her romantic ending as a martyr.

I had always wanted her to worry about me. To show she cared in any way. And I knew there would always be a little child in me, yearning for my mother's love. But I also knew I'd never get it. Not the way I wanted. She would keep us alive, she'd even kill and die for me. But love? I turned my back on her and left the room, shutting the door behind me.

XIX.

Midweek, Sabrina allowed me to drink her blood again, and it was as wonderful and explosive as the first time.

But like the last time, she had to intervene when I couldn't stop. She'd pounded on my back, pulling at my hair and ears. It was shameful to have such an appetite. If I wanted to continue feeding on her without hurting her, or even killing her, I'd need to get it under control. Sabrina was upset and I needed to please her. I needed her to keep supplying me. With each encounter I was learning more about this monster that had slept inside me for so long. I was learning to listen to it.

For example, on this third feeding the monster in me noticed Sabrina's desire. A sexual need deeply repressed, one she felt uncomfortable acting on. I knew she was aroused, a tang in the air, a shift in the tight space of her car. It was as if my senses were blossoming, transmitting finite details about Sabrina, teaching me about my prey. Whispering to me that the prey liked sex and they liked being loved.

Prey. Predator. I'd always known I was an outsider, but I'd had no idea how outside I truly was. I couldn't ignore that, with this new strength and awareness, came a crueler voice. It saw

Sabrina as something weaker, something like food, something that could be used. And I didn't want that. I wasn't like Hugh, taking advantage, using love and influence for his own needs. I was honored Sabrina would take on the risk. It was selfless and brave, and I was appreciative.

Since feeding from Sabrina, I knew I couldn't go back. My mother's watery, weak blood had kept me alive, but little else. It was like subsisting on broth. It seemed that, with Sabrina, I could get by with only a few solid feedings a week. I was learning how to adapt, how to work with this body of mine. I continued to keep my bedroom door locked and barricaded and my mother went unmolested by night. She was recovering. I started to feel hopeful that maybe everything would turn out okay.

That weekend Sabrina slept over and, after some drinking (pilfered Zinfandel from her mother's cupboard), when I felt she'd loosened up a bit, I touched her hair, her sleeve. She was uncomfortable though, not as receptive as she had been. It made me angry. I felt hungry and on edge. It had been four days and I didn't understand the problem. I sighed, louder than intended, and leaned back on the bed. She crossed her arms. Finally, when it was clear she wasn't going to speak, I asked what her problem was. I tried to sound understanding, receptive even, but I was sure it came off strained.

"Nothing. We could, I don't know, watch a movie, or talk. Why do we need to get right to that?"

She chewed her lip and avoided my eyes, striped socks tucked beneath her.

I forced myself to smile, though it probably closer resembled a big cat bearing its teeth. "We can do all those things after, Sabrina. I'm . . . hungry."

"It's just . . . the bites, they take time to heal. And they hurt after. I know we're figuring this stuff out, trying to understand, and I don't mind. I really don't. I just don't want to be your . . . milk cow, or some shit."

"Milk cow?" I tried to laugh it off, but my hackles were up. Please don't leave me, that voice inside whispered. "What does that even mean, Sabrina?"

"Like I'm only good to you for my milk, or blood, whatever. I want a friend, or a girlfriend, or whatever. We need to do normal stuff; we need to hang out together."

I stood and gave her space, "We are hanging out, aren't we?"

"No, Jane, I want more. We need to . . . I don't know, drive to the mall, or go to the movies. Eat pizza. You know, regular shit." She kept her eyes on the corner. "It can't just be me coming over here or sitting in my car while you drink my blood and then, 'Wham, bam, thanks, go home, Sabrina, I'll call you when I'm hungry.' Y'know? I want a friend. I want to have fun." She raised her head, hazel eyes red rimmed.

She was embarrassed and relieved at telling me the truth, I could tell. I didn't know what to say. I could remind her I'd never had friends, or that I didn't know what I was doing. But she knew that. She wanted me to be normal, but she couldn't understand that I was biologically an outcast. That her being withholding actually starved me. I tried not to get angry with her. My head was throbbing and a small voice deep inside groaned wretchedly. Tired of waiting, the monster in me stepped to the front.

"Sabrina," I said, my voice hard. She watched me intently.

"I promise you aren't a milk cow. And if you want to do all

those things, pizza and movies, all that, we can. You say when and we will. But right now I need you, I'm hungry. I really need you."

I willed her with my mind. Which sounds incredible, but my hunger, my dependence, melted her a bit. It pushed into her armor. I saw the frown soften, the sympathy in her face replacing the anger. A flipped switch. She nodded and extended her arm. I released the breath I was holding and went to her, my mouth instantly to her skin.

XX.

Interestingly, the revelation that I could actually control Sabrina made me want to be more careful with her. I thought of Hugh in the diary. I didn't want to be like that. I didn't want to use her and drain her with no regard.

So I made an effort. We went to a movie theater, my first ever. The theater was dark and noisome, filled with chattering teenagers. The air was heady with artificial butter and the acrid smells of over a hundred bodies. It was a slasher movie and told the story of a group of friends out camping that get attacked by a maniac. Each of the group gets dispatched graphically and horrifically for the audience to see, all but the virginal tomboy who manages to outsmart the killer and get away.

Overall, it was interesting. I'd never watched much horror growing up and I found myself scared for the characters, jumping in places, averting my eyes. I was filled with relief as the credits scrolled and the house lights went up.

As we left the theater, Sabrina kept looking at me and chuckling. When we got to the car she cracked up.

"What's so funny?" I asked.

"You. You were totally scared in there!"

"So? It's a horror movie. It's supposed to scare people, right?"

"But you're a vampire."

I flinched at the word, hating it. It evoked images of capes, coffins, crosses. Undead. I was none of those things. I was alive. My heart beat. I ate food. I slept. I could walk in the sun. I was a regular person. Sabrina noticed that I wasn't amused. Her laughter dried up.

"Sorry, it's just funny, is all." She ran a hand through her hair. "I thought you'd think all the blood everywhere was sexy or funny or something."

I opened the car door, and paused before getting in to respond. "That's gross, Sabrina. I don't want to see anyone get hurt. I don't like what I have to do."

A group of rowdy friends spilled out of the theater. They were boisterous, laughing and roughhousing, and watching them reminded me that I would always be on the outside. I couldn't even watch movies like a regular person. I thought Sabrina understood, that she got me, but I was wrong. No one could understand.

She tried to change the subject to lighten the mood, but I couldn't bring myself to play along. She swore and we drove home in silence.

XXI.

A few weeks passed and Sabrina and I fell into a routine. Once a week, we did something that she wanted to do: a movie, a meal, whatever. And bi-weekly, I got to feed off of her.

During this time, my mother showed marked improvement. Her face filled out, and she kept some weight on her bones. She'd even started to become more independent, bathing and dressing, fixing some of her own meals. We'd reached an odd impasse, her and I. Living in the home together, filled with mutual resentment and frustration but unable to go anywhere else. She made herself scarce when Sabrina came around, her disapproval plain. But she couldn't do anything about it, unless she wanted to put herself in danger or take up serial killing again.

It was a cold December night, a week before holiday break, and Sabrina was over. And I'd just finished, rising from between her thighs. We were both surprised and relieved by her period that month. The past few days had been mutually pleasurable for both of us and that made me feel good. I wanted her to be happy with me, to feel we were equals as much as we could be in our situation.

So on this night, she lay sated and smiling. I cleaned myself up and crawled into the bed with her, pulling the heavy covers with me and nestling up to her throat, enjoying the heat and steady thrum of her pulse. If I could purr, I would have.

We lay together, limbs intertwined. I was dozing when Sabrina blurted, "I want to talk about your father."

I sat up, instantly tense. "My father?"

I hadn't really thought of him outside of a character in my mother's diary. A person, a monster, who contributed in making me. I'd never imagined him as someone I would know, or have a relationship with. Sabrina plowed on in a rush.

"Hear me out. Right after you gave me the journal, like that same weekend, I started googling him. Just to—" she licked her lips excitedly, trying to find the words "—to corroborate your crazy story. And I found him! I just never told you. But I've been keeping track of his gallery, and of him ever since. I even found pictures online of him. He looks just like you." I could see she was both proud of herself and a little guilty at keeping something so major from me. I squeezed my hands together, even the idea of meeting my father filled me with dread.

Sabrina rushed on: "Anyways, after the movies the other night, I started thinking. You need to talk to someone like you. I'm trying to understand where you're coming from—I'm trying. You know I am. But I'm not like you. You need someone like you, to help you." She was thrumming with eagerness now. "His old gallery—the one that had your mom's show—isn't around anymore, but Hugh's got another one in Brooklyn now."

"I don't even know how to respond to any of that." My father was real. And Sabrina knew where he was. I got out of bed, suddenly ice cold and needing to be doing something. I pulled a sweater on, keeping my back to Sabrina.

"Well, he's like you, we know that, and he's your father. Aren't you even a bit curious?" She beamed up at me, entirely too proud of herself.

"I don't know. This is all too much, too fast. Last month I thought I was dying of cancer or something. And now I'm . . . whatever I am, and I have a father someplace? And you knew and didn't tell me until now." I paced the room. I was scared. How could Sabrina do this without talking with me? And how could she read the diary and want to find this guy?

"Winter break's coming up. And I have a crazy idea. I think we should drive down there and just check it out. It's only eight hours, maybe even six if we make good time. My cousin goes to college at Drew University. It's like an hour outside the city. She said we could stay with her. And—worst case—if we get too scared, we just go to the Statue of Liberty and come home. Don't you want to understand what you are, where you come from?"

I turned on her. Angry that she'd planned all this behind my back. "Why are you doing this? What's in it for you?"

She recoiled a little, hurt, but bounced back fast. "Because I care about you. If there are others like you . . . you wouldn't feel so alone."

"That . . . man . . . didn't want to be a father. He didn't want me. And he doesn't even know I exist. Why would he want anything to do with me now?"

Sabrina reached out of bed and took my hand. Her touch was incredibly soothing. I would never take for granted the simple act of touching, having been deprived my whole life. I felt greedy enough to take my other hand and place it on top, trapping her in between like a clamshell or a Venus flytrap.

"Just think about it. I know it's scary, so just think about it."

"Okay. Okay. I'll think about it." But I felt extremely ambivalent about the whole situation.

<hr />

I spent the next few days thinking about it, hard. On one hand, Hugh—my father—could be a monster. He could even hurt me, or worse. On the other, Sabrina could be right and this could be my only opportunity to talk to someone else like me. What if there was a community of people like me out there? A nest of vampires? Way too True Blood, too fictional. But still. I couldn't waste this chance. I needed answers, and Hugh was the only one who could give them.

I called Sabrina midweek and agreed to the trip.

XXII.

Remarkably, Sabrina's mother allowed her to take the car for our trip during winter break. Sabrina assured me her mother had a very trusting and hands-off approach to child-rearing, and once Sabrina spun my dramatic story of my dying mother and discovering a long-lost father, her mother was tearily handing over the keys and a wad of gas money.

What that poor woman must have thought of me. Sabrina had made a joke about me reminding her of Norman Bates and it hit a little too close to home. It took all my strength to explain that he was a killer of women, a human killer, and that I was something else. But I remembered the movie from late-night TV, the tall spooky house with a spookier-still old mother, the obedient only son. I could sympathize with him. The isolation, the resentment and the fear of making a change. For some, horrible and familiar was better than the unknown. I didn't want to be like that anymore.

On the Saturday morning we were leaving, I found myself sitting in the bathtub, the water raining on my head, terrified at what I was about to do.

It's not too late to say no, a little voice reminded me over and over. But this is what you prayed for, another chided. A change. Answers.

And finding Hugh would do that. Hugh. I careened through every emotion from numbing fear, to childish excitement sitting in that tub.

Later, when Sabrina's car horn tooted, I was as ready as I'd ever be. Duffel bag over my shoulder, I turned back to the den where my mother was propped up in her familiar chair, the radio playing a piano sonata. She stared at me, more lucid and alive than ever. All week I'd been pumping her full of protein and iron. She had some color in her cheeks and was holding onto some weight. She could even fill the stove with the wood I'd piled, plenty more than we normally went through in a week. The fridge was full of supplies to make sandwiches and soup in cans were stacked high on the counter. I left out huge bowls of water and food for Tommy the Cat and extra litter boxes. Clothes and blankets at easy reach for her. I still feared I'd return to find a body, decomposing in this exact spot. It was impossible not to, she'd been helpless for so long.

"I need to do this. I need to at least try to find him. I need to find out how I'm supposed to live like . . . this. It can't be the way we've been doing it all these years."

She nodded, blinking back tears, her hands squeezed into knobby fists. I closed the door and left it unlocked behind me. It had started snowing that morning, and already a few powdery inches coated the drive and yard. The air was crisp and filled with wood smoke.

The dark sedan idled, the headlights illuminating the falling snowflakes. Sabrina waved, beaming as I approached. I had to remind myself that this was, to her, a road trip adventure. A soap opera of monsters and mystery parents. A departure from her ordinary, normal, perfect family. I'd warned her all week that if we found my father, it was unlikely he'd be excited to see us. Would we even survive meeting Hugh McGarrett? Sabrina's smile evaporated when she saw me.

"What's up? You okay?"

I just nodded, trying to summon a smile.

"This is my first time leaving home. I hope my mom will be all right on her own."

Sabrina's eyes widened at the reality of that, as I tossed my duffel in the back seat and buckled myself into the passenger seat. She dropped the gear into reverse and accelerated, dirt and snow spraying.

"She's doing a lot better, Jane. There's a big bad world out there, and you're about to go explore it. Your mom will be fine."

Sabrina turned up the radio, the gnashing angry synth drowning out our voices as we drove onto the main road. I turned back once. The gate had been left open by a foot, and I was tempted to have her turn around so I could close it, before realizing the absurdity of it all. Let the gate be open, let the house exist without me to hold it up, to be its heart and eyes. I faced forward and allowed the miles of trees and houses to blur, letting my vision un-focus, floating above it all, tethered to my body like a balloon on a string.

The hours melted by, rural roads with few cars, all dirty from the slush and street salt. Miles of snow, dusting the trees and piled high and brown on the sides of the road. The roads slowly became highways like streams flowing into larger rivers. After a few hours we stopped for gas at a large rest stop oasis. The station glowed clean white amidst all the asphalt, the murky sky, the dirty snow. We sat in the car, the heat on full blast. We ate our over-processed fast food, the grease coating my mouth long after it was swallowed.

I sipped my coffee and watched Sabrina over the rim. My stomach felt empty still, the burger a greasy lump in my gut. She had a smear of ketchup at the side of her mouth. She chewed loudly and talked with her mouth full. Her hair was braided into pigtails. A streak of dyed pink was mixed into the shiny artificial blue black. Her hooded sweatshirt had the Misfits skull emblazoned across it. Her nails were painted pink to match the streak in her hair. Her right hand, squeezing the steering wheel, had three rings: one a skull, one a glass bauble, another a silver snake.

Sabrina was more like my mother than I was. Her clothes, her art, her desire to be someone. They both wanted people to see them as unique. My mother wanted people to see an artist. Sabrina wanted to be seen as an individual. How did I look from the outside? What did I want anyone to see? What would my father think of me?

That I looked like him, probably. A few days earlier my curiosity got the better of me and I asked Sabrina to show me a picture of him. He and I had the same big nose and thick eyebrows. The same dark brown hair and pale olive skin, the same shadowy brown-black eyes. The brown of wet rotting wood on forest floors.

But beyond a girl that looked like him, what else would he see in me? What did anyone see? Sabrina spent so much time cultivating a look and making a statement. But with my long hair and practical, thrift-store clothes, I looked nothing like Sabrina.

What did I look like to people? Poor? Weird? Would Hugh be ashamed of my appearance?

I turned to Sabrina. "What do I look like to you? If you just saw me in a crowd. What would you think of me?"

She stopped eating and regarded me strangely, mouth still full. "What do you mean? What got you thinking of that?"

"I'm going to meet my . . . Hugh for the first time. I was thinking about how much time people spend creating an identity. You make a lot of choices in what you wear. I don't. I was wondering how that works, how much real thought goes in. Hugh's a fancy guy. He likes nice things and art. How much of people's avoidance of me is how I look?"

I thought Sabrina might blow off the question, but instead she glanced at me quickly in between passing a few cars. "I guess, if I just saw you, I'd definitely think you were a little strange. Your clothes aren't current. But I think it's less what you wear and more how you carry yourself. You could be wearing anything, really. You seem . . . above that sort of stuff, I guess. Makes us mere mortals feel insecure. You don't wear makeup or jewelry. You're all dark and mysterious, and intimidating. I guess what I'm trying to say is, in a world of people who are trying to create an identity, the one who has a genuine one would always be an outcast, y'know?"

I sat back, staring out the dirty windshield at the other patrons of the rest stop. Such variety and bustle. Unruly children, stuffing food in their mouths, arguing. Young couples hugging, not a care in the world. Each person a vibrant, glowing beacon of life and energy. And I just sucked it in, like a black hole, stealing the light. An empty vacuum in space.

"He'll like you, Jane. How could he not? Fancy man or no." Sabrina said, squeezing my hand.

"Thanks, I hope you're right. I've always felt so alone. Shunned, even."

I nodded out at the parking lot. "Gazelles aren't friends with lions after all."

The discomfort in my gut had escalated a bit, after the hours in the car, being so close to Sabrina. I felt the first claws of hunger. I think Sabrina saw the shift, my gaze sharpening like a predator's.

"I just don't know how I'm supposed to just be like this forever, I want to just have a conversation with you without wanting to feed on you," I whispered.

Sabrina sipped her coffee and gave me a forced smile. I knew she didn't want to feed me either.

"That's what this whole trip is about. Finding someone like you, trying to understand what your life can be."

She packed up the rest of her food and tossed it in the back seat. After checking the coast was clear, she rolled up the sleeve of her sweatshirt. I'd never admit to her that there was an element of danger on both sides. That every time it was a little harder to stop, that the act of taking her blood was one of the few things that brought me pleasure. And more shameful still, the power over her life, the knowledge I could hurt her, was exciting. Her skin was salty from the hours of driving and greasy food. There was a trace of her perfumed body wash too. And laundry detergent. Beneath all that was her real scent, unique as a fingerprint.

I sank my teeth in. I could hear Sabrina's breathing hitch as I began to suck. I was instantly miles away, deep beneath the earth. I was safe beneath the ground. Above, I felt her moving above me, rustling like leaves around my head. Pressure on my skin, pressure on my hair, but all of it easy to ignore. Finally, a sharp, mind-clearing pain. Like a bucket of ice water had hit me.

I sat up, startled, and located the source of the pain. My hand throbbed. There was a perfectly round, pink circle, charred into it, and the stench of burnt meat filled the car. I looked at Sabrina, confused, my eyes watering from the pain.

She was gasping, her body pressed into corner of her seat, as far from me as the space would allow. Her skin was a pasty white, hazel eyes round and rolling fearfully. She held the smoking car lighter in her hand.

XXIII.

"You . . ." Sabrina squeaked, her lip trembling. "You need to learn to stop. I almost fainted. I was punching you, screaming at you, but you wouldn't stop. I got the cigarette lighter . . ."

She gestured at my hand. The ache had subsided some, but was still there. A wave of sharp, black anger consumed me. I wanted to hurt her for hurting me. I think she saw it. Her eyes opened even wider and rounder than before. She swallowed audibly. I leaned toward her, just a fraction, could feel my lips pulling back from teeth.

What are you doing? This is Sabrina, your friend. I forced myself back from her, as far as I could go. The taste of blood in my mouth turned from pleasure to something nauseating. What the hell was I doing? I would have killed her if she hadn't stopped me. There was no part of me that had worried about her safety while I was greedily drinking her blood.

I wiped my face on the rough wool of my sleeve and opened the car door. The gust of winter wind was welcome compared to the cloying, too-warm car. The smell of fast food, burnt skin, and blood was too thick.

I stepped out into the parking lot. I couldn't think of

anything to say. Or do. I just started walking toward the rest stop. Through the automatic doors, the lights were overly bright and Christmas music blared. I squinted, my senses rebelling in this vulgar hub of human life.

Inside the ladies room, I splashed my face with cold water and rinsed my mouth. My hands were shaking. I stared at the dripping face in the reflection, the eyes frenzied, the mouth cruel. My cheeks flushed with stolen life. I breathed deeply, in the nose, out the mouth, in again. Slowly, the rage dissipated. The burn on my hand throbbed, and I knew it would leave a scar. It only seemed fair, really, to wear the brand of my victim for once.

I wondered if Sabrina would drive away, strand me here at the rest stop. Realize that she had made a series of bad choices, starting with befriending a vampire. It would be better for everyone. This relationship wasn't good for her. Here she was, always trying to help me and I was hurting her. I came to two depressing conclusions: I knew she'd keep letting me use her, and I lacked the fortitude to stop her. Pandora's box was open, and now that I knew what feeling good was like, I didn't want to stop.

Unsure what to do with myself, but not ready to talk to Sabrina, I slid down onto the dingy floor and stared off at the tile pattern. Periodically, women would come by to wash their hands. One glance at me and they'd scurry out.

A janitor entered with a trash barrel. As she changed the trash bag she met my eyes and smiled warmly, wished me happy holidays and started to leave. I was so surprised by her friendliness that I stood and called out to her.

She had soft eyes and distinct laugh lines. I asked her to repeat what she'd said. She smiled incuriously and said, again, "Happy Holidays." I nodded, astounded, and said it back.

Even more remarkable was when she reached out and gave me a supportive, almost motherly squeeze on the arm. She touched me willingly, without an ounce of fear. I smiled back, genuinely, before backing out and leaving the gas station.

So Sabrina wasn't an anomaly.

I knew, with my crocodile-predator brain, that if I forced that woman, she would have given me blood. I knew that I could have controlled her.

The science of this was making me curious. Maybe in a bigger city, there would be others who'd be welcoming and want to be near someone like me. Suddenly I felt a surge of hope that maybe I wouldn't have to be so alone, so loathed by everyone. The janitor's simple greeting had opened the world up a little wider, given me new options. I felt cautiously optimistic.

Sabrina's car was still in the parking lot. The wipers weren't on, so the windows were blanketed out with a layer of snow. I yanked open the door, trying to contain my new discovery and what it might mean. I had to remind myself I left this car after nearly killing her and getting myself burned for it. I was guilty and sorry, and needed to look the part. Sabrina sat slumped on her side still, head resting on her fist. Eyes staring out at nothing. The radio was on, and the car was overly warm. She didn't so much as glance at me. I slowly reached over and turned the heat down before clearing my throat.

"I'm so sorry. I hate that I hurt you again. I hate that we keep having to have this conversation. I will learn to control it."

She turned to me, eyes red-rimmed from crying, skin chalky. Even her lips beneath the gloss were pale.

"I don't know if we can keep doing this, Jane. I think you're just going to kill me one day. Maybe soon. Even if you don't mean to."

Sabrina pulled her sleeve back. The wound was bandaged with some gauze and tape. But her forearm was bruised, perfectly outlined handprints encircling her arm. I gingerly reached out and touched her. She flinched, but only a little.

I thought of my mother's journal, her complicated relationship with my father, how she loathed what he did to her body. But now I could see Hugh's side so much clearer: sure, the victims got some scars, but without them we'd die. I needed to be better about controlling myself, but more than that, Sabrina needed to know it was worth the risk. She needed to be reminded that she was keeping me alive, that I needed her more than anyone else. I took her hand and held it to my chest where my heart was beating, healthy and vital.

"You're braver than I could ever be and I need you. Without you I would have literally died. I don't know what else to say. Please don't lose faith in me." Sabrina's eyes teared up and she lifted her chin, breaking eye contact. "I don't want to hurt you, but there's something in me capable of killing you." I paused, debating on finishing my thought, the truth in it leaving me queasy. "And enjoying it. Hopefully Hugh can help me control the hunger. Control myself. Sabrina, you're more important to me than anyone else I know."

I willed her to understand, to believe me. Using that connection between us, I pushed. Her frown softened. She wanted to be needed by someone. But I knew she wanted more than that. I leaned forward and our lips touched. Sabrina released a sob and kissed me back furiously, her hands wrapping around me, pulling me close. I could feel the hot tears on her cheeks, on my own skin. Feel the conflicted emotion pouring out of her. We kissed deeply, the embrace becoming more intimate, all hidden away by the cover of snow in the parking lot.

Afterwards, she drank a large bottle of orange juice and took an iron supplement. We got back on the road, which was fairly clear as the snow was letting up. Sabrina was smiley again, trying to keep conversation light, but it felt forced. I worried that I was taking more than her blood.

XXIV.

The highways widened ahead of us, red taillights sparkling as night fell. I rolled the window down, my face pelted with needle stings of snow. My senses had become noticeably more acute as the weeks passed—my nose especially. I was in tune to the scents on the wind, even the sensation on my skin. My ears catalogued every sound.

If I found Hugh, would we be able to talk about all this?

Hugh. My father and a monster. Even the thought of him made my palms moist. Would he like me? Would he take me in? Would he try to kill me? There was no way to know the future and I needed to get a grip. Sabrina yawned loudly, the yawn turning into a groan. I welcomed the distraction. She'd been uncharacteristically quiet as she drove for the last few hours. I angled toward her, turning the music down a bit.

"You okay?"

Sabrina rubbed at her eyes and glanced my way. "Yeah. I'm just in the zone, focused on the road. Deep in thought."

"Any thoughts you want to share?"

"I'm thinking about how we need to make a plan."

I regretted my playful tone instantly, knowing the thoughts were more than likely about the danger of my father killing us. I wasn't ready to think about Hugh, whether he would welcome us, chase us away, or worse. So I just sat there in total silence, until Sabrina sighed, sounding annoyed.

"We need to plan, Jane. More than just drive down there."

"I know. Okay. So, we drive to his gallery and confront him?"

Sabrina sighed again and glanced at me. "It's not some paternal reveal talk show, Jane. Confront seems a bit . . ." she floated her hand around looking for the word ". . . aggressive. For a vampire. I think going to the gallery is best, since there'll be plenty of people around. And it'll be safer."

"Safer," I repeated.

"My cousin, Isabelle, is expecting us to show up at her place late tonight. So, I figure you go into gallery, and I'll hang back, stay out of sight, and be ready to dash if we need to. And who knows, he might be excited to see you."

I pressed my palms to my eyes. "I doubt it. You read that journal. He was not particularly pleased about having a baby."

"Oh, young, naïve Jane, your mom was what? Twenty? And they'd been dating for like two months. And she was essentially his bloodbag girlfriend. Why would he be excited about a baby vamp with some girl he was probably using?"

I was unsure how to respond. My long pause earned a quick glance from her. "A lot of guys freak about pregnancy scares. Normal guys. But there's a big difference between the idea of raising a baby, and a ready-made almost-grown daughter showing up. He might be happy to meet you even."

"Maybe."

"Granted, he may also freak out and try to kill you, like Highlander rules or something." When I looked at her quizzically, she continued: "My dad is obsessed with Highlander. We even have the collectible swords. Anyways, they're immortal. Have a whole 'there can be only one' thing, where they have to kill each other for territory or power. I don't know what vampire society is like."

"Or if there even is one," I said quietly. "Maybe they're just loners. Like spiders."

"Maybe. We have to be smart either way. We know Hugh has been around and can be dangerous. So, we just need to be smart about everything. Trust our guts."

We fell into silence, both lost in our own thoughts. I tried to imagine Hugh raising me from a baby. Would he have brought in blood nurses for me? Put little blood bags with bottle nipples on them for me in a crib? It was a garish image. Would my life have been better with a vampire dad raising me? It was hard to say, since most normal childhoods would probably have been better than mine. The more I thought about the care and maintenance a baby vamp would have needed, the more I could understand why Hugh wouldn't have wanted one.

Time passed. I'd been staring at the tree line, entranced, when Sabrina blurted: "New subject. Let's talk about us. Or I guess me. I was always suspicious that I liked girls more than boys. I never really gave it a name, you know? I think I was scared to. But with you, the second I saw you, I was drawn to you like a ship caught in a tractor beam. It was kind of scary."

My heart sank. "What if it's what I am and not who I am that draws you to me? What if this is more than liking another girl?" I paused, trying to shape the theory. "What if I'm doing something to you?"

I couldn't help but wonder where the line between attraction and biological imperative was with us. I could control Sabrina and make her do things, after all. Maybe I compelled her from the very beginning? The hungry and desperate thing inside me manipulating her from the start.

Sabrina scrunched up her face. "No, I don't buy it. I was the one pursuing you. I was the one who sat next to you. I was the one who offered you the ride. I practically forced myself into your house. I brought out the booze and made you dance with me. You might think you have this whole supernatural Dracula thing, but if we're being honest, I was very willing, very forceful. Hell, I might be the Edward here."

"Edward?"

"From Twilight, you know, stalkerish boyfriend, watches Bella sleep? Follows her around? Have you ever read a vampire book before?"

I could feel my cheeks flush. "Dracula, for school."

Sabrina released a braying laugh. "You are really bad at this! I'll give you a reading list when we get home. Catch you up. Twilight can be last on that list, since it's basically about creepy old virgins who go to high school forever."

I poked my finger through a hole in my sweater. "Deal. But let's be serious for a second, because I'm still worried that I'm making you like me. I guess . . . maybe it's easier for me to think I've compelled you to be with me. I don't see any reason anyone would like me otherwise. Seems like I'm a lot of trouble."

"Jane, enough already. You keep saying shit like that. You

need to give yourself more credit. Seriously. So what about me? Were you into me right away like that?"

I knew I couldn't be completely honest and tell her the truth, that the thing in me used sex to get to her blood. I worked the thought like a piece of clay. "I never thought much about love or boyfriends. Or girlfriends. But the first time we touched, I liked it. Didn't know what it meant, maybe?"

"It's probably more complicated for you. Food and sex. Since you need to get close to your food, and the easiest way would be if everyone was naked and distracted." Sabrina waggled her eyebrows suggestively and my face felt hot, like she'd pulled the thoughts from my head.

"Yeah. Though I don't like thinking of you as food."

Sabrina's face grew a little more serious. "Do you think you could kill someone? Drink them dry?"

I'd had a feeling we'd be heading this way again sooner rather than later. I sighed. "Do you want an honest answer?" She nodded. "Yes. I think I could. It's why I can't think of you as food. I can't forget that people are . . . people. That you matter. I get lost in the blood—it's so nice there, like an oasis in the desert. I've spent my life starving, subsisting, and the temptation is very strong. Even though I care about you and respect you. The thing in me, it doesn't care."

"Guess that's the price of being what you are. It's not your fault though. And besides, it's my fault for being too delectable." She grinned, but it didn't reach her eyes.

I was curious about how much Sabrina believed what she was saying, and how much she wanted to believe it. How many times would this happen before she got sick or died? Was my mother an anomaly for leaving my father?

"You think you would have figured out what you were if I hadn't moved here?" asked Sabrina.

"Honestly? I would have killed my mother without a doubt . . . but after that? I guess I would've just died. I wouldn't have thought I would need . . . what I need." I scratched at my scalp, my bun suddenly feeling tight.

"Would it have been better?" Sabrina asked. "To waste away? You and your mom dead in that old house? That's pretty bleak, Jane."

I shrugged. "My conscience would have been clear. I would have died thinking of myself as an innocent and tragic victim of bad luck. . . ." My voice cracked and I swallowed. "I have to live with myself, now. It's a horrible trade-off. If I want to feel good, feel alive, then I have to get what I need. There's no winning: do I stay sick but innocent, or healthy and a monster?"

"That's all pretty dramatic, Jane. People aren't as innocent as you make them out to be."

"Maybe. I think that's what's most terrifying about actually meeting my father. Does he even like people? Or does he think of them as food only?"

The snow had started up again, not too heavy, just fluffs that melted as soon as they touched the warmth of the windshield. The sky was darkening, the headlights cutting through the gray and the gloom highlighting the crystalline flakes as they plummeted from the sky. We started seeing signs for New York City, and with each one that streaked by, the twin sensations of excitement and trepidation grew.

Cutting through the winter gloom the city shone golden,

alive. I had seen the cityscape thousands of times on television and in magazines, but to see it with my own eyes, the sheer size of it, was unbelievable. Sabrina and I both laughed giddily as we drank it all in. There was something in me, an impulse that yearned to jump out of the car and vanish into the throngs of bustling bodies. I wanted to be absorbed into the endless energy that kept the city alive.

It was full night by the time we made it through the traffic and into Brooklyn, driving along the crisscrossing labyrinthine streets. Sabrina drove nervously while I kept an eye out for any wayward pedestrian or cyclist.

We finally drove under the Manhattan Bridge, the giant structure was dark and awe-inspiring from beneath. The river was black, glistening as it reflected the city. Under the bridge the cobbled streets were eerily quiet. Sabrina and I hadn't spoken since we crossed under the bridge, the city demanding all of our focus. After a few wrong turns on dark streets, we found the address on Jay Street. We parked, semi-legally, idling in front of a glowing gallery nestled in a tall brick warehouse.

"Well, we made it!" Sabrina said and clapped her hands together. She fished her cell phone out and stepped from the car, calling her mom to check in. My eyes were glued to the doorway of the gallery, and what lay beyond it.

When Sabrina got back into the car, I asked, my mouth gone dry, "So you think I should just walk in there, and try to find someone who looks like me? Thought you said confronting a vampire was a bad idea. And how do we even know he's in there?" The longer we sat there, the more I thought we'd been too impulsive and that this was all a terrible idea. I should be home, in bed with my cat.

Sabrina watched the gallery door closely. "We know he's there. And, it won't be a total confrontation."

"How do you mean?" I whispered, even though no one would have heard or noticed us.

"Because I emailed him," Sabrina said sheepishly. "I thought it'd be better not to tell you."

"What?"

"We came down tonight because there's a big opening. We knew he'd be there, and there'd be lots of witnesses. And I sent an email to him at the gallery, just basically saying that you were someone from his past, a friend of Vivian DeVry, and that you'd be at the show, and that you wanted to speak with him," she replied.

I was at a loss. He already knew I was coming. Sabrina had it all planned out.

"So, you go in, find him, I'll go in totally separate, and keep an eye on things. It gets scary or weird, you bolt, get to the car, and we go to my cousin's dorm in Jersey."

"How will you know if things get scary or weird?" My mouth was bone dry, the panic creeping up and threatening to choke me. Things had gotten too real, too fast.

"Hoot like an owl," Sabrina said with a shrug. "Nothing crazy, just like HOO HOO."

I laughed despite my nerves, or maybe because of them.

"Okay, not my best idea. How about you cough loudly? Pull a fire alarm? If you had a cell phone you could text me but you don't."

"Did he answer? I mean, did Hugh answer? The email. You

wrote as me, I assume."

She nodded. "Of course. We don't want him to know about me, right? Not until we know if it's safe. I made you an email address, since it's ridiculous you don't have one. And said I was you."

"And he said . . . ?"

"Looking forward to meeting you."

I gaped at her, shocked yet again that she had held all this information from me.

"Don't be mad, Jane. I just didn't want you to lose your nerve, or worry about a full-on ambush."

"But you told him! You gave up any advantage we had to surprise him."

Sabrina rolled her eyes at me. "Jane, we aren't going in there to stake him! You're going to meet you damned father. What advantage is there to surprise? Again, it's not some daytime talk show. This is your life—this is talking to another creature like you and getting some advice."

"And what if he's dangerous? What if this is all a trap?"

Sabrina smiled. "Then you use this." She pulled out a steak knife from her purse. "I brought one for me too. They're my mom's fancy Wüsthof knives. She'll kill me if she finds out I took them, so just don't lose yours, okay?"

"I think losing a nice knife is the last thing we should be worrying about." I gingerly wrapped the knife in a glove and tucked it into my pocket.

At eight o'clock, we began to see people heading for the lit doors, stamping the snow from their shoes, shaking out umbrellas and scarves. The place was filling up fast. It was now or never.

XXV.

"Okay, show time, Jane," Sabrina said, pulling down the sun visor mirror, inspecting herself. "You go in, check it out, try to find him. I'll wait five minutes, watching from the window and then go in. I'll act like I'm on the phone or something. Once I'm inside, I'll just blend in."

I gestured to the doorway, my voice barely above a whisper. "How on earth can we blend in? We're teenagers." I was almost worried Hugh could hear us conspiring in the car. How good was vampire hearing, anyway?

"Put this on. . . ." Sabrina rummaged in her bag. She pulled out some lipstick and handed it to me. She then wiggled out of her sweatshirt. ". . . secret is to just act like you belong. Look at some art, try to sneak some wine, and if we can't find him, then we ask whoever works there to leave a message. Then we wait for him to contact us, or you."

I applied the bright red lipstick in the visor; it made me look like a different person. "I don't know if I can do this, Sabrina. I'm scared. Do I even look okay?"

A rectangular strip of light shone out onto the snowy street. Shadows of the people inside flickered on the ground. Any of those outlines could have been Hugh. My nerve was failing—we were being silly and impulsive. I glanced over as Sabrina wriggled awkwardly into a tight black dress. She'd undone her braids, her bottle-black hair gleaming wetly in the sodium streetlights.

"You look great. It's now or never, Jane. We need to do this. If he knows anything that can help you . . ."

I nodded and opened the car door, the snow blowing in ferociously. We stepped out onto the icy street. Above us, a subway streaked overhead, cars clattering. A garbage barge slid along the oily waters nearby, a flashing light bobbing on its roof as it let out a sad siren to anyone listening before it passed out of view. I was in a strange city, far from anything I knew. My chest was tight, and the snow accumulated fast on my shoulders. It should have motivated me to get moving, head toward the gallery, toward light and warmth. But I was terrified.

Sabrina stood on the other side of the car. "You can do this, Jane. I'm here. If it doesn't work out, we take off, get pizza, it's all fine."

I took a few more breaths, forcing out the fear as much as I could. My lungs felt a quarter of their size. I wondered if this was what a panic attack felt like. Sabrina came to my side, taking my hand in hers and squeezing it. Her support got me moving. She laced her arm through mine, half walking and half dragging me.

The door was clear glass and metal. Printed on it was McGARRETT INC. I stared at the name and felt faint. My father.

Sabrina opened the door and ushered me through. "Hoo hoo," she whispered. "But seriously if you're in real danger, you scream, stab him and then you tear out of there. Get to the car. Good luck!"

And then I closed the door and I was inside, alone.

The space was blindingly white, the exposed ceiling the only remnant of the industrial space. Lights hung down, angled to shine on the paintings throughout the room. The paintings themselves were enormous, abstract, and very white and blending into the walls. Each had a violent, almost intimate splash of red that instantly made me think of blood on bedclothes. Instantly a flash of hundreds of mornings hit me: finding my mother bloodied, stains on her sheets, her towels. Blood soaking miles of white linens, drowning in seas of bleach. The paintings suddenly overwhelmed me, and I shut my eyes.

"Intense, isn't it?"

I turned, startled by the voice. It was a petite woman, Asian features, white-blonde hair, dressed in an oversized white dress shirt and black leggings. Her high heels were red. She matched the paintings. Her mouth was large and cherry red. When she smiled, it revealed very white, somewhat crooked teeth. I stared at her for a moment, still not accustomed to people talking to me of their own volition.

I knew instantly that she was like Sabrina, like the janitor at the rest stop. I turned to Sabrina, but remembered she was still outside, no doubt casing the place for signs of my father. The red-lipped woman stared at me expectantly.

"Yeah, it reminds me of . . . some unpleasant things."

The woman studied the painting thoughtfully before returning her intense gaze to me. "I call this one The Dowry.

The white one on the other side is called The Virgin. They're companion pieces. The before and after."

I nodded, looking at the painting again, summoning memories of my mother, and the scores of art books I'd looked through as a child, trying to find a common interest we could share. I hoped it would allow me to talk to the artist without sounding like a gawky kid.

"My name is Natsuki." She studied me so intensely I resisted the urge to squirm. She had come straight to me in a room full of people. Did that mean she knew what I was? Would she want to see my invitation? I cleared my throat and calmed down. She could just be curious what a young stranger thought of her work.

I tried to look at ease and responded, "I'm Jane. Nice to meet you. You have . . . you have a real talent. I was immediately emotionally struck."

Natsuki didn't retract her probing stare, a perfectly shaped sliver of eyebrow arching.

"You look so familiar to me, Jane. Have we met before?"

I shook my head, looking over her head and scanning the room for Sabrina. I didn't see her, and a flutter of panic rose in my chest. Natsuki seemed to sense the change and turned as well, looking across the crowd. Her long, loose white-blonde hair fanned out as she spun. It smelled like lilies.

I blurted, "I'm just looking for my friend. Supposed to meet me here."

Natsuki spun back to me, her smile easy but also unnerving.

"She'll turn up, I'm sure. It's not a very big place, but it's filled with interesting people to ensnare her. Now tell me, Jane, how is it you came to be here at my show?"

Suddenly her warm hand was touching the small of my back, startling me, as she guided me toward the next pair of paintings.

"Oh. I'm very interested in art. My mother was a, is a . . . a painter as well."

"Oh? Would I know her work?"

I stumbled now. I searched the room a bit more urgently for Sabrina but couldn't spot her or hear her voice over the music and overall din. My heart hammered.

"Probably not, but she did have a show with, uh, Mr. McGarrett, a long time ago."

Natsuki raised her eyebrow again at that. "Really? How interesting. . . ."

With the speed of a snake her left hand shot out, and the glint of a large diamond ring waved to catch someone's attention. I followed her outstretched arm, trying to see who she was signaling to. From my angle, I could only see the side of a man's head, his brown, silver-shot hair, and his tall broad stature.

As he drew nearer, and I could see his face, it felt like all the air had been pushed out of my body. My blood froze in my veins. The man appeared to have a similar reaction, stopping mere feet from me. It was as if the sounds and bustle of the room dimmed, and it was just the two of us.

There was no question I was his daughter. The brown hair, the dark eyes, the nose. His face was blank and the color, what little there was, visibly drained from his face. All of this happened in seconds, but he recovered in a flash. A tight smile replaced the shock. His whole demeanor shifted as he came up, sliding a familiar arm around Natsuki.

"You summoned?" The man said this with a grin, his British accent subtle. He gave me a quick once-over. I sucked in a breath and tried not to gape. I'd forgotten to be smooth, forgotten decorum at all. His smile was false, even hostile, as he appraised me. The seconds stretched between us.

"Yes, Hugh, this is my new friend, Jane. She's a fan of my paintings. She found them particularly moving. Barely got in the door before being snagged by The Dowry. It's exciting seeing someone so young so passionate about the arts, no? She was telling me that her mother was an artist, and that you hosted a show of hers . . . when was that, dear?"

My whole body was I fight or flight mode, and I desperately wanted to flee. Breathe, breathe. Where is Sabrina? I looked around one last time, forcing myself to breathe.

And miraculously, I found my courage. My eyes met Hugh's. Hugh—my father. Dad? I had no idea how to think of this stranger. His expression was unreadable, intense. I decided to go for broke—this was why we'd come here, after all.

"About eighteen years ago."

I let my words hang between us heavily as my gaze locked on his. Natsuki's brows shot up as she turned to him, the pieces falling into place. She seemed to be enjoying the tension. "What's her name? This mother of yours?" she asked.

Hugh's face was a deliberate blank.

"Vivian DeVry," I said clearly.

"I got an email that you might be coming. How wonderful you were able to make it," Hugh said coolly. I knew nothing about him but the scribbled ravings in a diary. Had I made a terrible mistake? He could be dangerous. He could be anything.

From the corner of my eye I finally spied Sabrina. She was about ten feet away, which felt like a thousand in that instant. I ignored her, not wanting Hugh to notice her, and turned back to him. Hugh was about to speak when we were interrupted by a stocky bald man in horn-rimmed glasses and a tall, older man with dark skin and long dreads. They wanted Natsuki's attention.

As she turned to them all smiles, Hugh took my arm. It was a casual, even friendly gesture, but I could feel the force beneath it. He steered me through the crowd quickly and without raising alarm. Along the way he would nod or greet someone, but our trajectory was as clear as if people were making a path. I thought about the knife in my pocket. Or about hooting like an owl.

We passed the bar and a restroom before Hugh opened a door to a smaller gallery space. Before I could decide, he pushed me inside before closing the door and turning, his body tense. The room's walls were painted black or dark gray, and the room was very dark, except for a single light shining on a small white sculpture on a white pedestal. Two benches in black and chrome faced the sculpture on either side of the room. The sculpture was of a figure, a woman, with sagging breasts and sagging head. At her feet was a still baby. Too limp to be sleeping. It made me uncomfortable and I couldn't look at it. As uncomfortable as Hugh, who was still quite near, was making me.

XXVI.

"*Guess* Vivian lied to me."

Hugh's voice was cold, but there was a hint of something else there: surprise, maybe? I watched him warily, moving to the other side of the small room to give myself some distance, keeping the grim sculpture between as some protection. He paced, catlike, his eyes constantly returning to me. Unsure how to proceed.

"Is she dead?" he asked point blank, stopping his movement abruptly. The sudden stillness was unsettling.

"No."

He stared at me, astonished, as he eased himself onto one of the benches nestled in the corner. He was almost entirely in shadow.

"Really? That's remarkable. So, she sent you here?"

"No, she didn't send me. I never would've found out about you at all if I hadn't discovered her journal. She never mentioned you once. I came to you because I have no one else to turn to. She's been dying slowly all these years. I need to understand . . . what I am."

I felt exhausted, the fear fizzling to a more familiar despair, as if the ground was finally opening up beneath me. I came around the sculpture, closer to Hugh, praying that my voice would stay firm. I stared at the glossy cement floor, and I could feel his eyes on me as I looked down.

"You know what you are," he said.

"I need to know how to survive, how to do this." I gestured at my body. I saw a flicker of something in him then—remorse, pity even. If nothing else, even if he hated me, even if he kicked me out, or worse, at least there was someone who understood. I wasn't all alone.

After a long pause, all the while watching me, he made a frustrated-sounding noise. "It's not like there's a manual. And from the look of you, you seem to be doing all right."

I felt my eyes well up. I didn't want to cry. Be strong, Jane. Hold your head up.

Hugh seemed like a man who easily stepped over those he thought were weaker. I wouldn't let him think that about me. Not even a snarky thanks for nothing would pass my lips.

"Well? You came all this way. That's it?" he said.

"I just hoped there was more. More than just finding people and feeding on them. I wanted to—learn, I guess."

Hugh laughed mirthlessly. "I don't have anything to teach you, Jane. I do what I need to survive, and so will you. I didn't want a child for this exact reason. It's hard enough keeping myself fed, let alone someone else, a kid for that matter."

Do not cry. But I was tired and this was my exact fear, that he wouldn't want to help me. Tears falling, I nodded, not trusting my voice. I turned and walked toward the door.

"Jane." My hand was on the knob and finally I turned back to him. My disappointment was transforming into anger.

He'd risen, arms crossed. "Look kid, I'm sorry I don't have better answers for you." And something about how smug he looked pushed me over the edge.

"I'm so sick of being treated like a mistake and an inconvenience. I know you didn't want a kid, and ultimately my mother didn't either. All I came here to figure out was how to survive being a monster, being a fucking vampire. I need to understand what I am. And for some reason I thought you could help me. God, you and my mother were a perfect match. Selfish, cruel . . . you're acting like I need you to go to a daddy/daughter dance or something. I am so sorry to impose. I'll just keep flailing around in the dark trying not to kill anyone."

I yanked the door open, but his arm shot out and he grabbed me. I snarled at him, trying to pull away. Hugh's hand tightened and he pushed me against the wall with a thud. Just like the journal. He did this to my mother all those years ago.

Panic crept up into my throat, tempting me to call out. Hugh leaned in close, eyes cold like a reptile. Polished onyx. Spilled ink. The same eyes I saw in the mirror every day. His breath smelled of liquor, and beneath that, the coppery hint of blood.

"I can't have you running out there and causing a scene. This is my business. You need to calm down."

"And you need to take your hands off me."

His stare bore into mine, nearly nose to nose. I sniffled, I was scared, but I meant it—I wanted his hands off me. He couldn't just toss me around and rough me up like some disgruntled abusive tyrant.

He let go. My arm ached where Hugh had grabbed me. I rubbed it absently, glaring at him. He stepped away and actually appeared embarrassed by his violence. He swore at the floor, then walked off across the gallery space.

"Sorry about that. Come along, if you want." I reluctantly followed Hugh through to his office, where he'd taken a seat behind a large glass-topped desk. He gestured for me to sit across from him, and after a bit of indecisive panic, I walked over and dropped into the chair.

"I need a drink." Hugh reached across his desk and pulled the top off an ornate, crystal decanter, and poured some amber liquid into two small glasses that were arranged on the corner of his desk. He slid one toward me. He took his and shakily I reached for my own. I had a sudden, impractical fear of poison, but I pushed it aside and took a sniff. It was pungent, the alcohol instantly making my eyes water.

Hugh smirked at me. "I assure you, it's very good whiskey. I think we both could use a belt or two. Cheers."

He slugged it back with a quick tip of his head. I stared at my glass before trying to imitate him move for move. I tried to mirror his confidence as I swallowed it. The whiskey seared my throat, the burn instantly reminding me of that night with Sabrina. I gasped and coughed while Hugh laughed, pouring himself another. He offered one to me but I shook my head.

The silence stretched, but it was less hostile. I glanced around the room—one wall had a large nude painting of a woman floating in water. Another wall had a black and white photograph of a goat skull. The other wall had a floor to ceiling bookshelf sagging with art books. There was no window. I tried to imagine Hugh working here all day, living his life all this time, while I led mine a few hundred miles north. And we never knew the other existed. I risked a look at him. Hugh was staring up into the corner, miles away. Finally, he cleared his throat, sat forward and steepled his fingers, regarding me over them.

"I handled this badly . . . Jane. And I apologize for being so brutish a moment ago. You're right. It's not your fault that you were born, nor is it your fault that you don't know who you are or where you come from. It just caught me off guard. Frankly, I haven't thought of your mother in years. And that ominous email had my hackles up."

I shifted in my seat, strangely more uncomfortable about his apology than anything before.

"Okay. I guess I could have handled the situation better too," I said. "I could have tried to call you, but I was afraid you wouldn't see me or you wouldn't believe me."

He laughed at that. "You know me better than you think. I probably wouldn't have." He crossed his legs, picking up a round stone paperweight and tossed it from hand to hand.

"Vivian was an amazing artist and had such lovely red hair. Does she still paint?"

I shook my head, eyes on the floor. "She's too sick. She been bedridden for a long time."

"And where do you live? Surely not in the city? I vaguely remember gossip that . . . your . . . mother had moved home."

"No. We live up in northern New Hampshire."

He wrinkled his nose at that, sipping his drink and looking back to me now. "Rural?"

I nodded. "Quite."

"My condolences. It's hard for people like us to find friends in small towns, I can imagine. Like finding a needle in a haystack."

"I found one," I said, stopping myself before I said anything more.

"One?" He chuckled. "Explains why Vivian isn't in good shape, I imagine."

My face heated with shame. I glared at him. "That's why I'm here. Tell me about people like us."

"It's not a close-knit community. We are pretty territorial, and there are a limited number of willing donors, as you've noticed. So, we tend to stay clear of each other. But respectfully. We can reproduce, but it's rare. And the mortality rate is high, for babies and especially mothers."

There was a knock on the door. Hugh frowned but called out a response. Natsuki peeked in, a smile on her face. I didn't like this woman. Despite the blonde hair, she reminded me of a crow. Her eyes glittered as she glanced between the two of us.

"Yes?"

"Just checking on you, dear. Some people are asking for you."

"I doubt it."

"They are!" she said, petulant. Her nosiness was obvious and unattractive.

"I'll be out soon. Thank you, Natsuki," he dismissed her evenly. She nodded, her curiosity appeased, and closed the door.

"She knows about you, doesn't she? What you are. You feed off of her. Don't you?"

Hugh sighed. "She does. She's my fiancée." He saw the shock on my face and chuckled, leaning back. "Natsuki is a brilliant artist. Not only that, but she's from a very wealthy family, and she has a profitable career here and in Japan. It would be foolish not to marry her, don't you think? A bad business decision."

I flailed around for a response. "Do you even love her?"

"That's a gauche question, Jane. You don't know me."

"You don't know me either," I snapped, and would have continued, but Hugh held a up a hand.

"Of course I love her. But for you and I, love means something different than to regular humans. I would have never started my first gallery if not for the money left me by my first wife. You will understand all this as you get older."

"Did you love my mother?"

Hugh didn't hesitate. "I did. She was a vibrant woman." But he was lying, I could see it plainly, and besides she wasn't rich, she was just a means to an end. I didn't know if I wanted to cry, or leave, or scream.

He glanced discreetly at his watch and got up, taking the choice away from me.

"I really do need to get out there. Duty calls. You should leave me your cell, or the hotel you're staying at."

I dropped my eyes to my chest, too quickly.

"Uh . . . maybe we could just set a time to meet again? I don't have a phone."

He opened a drawer and dug around in it. "It's snowing and below freezing outside. Where did you plan to stay, Jane?"

"Don't worry about it. Just tell me when and where and I'll be there." I didn't want to give him any information about Sabrina, or her cousin's dorm.

Hugh cocked his head. "You really had no plan past finding me? Well, I guess the least I can do for a surprise illegitimate child is offer you a place to stay for the night."

"You really don't have to," I protested. I had the feeling that Hugh did very little out of the kindness of his heart.

But Hugh held a hand up in protest. He then produced a set of keys out of the drawer and slid them to me across the desk. I stared at them confused.

"You're very lucky that I have a small apartment down the street for visiting artists. Natsuki is local so no one's using it right now." He scribbled on his business card and slid the address across the desk as well.

"I've got a place to stay. It's a generous offer, but I don't think so."

"I insist, Jane. If you're in the city, I would prefer to know where. It's close, and then we can talk more under less pressing time constraints."

I opened my mouth and he cut me off: "Take the keys, Jane. It's freezing and snowing. I know you don't know me, but you can trust me."

I took the keys, unsure what to say.

Hugh came around the desk and coolly smiled at me. "See? I can be a nice guy."

I felt like he was teasing me. Like I was one big joke. I didn't respond, just stood and turned away.

"Oh. Before you leave. One question." I stopped. "Does anyone else know where you are? Or why you're here?"

My blood chilled. Hugh's forced casualness felt like a threat. I didn't want to give up Sabrina, but couldn't think of a deft way to lie to him off the cuff. "My friend, who drove. And her mother. And my mother up north." He nodded, reassured (or pretending to be), passing around me and out the door.

After composing myself, I followed him out, heading back into the throng. The crowd had doubled since I went into the office. The reek of alcohol, perfume, and sweat were thick in the space. I tried to find Sabrina, and, after standing dumbly in the middle of it all and turning in a slow circle, I finally spotted her. She was at the hors d'oeuvres table, hands filled with finger foods.

XXVII.

"*What* happened?" Sabrina hissed, her eyes scanning back and forth. We were pressed into the corner near the bar, the busiest part of the gallery. "I saw you two talking and suddenly Hugh dragged you away. I tried to follow, but that blonde Asian lady cornered me and I got stuck talking to her. I didn't say anything . . . but she was really nosey."

A tinkling of silverware on glass caught our attention. Everyone was now facing the opposite corner of the room, listening to Natsuki thanking everyone for coming. I used the opportunity to leave the gallery, Sabrina at my elbow. My father's gaze met mine as I opened the door to leave, but it gave nothing away. Natsuki followed his gaze and that same damn eyebrow rose. She kept talking, but I could feel her eyes on me even after the door was closed and we were out on the street.

I told Sabrina what had happened as we trudged through the snow to her car. After brushing it off, we drove the few blocks to the apartment scribbled on Hugh's business card. When we parked before the big nondescript brick building, the feeling I was leading us into a trap kept me from getting out of the car. I stared at the banks of black windows reflecting the city. The snow fell undisturbed on the streets. It felt deserted and post-apocalyptic out there. I had always imagined every inch of New York City was constantly buzzing and thriving with life, like an ant's nest, or a beehive. But this street was completely still.

"He wanted to know if anyone knew I was here, and I told him you were with me. I didn't want to risk lying. And I figured it was safer if I told him someone knew we were here," I blurted.

Sabrina frowned. She lit a cigarette and rolled the window down, expelling a plume of smoke.

"I don't know if we should stay, Sabrina. I can't figure Hugh out. I don't know if we're safe here. I think maybe we should go to Isabelle's. Can you call her?"

As Sabrina talked to her cousin, I stared out the window, lost in the thought. Hugh was real, and there were other vampires in the world. But if they were all like Hugh, I might not like or want to be around any of them.

Sabrina raised her voice into the phone and pulled my attention back into the car. "What do you mean you aren't at school? At a party? In Philly? You said we could crash with you! Remember?" Sabrina rolled her eyes. "Yeah, we are in the city. This is super shitty—there's a blizzard on in case you hadn't noticed! And, hello? Now we're homeless." She swallowed loudly, and glanced at the apartment building. "If we end up dead because of you, I'm gonna haunt you forever. And no, I am not being overly dramatic. Thanks for nothing. Yeah, have fun." She hung up her cheeks flushed. "Asshole."

I raised my eyebrows.

"My dumbass cousin went to some house party in Philly and won't be home until Sunday night. I can't believe her. So, okay . . . we could try to get a hotel, see if my mom could call in a credit card. Or we could sleep in the car?" She looked at the backseat frowning. "It's gonna be below freezing, so that's probably a bad idea."

"So, what should we do, Sabrina? Drive back tonight? I don't want to lose the opportunity to talk more to my father, even if he is also a huge asshole."

Sabrina chewed her lip, "Maybe we risk it and go check out Castle Dracula up there? We have knives, we can protect ourselves. If it's too scary we bounce . . . and I dunno, park in a pay garage and sleep in the car or something."

"Ugh, I don't know. A part of me—and this could just be the lost little girl who wants loving parents talking—thinks he's trying to be nice but lacks normal social graces. Like me. That maybe he offered us a place to crash because he didn't want us to freeze to death. We're kids on his doorstep, after all."

"So, are you talking us into or out of going up to the apartment, Jane?"

"Umm, I don't know. He's a killer! I'm sure of that. He basically confessed to marrying and killing women for their blood and money back there. It was creepy."

Sabrina smoked and thought. She squinted up at the building, then down the street for signs of anyone. For signs of Hugh. Finally, she said, "But maybe that isn't so weird among your people. What does your gut say?"

"My gut?" I blinked.

"Yes, your intuition. Do we go in and check it out? Or should we just drive away?"

I covered my eyes and groaned. "I just worry he doesn't think like . . . people. You wouldn't get it."

"Oh, because I'm a mere mortal and all that?"

"Don't joke, Sabrina. I'm totally serious. I know nothing about this guy. I'm worried that I'm so desperate to connect with someone like me, to share this burden, that I could put you in danger."

"This is what we came for, Jane."

"It may not be worth it," I said. I didn't want to be like my father—I couldn't be so cavalier about loving someone to death.

Sabrina was silent a moment, taking a drag off her smoke. The coils escaped from her nose and mouth, serpentine, toward the sliver of open window. "I care about you, Jane. But you piss me off. I think we should risk it. We drove all the way here to find this guy! You want to just sit there in that house of yours with your mother until the whole thing collapses in on itself?" She turned and glared at me. "You'd rather lie there wasting away in the debris than actually take control of your life! You got dealt a bad hand. Like it or not, you need blood to live, and you need him." She pointed hard out the window, at the building.

"You need his help. People aren't meant to live like you do. I'm saying this as your friend, or your girlfriend, or whatever I am."

"I'm not 'people,' though, am I? I'm not even human, really. Maybe I deserve whatever I get." I sucked in a breath, unsure whether to yell at her, or weep. "Plus, I just don't think I can survive being disappointed. At least if I went home . . . I know my mother. I know we'd be safe. I know that life."

"But you can't go back to that life now. Do you think you can just ignore everything you've found out? Wake up, Jane!" Sabrina was really yelling now.

I recoiled. I didn't trust my father. I didn't trust his generosity, but at the same time, there was no other real choice. Especially if I wanted any kind of a different life.

We sat in silence. I watched, though unfocused eyes, the blobs of city lights as the snow on the windshield melted away. Finally, I opened the door and crunched out onto the pristine snow. Sabrina followed and we both grabbed our bags.

The building had an enormous industrial door. I tried the key, and it swung open easily for its size. I had expected a dramatic creak and the need to throw my body weight against it, but it opened without complaint. The hallway was generic, a greenish buzzing light above, and a large empty space that echoed as we stepped into it. To the right was a row of mailboxes, to the left a painted black stairwell.

The apartment was on the fourth floor, so we climbed the stairs, Sabrina audibly breathless by the time we reached the top. I was unaffected, felt as if I could go up two or three more flights before noticing. Her healthy blood was changing me. I noticed it more and more. My senses, my body, in some ways even my emotions. Would I have taken this trip even two weeks ago? Unlikely. Would I have made it up this many stairs without puffing? Doubtful.

The hallway was concrete, the door stainless steel, the walls painted white. There was only one door along the hall that I could see, but to be safe, I knocked. We waited. Sabrina leaned against the wall to catch her breath, encouraging me to unlock the door. It gave easily, the door swinging open into a dark space spilling out stale air. It was cold.

I hit all the lights and one by one the tract fixtures above went on, illuminating a large rectangular room with mammoth windows overlooking the Manhattan skyline and the bridge.

"Holy shit," Sabrina said and ran to the windows, pressing both hands against the glass to look at the view.

I walked carefully around, noting the simple cream sofa and chair, the large kitchen with wooden stools, the modern polished cement floors. There was a flat-screen TV mounted on the wall above a fake mantel and a half-dead houseplant beside it. A few paintings, mostly abstract, hung on the wall. There was a small bathroom with a shower and toilet in black and white, and a good-sized bedroom with a large bed, bare mattress, and a small desk and chair. The space felt like a hotel room, enough furniture to be comfortable, but not enough to feel at home.

Sabrina plopped into the living room chair. "This is nice. Better than Isabelle's dorm, if we survive."

I felt awkward in the space, as if it were riddled with traps or hidden cameras. The whole situation was off. It shouldn't have been this easy to find Hugh. We should be lying uncomfortably on a dorm floor an hour away. This all felt like a dream.

After sitting in tense silence for a while, Sabrina demanded more stimuli and turned on the TV. Some reality show she liked was on, so it took the focus off me.

I flipped through an art book displayed on the coffee table and wondered at the drink ring on the glass-top surface. Did Hugh come here and visit clients? Did he come here to drink blood? I forced myself to stop obsessing and tried to relax. At least for the time being we were safe and comfortable, and the trip so far had been a success: we found my father, we weren't sleeping in a car, and he didn't immediately try to kill us. And on top of that Sabrina was right: I had to keep marching forward. I couldn't go home emptyhanded. The stress of the day slowly caught up to me, and before I realized it, my eyes had closed.

XXVIII.

Something woke me—a feeling, more than anything. I hadn't planned on falling asleep. I bolted up in panic, scanning the well-lit room. It took a moment for everything that had happened to flow back. I saw Sabrina sprawled in the chair, snoring softly. The TV was still blaring, some late-night infomercial.

I was about to stand when Sabrina made a sound of protest and twitched in her sleep. Her arm was draped over the edge of the chair—I followed it down to the floor, where a dark shadow knelt. Quietly suckling. I must have made a noise. The shadow's head shot up, mouth red, eyes nailing me to my seat. Hugh.

He rose and, before I could move, was suddenly looming over me. I slid away from him, off the sofa, falling to the floor. I got tangled in the throw, about to yell, when he signaled for me to be quiet and gestured toward the bedroom. Without a word, I followed, confused, as if on a leash. I looked back at Sabrina once. She had turned onto her side, injured arm pulled in like a bird wing, but otherwise seemed unharmed.

Once in the room I closed the door. I was surprised how much sound was blocked by it. Or maybe I shouldn't have been surprised, given what Hugh was. The television was nearly silenced.

I glared at him. "What the hell are you doing?!" I hissed, trying to contain my anger.

He smiled at me. Smiled, almost playfully, and came closer to me. I stayed near the door, ready to flee at a moment's notice. "I didn't mean to wake you, I just wanted a taste."

He passed me and opened the closet, pulling out a stack of linens and set them on the bed. I was angry but paralyzed, powerless to proceed. He stared at me, expectantly.

"That's my friend in there! You can't just walk in and bite her!" I sputtered, unsure what the appropriate response to this horrible situation was.

"You need to calm down. And quiet down."

I narrowed my eyes at him.

Hugh rolled his eyes, as if annoyed this was still a discussion. "I'm not going to apologize. You came here to learn about us. Now you know—at the core we are opportunists. We have to be."

"That's not a good enough reason to molest someone."

"I didn't take much at all, I promise. Barely two mouthfuls. Please sit."

I eased onto the edge of the desk chair, prepared to spring up. I felt itchy, but Hugh was still taking his time.

So I watched him. He was tall—not overly so, but enough to intimidate. Square jaw, lined face, coffee-brown eyes that gleamed in the dim lamplight. They were inhuman, too much like a shark's or an insect's. I was close enough to reach the door if I needed to, but it didn't comfort me. He settled onto the corner of the bed.

"How long has she been with you?" Hugh said this casually as he laid his hand on the pile of sheets, smoothing them.

I thought about it. "A month, maybe a bit more."

"And she knows what you are? So quickly?"

I nodded. "She found out when I did. . . ." I didn't know how much to say, what to tell him. I wanted to be honest, but he frightened me. And I was still so angry at him.

"How is that possible?" Hugh asked.

"My mother kept it from me. I didn't know. I guess I chose not to know." I tightened my jaw. "But it's my turn to ask a question. Why sneak in like that?"

"Honestly? I was curious. Curious to see if you would trust me enough to come here, and when I came in and saw her lying there, I was curious what she tasted like." He shrugged. No shame. "As I said, this is what we are, what we do."

"This is not what I do," I answered stiffly.

Hugh raised his shoulders, cavalier.

"Are we . . . even human?" I blurted, heat crawling up my neck.

I expected him to be angry, but he leaned back, pursing his lips, thoughtful. "At least partially, yes. Your mother was human. And we live, we age, we die. We aren't immortal like in the movies. But we can live longer than regular people, and we are tougher than regular people. We just lack something, some wholeness. We need the blood and the lifeforce of others."

He crossed his arms. "I'm no geneticist. All I know is the vampire gene, or whatever it is that makes us what we are, travels down from either parent. Our infant mortality is high, but we tend to breed true. Unfortunately, when we reproduce, it often kills the mother because she has to give everything. Mothers carrying vampire babies basically are drinking for two." He paused, meeting my eyes. "So, it's smart to go the Sapphic route with your little friend out there. Since becoming a mom is pretty much a death wish. I killed my human mother. It's normal for us." He smirked. "It does happen in nature, to octopuses of all creatures, but I digress."

He was so blasé about his mother dying that it left me speechless. I pictured my mother, sitting beside a cold stove, congealing oatmeal in a bowl before her. I had been so consumed with finding my father, finding the truth, that I'd left her alone. Now I couldn't believe I'd done it. I squeezed my eyes shut, breathing out. She might not have been mother of the year, but to be condemned to a slow death by her child seemed especially cruel, for anyone.

I dragged myself back to the moment. I was so tangled in my guilt I'd missed what Hugh was saying, so I tuned back in. He didn't seem to notice, anyway. I was getting the impression he liked to hear himself talk.

"My mother died when I was about five. My father kept nannies and tutors in the house, all of them like Natsuki, or your mother, or your little friend out there."

"Her name is Sabrina," I said.

Hugh smiled at me like he was pacifying a baby. I clammed up and he plowed along as if I'd never spoken.

"My father would marry and move, marry and move. Always wealthy widows, or young women with sizeable dowries. This is our way. His mother, my grandmother, was a many-times-over widow before she died when my father was little. That's just how it's always been with our people. It has to be, if we want to survive."

"Why?"

"Surely you've noticed that most people have a real aversion to our kind." I nodded. He pressed on: "Self-preservation. And for that reason, we aren't good at being the face of a business. We work better behind the scenes. We aren't naturally creative either. But we're good at pulling the strings. My theory is we are too concerned with filling our bellies to be great artists. But we make excellent muses, and wonderful maddening obsessions, and even better grieving widows and widowers." His eyes twinkled at his own cleverness.

I swallowed. "What do you mean?"

"That you're young. And ignorant. It's not your fault. If you had grown up as I had, you'd be more accustomed to my humor."

"I could have grown up that way, if you'd stayed with my mother," I said venomously.

He chuckled. "You seem like a nice enough girl, but I didn't want to be anyone's dad, let alone a little bloodsucker I'd have to take care of. No offense."

"None taken."

"And clearly nature finds a way, even though you made her sick and basically ruined her life, she had you and raised you. Honestly, my father could barely look at me growing up, and I didn't want to be like him. Didn't plan to pass the bloodline along."

This was what I'd come for. This was the truth, the one I

dreaded most of all. Over and over in my head I thought: I want to go home, I want to be in my own bed. I strangely missed my mother's silence compared to this pragmatic indifference.

"Is your father still alive?"

"My father lives in Edinburgh now, an old gargoyle with a harem of very pale nurses. My mother was from Greece. They met on holiday, and after a whirlwind affair she ended up pregnant and the rest is history. I was like you. Unplanned, unwanted, even. But my father stuck around, cared for my mother and me until she died. Tolerated raising me. He must have loved her most of all to do that. Do you understand?" Hugh caught my eye, and there was a flash of something almost human in his face. A sadness for his mother perhaps? A kinship for being unwanted like me?

"But even with all his love, she lived only until I was almost six. So how is it that Vivian is still with us now? She must have been bringing in . . . help."

"Hitchhikers," I murmured, feeling as if I had just broken some secret trust.

"Really? I never would have thought Vivian to be so ruthless. She must care deeply for you."

I snorted, an ugly sound. "I don't think it was love that motivated her. I think she had me to spite you. I think she wanted to prove something. She didn't want me. I've brought her nothing but sadness and sickness. Like you said, I basically ruined her life."

Hugh nodded, but there was no real sympathy there. "For anyone to truly love us, they must give themselves. We need them. It's what we are. And they need us in a strange way. They are unique. You have noticed how hard it is to really connect with other people?"

I lifted one shoulder in a defeated shrug. "I feel like I've spent my entire life trying to find someone who'd even make eye contact with me. I never realized how strange it was until Sabrina came along. My doctor as a child, my mother, Sabrina, and a janitor. Four people in seventeen years."

"You'll get used to that. Most people will cross the street to avoid us. So, you need to treasure and nurture those who don't run. You need to be in a city—more people equals more friends. That's why I surround myself with artists, and believe it or not, people in high finance. Those communities have more of our kind of people. They're drawn to us: they want to be victims. They like the risks and they take care of us in turn. It's an ecosystem, Jane."

"I don't want to kill anybody." I folded my arms tightly. "Can't I feed off animals or something? Like get crates of rabbits or guinea pigs or . . ."

Hugh shook his head. "Unfortunately, no. It wouldn't be so bad if that were true. But what we are missing is so much more than blood. It's them. Humans. It's their life, their essence. We take everything."

I was numb. "So there's no way to get what I need without killing?"

"You'll take it all and then there will be another," he replied.

I stared at the blank wall, thinking of Sabrina beyond it, my heart aching. "That's so horrible."

"Jane, I don't do it because I'm cruel. But it is what I am. It is what you are. I want to live. Don't you?"

"But . . . my mother got away. . . ."

"The only thing that saved your mother was you, inside her. I hoped if we caught the pregnancy early enough you wouldn't have gotten into her head, but nature is a strong thing. Without a hungry fetus inside her, she would have stayed with me."

"Why does it matter if she left, if there was always someone else waiting in the wings?"

"Because she was mine, and she did have a real talent." The way Hugh spoke about my mother was macabre. To him, it seemed like we were all little more than animals, driven by our biology. I swallowed. Would I be this detached one day? Silence stretched between us.

"You really don't remember how many people you've . . . loved?"

"Why would I want to? If I really counted back, I suppose I could." He paused. "Look, I know at this point in your life it seems unfathomable to forget someone like Sabrina. But she is your first love. You will understand with time. They come to us, they seek us out. Even when we hurt them, they come back. Surely you've noticed this? How they return even after they swear they won't. Even when they hate us, even after we take too much."

I couldn't stop myself from thinking of earlier today—how angry Sabrina had been, how terrified. But she'd come around. I had thought it was because of what we shared, but—

"It's almost—" I hated to say it, hated to think it, but I needed to. "You're saying they want to be victims."

Hugh grinned. "Now you're beginning to understand. They find you. They want to connect with us, they want us to love them. They want what we give them."

I hated that I believe him, but what little I'd experienced said it was true. "But we give them nothing. . . ." I felt like I'd been stabbed in the gut.

Hugh began to pace, seeming too big in the confined space. "Not true. We need them to survive. Maybe that's what they want. To be needed. Most people want love that ravages, that consumes, that devours. We live because they let us. It's romantic, in a way. The ultimate sacrifice."

"Then maybe I should just kill myself," I said.

He waved me off. "That's a bit extreme. But—do what you want."

"Wow. Thanks, Dad."

He gave another of his long-suffering sighs. "Just keep in mind that we are a tough little species. We want to survive. And trust me, it gets easier over time. You need to unlearn your idea of what a normal life is, or a normal relationship. Once you do, you won't feel so bad."

"You don't know me. You have no idea what I feel."

Hugh laughed fully now, walked up to me and bent to face me where I sat on the bed. "I can see your eyes, Jane. They are a killer's eyes. I can see the lie that you cling to so desperately. You will kill that girl out there, and before she is even cold in the ground, you will have another. Or a few at the same time. And each time it happens, you will grieve for that love, but each time you will be too hungry to stop. We have to keep moving on to survive. In time, their loss will be like the changing of the seasons or the inevitability of the tide. It will just be. How. Things. Are."

He stepped away, resting his hip on the desk. His legs crossed as well as his arms, posing like a menswear model. To see him, you would have never believed that Hugh hunted people, that he killed people. "You came here for the truth Jane, that's the truth."

In a flash, I could clearly picture the life my mother would have had if she hadn't become pregnant. The one where my mother remained his plaything. She would have withered away until there was nothing left, inside or out. Hollowed out and fragile as blown glass. Fate had marked her the moment she crossed Hugh McGarrett's path. Her life had been forfeited a long time ago.

And then there was Sabrina, sleeping peacefully, curled up with a blanket, trusting me. She had known me for less than a month and already she had opened her veins and her heart. I swallowed, a stone lodged in my throat. I had so wanted her to like me for me. To care for me because I was a person who deserved love. I didn't want to face the reality that the one person I'd really connected with was compelled to be with me out of some strange suicidal pheromone.

I could feel Hugh watching me. I ignored him, tried to shut out everything in the room, in my mind. Blot it all out.

"It's a terrible life. Cruel and . . . lonely, no real friends or real love," I whispered. I finally met Hugh's stare.

He frowned and moved away from me, stalling. He tried to act like a seasoned nonchalant killer, but I'd hit something vital. "Any life can be those things, Jane," he finally said, his voice softer than I expected.

He had responses for my anger, for my childish disappointment, even, but it was clear that the truth spoken plainly disoriented him. It brought out a sadness. I could almost feel the shift in him, as if the room's temperature had dropped a few degrees. He sat back down on the bed, the mattress settling.

"It's not terrible. It's just not as easy as regular people have it. This is who we are, this is what we are. We aren't serial killers, we aren't maniacs or sadists. We are just trying to survive, and if we could drink animal blood, or synthetic plasma, or take a pill, obviously we would. But we need that love, that energy. It feeds us almost as much as the blood itself does."

I leaned forward resting my elbows on my knees.

"I don't want to kill my friend. So what do I do? Is there any way to survive and avoid doing that? Any way at all?"

"Sure." He said it so easily that my head shot up, eyebrows high.

"But you told me that—"

"You let her go."

Hugh opened his hands wide. "And you find another, someone you care about less. That's all. If you stay near each other it will continue. The only absolute way is to send her away from you."

I choked. "If I send Sabrina away . . . there's no one else. My whole tiny, shitty town treats me like a pariah."

The unspoken fact was I didn't want to send Sabrina away. She was my friend, my only friend. We'd barely spent any time together and already I was supposed to send her away, and be alone again, or eventually kill her.

Hugh regarded me thoughtfully, hand over his mouth, rubbing the stubble at his chin. "I suppose you could stay here for a while. It's a big city, and you wouldn't be alone long." He stood.

My eyes welled up. I exhaled a shaky sigh, forcing myself not to cry. I avoided Hugh's eyes. "Thanks for the offer. But my mother needs me still. She can't be left alone. And if I break it off with Sabrina I'd be all alone." I felt utterly hopeless.

"Just think on it. Look, you came here for answers and I am trying to be straight with you. No kid gloves. Think about what I've said."

"I will. Thanks," I croaked.

"Good. Anyway, it's quite late. And you look like a patch of rough road, so why don't you get some sleep? Tomorrow, explore the city, spend some time with your friend, think about things. We can have dinner tomorrow evening, and talk more." He walked to the door and opened it. Looking out at Sabrina sleeping, he turned back to me. "Obviously, the dinner invitation is for you alone."

I stared at the empty door frame long after he left, numb. Eventually I made up the bed, then changed into the sweats and woke Sabrina, helping her groggily settle into the bed. She was asleep before she hit the pillow. I snuggled in, fitting into place beside her, my knees behind hers, my chin at her shoulder. I loved the way her body felt pressed to mine, the warmth she gave off, the life. I wrapped my arms around her soft middle and squeezed. She sighed, content, and shimmied closer. My heart felt heavy, but I was finally able to fall asleep, lulled by the steady thumping of Sabrina's heart.

XXIX.

Sabrina had woken early in the morning, griping about the sunlight being too bright. I kept my eyes shut and pulled the blankets over my head, burrowing down into the bed. I heard her walking heavily over to the windows and the shuck sound of the curtains closing. The room was once again dark. She crawled back into bed, nuzzling up to me, and we both fell back asleep.

An hour or two later we woke for good, fairly well rested considering all the stress and travel of the previous day. Sabrina called her mother on her cell, reporting that Isabelle had screwed us over, but that Hugh had offered us a place to crash.

"Yes, Mom, he's super nice, and rich." She rolled her eyes at me and pointed at the phone. "It is like a fairy tale! Let me give you the address."

In case we never came home, I caught myself thinking darkly.

Sabrina walked into the bedroom but I could still hear her talking, mostly about the traffic and the neighborhood. It was an easy conversation, and I was suddenly overcome with envy. How I yearned to have that conversation with my own mother. To have a mother who cared, who just wanted to have a normal

"Are you all right?" check-in on the phone. But Vivian DeVry existed so out of time and out of the norm that I couldn't even picture her using a land line much less a cell phone.

I got in the shower. I ran the water as close to scalding as I could. Another punishing shower. I would be red as a lobster if I kept this up.

Once clean and dressed I emerged to discover Sabrina was done on the phone and ransacking the cupboards for food. She managed to find some cereal bars and a jar of instant coffee, so she put the kettle on. I sat on the stool, elbows on the granite island as I watched her putter around the kitchen. She hadn't heard me come out of the bathroom and I took the time to watch her unobserved. Had she lost weight since last month? Her cheekbones were a bit hollower and she had dark circles under her eyes.

Was her hair less shiny? She was singing to herself, her hips swaying as she pulled down two coffee cups. She jumped and squealed when she finally turned around.

Clutching her chest, she scowled at me. "Jesus, how long have you been there?"

"Just a minute, patiently awaiting the feast you've prepared."

With a dramatic flourish Sabrina placed a small plate in front of me with a granola bar on it. I laughed and unwrapped the foil, biting into the bar. She poured water into coffee cups and added a spoonful of instant into each one. Then she settled onto a stool beside me. I noticed her watching me with anticipation.

"Well?"

"Well, what?"

"I know your dad showed up here last night. I woke up and heard you guys talking. I didn't eavesdrop or anything, but I know he was here. So . . . what the hell happened? Tell me everything."

Her eyes were wide with excitement, an eager smile on her face. All I could picture was his hulking shape over her, stealing her blood while she slept on, oblivious. I debated telling her, but decided against it. She wouldn't understand. I barely did. Her anxious curiosity had me scrambling to find a positive spin on what was essentially my doomed condition.

"Well, it was interesting to meet someone like me. And it was awkward. Hugh's my father biologically, but he's also a stranger. So it was strange."

"Okay, so you met a strange stranger. That's all?"

She was teasing, but she could sense my hesitation. I didn't want to tell her what I'd learned. I especially didn't want to tell her she'd probably die if we stayed together. The granola bar turned to chalk in my mouth. I swallowed it, cleared my throat.

"It just wasn't a very encouraging evening. Basically, there's no magic bullet that makes me not need blood. Human blood. If I want to live, that is."

"Oh, shit. That sucks. Are you okay? How do you feel?" She asked this without the earlier mirth, suddenly serious, her hazel eyes peeping out over the cup, looking very young without all the harsh makeup.

"It made me feel terrible. I don't want to be like this."

Sabrina's face fell. "I was really hoping there was something, some herb, or some secret blood bank, or cabalistic doctor network or something."

I nodded wistfully and rested my head on my fist. "Guess only the real stuff straight from the source works for us. He wants me to have dinner with him tonight. Just me, though. Would you be okay on your own?"

She was clearly hurt, but anyone arguing for an invite to an evil vampire's dinner might need some re-evaluation.

"Of course. He's your father. You guys have a lot to catch up on. Not just the, uh, blood stuff, but the real father-daughter stuff. I get it."

I highly doubted Hugh and I would ever have a close father-daughter relationship. Something told me he'd only been hospitable and indulgent so far because he didn't want us to screw up anything for him. But it meant a lot to me that Sabrina didn't push.

As repugnant as I found his way of life and personal philosophy, I needed to learn from Hugh. And as hard as it was for me to admit, it was a relief to be around someone who understood where I was coming from. He might believe there were no other options, that we had to move from victim to victim to live, but surely there were other ways to survive. Dr. Blake had kept me alive and healthy with transfusions when I was a kid. If I could find a discreet doctor, or a scientist . . . maybe I could find help to manage this condition. I refused to accept Hugh's version of things.

I felt a swell of hope, tinged with anxiety at the prospect of seeing him again. If I did have to send Sabrina away, then I wanted the time we had left to mean something. I wasn't sure where our attraction began and biology ended, but I owed her regardless. She'd taken a risk on me and genuinely cared for me. She'd forced me to face my nature, and she'd brought me to find my biological father. She'd made the world and my future suddenly so much larger and full of possibilities. And for a little while I'd felt loved.

"I think we should go out, do touristy stuff, make it more of a vacation. Let's see some sights, and just have a normal, fun day, okay?" I tried to make my smile reach my eyes, for her not to see the sadness behind them.

Sabrina nodded excitedly and jumped off her stool. She put her arms around me in a tight hug. After a beat I hugged her back, a knot in my throat. She pulled away to look into my eyes, and when she spoke her breath smelled of coffee and raspberry. "That sounds like a great idea."

And she leaned forward and kissed me confidently on the mouth. My body seemed to rev up at the touch, my heart rate increasing, my senses unfolding, pulling in everything around me. I felt like a flower opening up for the sun. Hugh's words were in my head then. This was the lifeforce, the love he talked about us needing; I was stealing something with this kiss. What I stole was hard to name, harder still to describe. I was drinking in her energy, her essence, her . . . soul. That black snake in my gut was fattening on her touch. I was disgusted, yet unable to stop myself. This was not affection, this was predation. My father had insisted that it was more than just blood that sustained us, and he was right. There was a nasty undercurrent to even this simple kiss. And as much as it made me sad, stealing Sabrina's lifeforce gave me pleasure right to the core.

She finally broke the kiss, breathless and wobbly, her smile big. But I wasn't fooled. I could still see the circles beneath her eyes. Her complexion was pasty, her skin tight across her skull. Her pupils were large and she almost seemed drugged. With a playful peck on my nose, she danced away toward the bathroom. My smile stayed in place until the door closed. I could feel the tingling along my skin and mouth. She was inside of me. I knew my cheeks would be ruddy, my skin clearer and more luminous. My father was right. Whether I liked it or not, I was stealing her life. I touched my fingers to my mouth, revolted.

That day, we set out to see the city. "Let's start with the classics," Sabrina had said. "All the typical touristy NY sights, also the freest, since we don't really have any money."

First, we headed to Times Square. The subway was packed and jostling with the combination of morning commuters and out-of-town visitors. I had never seen such a variety of people, a veritable sea of faces and voices. I'd never really understood the smallness of my old world until now.

"You need to relax," Sabrina had to keep whispering in my ear.

Unfortunately, the natural aversion people had for me was amplified in the confined space. Even the most cramped subway car would clear out around me. A seat would miraculously appear wherever I stood. Just a shark swimming through a school of fish. A distinct invisible barrier surrounded me wherever we went. Sabrina had either stopped noticing entirely, or didn't care anymore. "Don't look so glum, Jane, I think being able to get a seat anywhere is a definite perk." She snagged the vacant seat with a grin. I held the pole and tried not to take it personally. I pictured Hugh riding these trains, standing by the doors, newspaper in hand. Completely oblivious to the near panic, the animal-brain compulsion, people scrambling as far from him as possible.

Times Square was garish and loud. The streets were packed to capacity, more like pipes clogged with hair than walkways. Rainbows of shopping bags swinging, the sharp edges jabbing into our shins. There were babies shrieking, store lights flashing, car horns honking. And every look that turned my way was desperate to escape my gaze, mothers clutching their children tighter, others scrambling to cross the street. The honking horns and strobing lights, the smell of refuse, the smell of humanity, the miasma of fear and hatred directed at me.

"It's too loud, too much," I said to Sabrina, finding the world at too high a decibel. I waded through the crush to an alleyway. I needed to get away from the press of bodies.

In the alley, the air reeked of garbage and urine, but at least I could collect myself. I leaned against a wall, breathing as deep as the foul space would allow. My hands trembled. Sabrina crowded me, worrying like a hen. I pushed her off, harsher than I intended.

"I'm sorry. I just got overwhelmed."

She nodded, looking back, watching the stampede, voices blending into one cacophonous noise.

"Yeah, it's pretty crazy around here. I don't like it much, myself. Let's go someplace less busy."

We decided to go north to Central Park. It was cold and had started snowing again, and we hoped that would chase off most of the park goers or tourists. The traffic, both humans and cars, petered out as we walked. The buildings became more residential and my revved up nerves finally started to relax.

"I think you almost had a panic attack," Sabrina said after a few blocks of silence. She stopped to light a cigarette and was puffing along, the steam of her breath mingling with the smoke around her face. It was midafternoon now and the snowflakes were fat and fluffy, the sky gray, heavy with the threat of a serious storm.

"Yeah, I think so. It's hard to be loathed by a whole city at once."

Sabrina smiled and took my hand. She seemed so brazen in the act, staring around defiantly, wanting someone to see us, wanting someone to care. No one did. The city moved in a blur and there was a strange camouflage in that. Just two more stars in an infinite galaxy.

We finally reached the park. Stopping at a coffee truck, we bought two cheap, watery coffees, more for the warmth on our hands than anything, and then trudged into the park. As the temperature dropped and the snow accumulated, the park started emptying out. We walked farther in, taking spindly trails, going deeper into the woods. We eventually came to a pond. The water was slick as oil, a few winter birds gliding effortlessly along the surface. It hadn't frozen over yet, but the banks were white and round. There was a heavy silence here, which seemed strange in the heart of a sprawling metropolis. It was like a mirage. Above us, branches and sky—no buildings to be seen in any direction.

Sabrina found a bench and dusted off the thin layer of snow. The seat was so cold that it immediately seared through the thin fabric of my slacks, but it was worth it. My legs ached from the miles we'd walked. She took my hand in hers, the skin of her fingers red, mine pale and bloodless. Both numb. We didn't speak for a long time, just sat watching the birds. It felt so far from everything.

I closed my eyes and breathed, smelling the dark marshy water, the fowl skimming the top. Had I always been able to parse smells? Maybe I just never noticed.

I could sense Sabrina wanted to talk. Everything about her, from the tapping of her foot, to the thrum in her body, intruded on the tranquility around us.

Finally, after allowing myself an internal sigh, I turned to her. "What is it?"

She avoided my eyes. "Nothing really. We've been so busy all day we just haven't really talked at all. I'm just wondering what'll happen now. Like what if your dad wants you to stay here with him?"

"What if?"

"Well, would you?" Sabrina worried at her lip. I was hypnotized by her wet mouth and dark plum lipstick. She prodded me and I met her eyes.

"I don't know. This isn't my home. But I kind of hate everything back in Hob's Valley. My mother should be in a hospital, if I could make sure she was settled, and I could do something about my cat. Maybe then I could stay here."

"And you're sure I can't come with you tonight, even as moral support?"

I shook my head. "No. He was very clear on that. I'd feel better if you weren't there. And it'd be safer for you. Hugh is not a good person—hell, he's not even really a person at all—and I don't trust him around you."

"You think he would hurt me?"

I know he would, I thought to myself as Sabrina shimmied along the bench, bumping into my hip. I felt the warmth of her body against me. I was greedily sponging it up. Even through her clothes, she wasn't safe.

"He doesn't think of you as a person. People are a means to an end. I don't want you to feel that way. And he specifically asked that I come alone." I risked making eye contact.

"No problem. I'll stay in. Get pizza and watch TV. No big deal. Really, I'll be fine."

Sabrina wrapped her arm around me, pulling me close. I rested my head on her shoulder, watching the snow fall soundlessly. The smell of her skin, of her sweat at the collar, brought my inner monster roaring to the surface. I nuzzled at her, not even meaning to. I wasn't even hungry, really. I think I craved comfort more than sustenance. She stiffened, and I could feel her anxiousness. I willed her to be calm, to be unafraid, and miraculously she relaxed, leaning into me, and whispering her permission into my hair.

The flesh at her neck parted easily for me, the blood trickling in, driving me mad with its complexity. I slid my tongue into the wound, teasing out as much blood as I could. I didn't want to take too much; it was a long way back to the apartment. And Hugh and I had both been at her in the last two days. But even knowing that, intellectually, another voice whispered that I could do whatever I wanted. That it was time I got a little more selfish, that I started taking care of myself since no one else would. It was an ugly voice, and it brought me back. I pushed against it, sealing up the door in myself. I needed to take control. I needed her to trust me.

So with all my strength, I pulled myself from her, wiping my mouth shakily. Sabrina was paler, and shivering, but she looked otherwise okay. She smiled, her lips a bit chalky under their paint, her eyes a bit unfocused. I reached out and tucked a strand of wayward black hair behind her ear and I felt proud that I'd fought the thing in me and won. I kissed her, impulsively, feeling alive and happy, and complete for once. She laughed, and wrapped her arms around me. I snuggled in under her chin, her head resting on mine and sighed contentedly. I wished we could stay there, entwined together, forever.

I didn't care if it wasn't real, if Sabrina was drawn to me by something out of our control. I'd let myself believe the lie, for now. I needed her to care for me. I needed her to see me as a person, not a ghost, not an addiction, not some sort of symbiotic parasite. I didn't like the thought of Hugh being right, but I understood holding and being held—that I was starved for more than just blood. I needed Sabrina's love and touch just as much. We stayed on the bench until the fading light and the cold pushed us out of the park and back toward Brooklyn and my father.

XXX.

It was snowing heavily by the time we stepped out of the subway in Hugh's neighborhood. On the way to the apartment we stopped at a well-lit, warm pizza place and Sabrina bought two gigantic slices soaking cheese and grease into the small paper plates they were balanced on.

When we got to the apartment it was full dark, the city twinkling magically in the distance. Sabrina ate the remainder of her pizza on the sofa, flipping stations. I wondered if I was dressed all right. I was anxious. It felt foreign to watch the door, to watch the clock, to pace. Finally, I decided to change, opting for a pair of dark pants, a turtleneck sweater, and my grandmother's tweed blazer from the previous day. I pulled my hair back into a tight bun and on impulse took a bright red lipstick tube from Sabrina's makeup bag and put it on. The effect was dramatic, my mouth now a deep red gash, my teeth white and sharp when I smiled. I stepped from the bathroom, Sabrina glancing my way and doing a double take.

"Wow," she mumbled, checking me up and down. "You should wear makeup more often."

I blushed, embarrassed at the attention. After pacing the length of room, I finally sat on the edge of the sofa. We watched a dance competition show, Sabrina chuckling and mocking the contestants. I tried to engage but it all seemed so pointless, and my eyes kept going to the door, to the clock. Hugh had never given a time, he'd just said dinner. Sabrina could sense my nervousness, periodically quirking her eyebrow at me during commercials.

"Calm down," she said, flipping channels.

"I don't know why I'm nervous. I don't even think I like the guy. It's pathetic that I'd be anxious to see him, right?"

"Not really. He's your dad. Most people spend their lives looking for or trying to connect with their parents, even when they don't like the choices they've made."

"Wow, that was a very profound piece of advice."

Sabrina gave me a lopsided grin. "My mom watches a lot of self-help talk shows. They're mostly about mommy and daddy issues." She scooted along the sofa, snuggling her body against mine. She reminded me of my cat. I hoped Tommy was okay and had enough food and water, which inevitably made me worry for my mother. I'd somehow not thought about her for almost a whole day.

Please take care of each other, I silently prayed. Please don't make me regret coming down here. Stop it, I scolded myself. Stop worrying yourself to death. I relished Sabrina's closeness instead and wrapped my arms around her, breathing out the stress. I tried to ignore my father's assurance that I'd kill her. No. I won't let it happen. I let the defense repeat in my head over and over. That's him. Not me. I fed off her in the park today and stopped myself. It's just a learning curve, but I'll get it. Sabrina practically purred with contentment. I was so relaxed that I actually began to doze. Time moved, snow fell beyond the windows, and I tuned out the banal conversations on the television.

When the buzzer sounded, I jumped. Sabrina rubbed at her eye with a fist, smearing makeup. I spun anxiously back to her, adjusting my clothes and hair.

"You look fine. Should I stay in here or go in the bedroom?" she asked.

I didn't have a chance to answer. The door was being unlocked, and Hugh then stepped in. Tall, intimidating, vaguely Mediterranean features, not traditionally handsome. He wore a black wool topcoat, the shoulders dusted with rapidly melting snow. His wet hair twinkled with it in the kitchen light. He looked me up and down and then shot a glance to Sabrina, still as a statue, standing near the sofa.

"This is my friend, Sabrina. This is Hugh McGarrett. My, uh, father."

He didn't make any move to draw nearer, or even look directly at her, before turning back to me.

"Are you ready to go?" he asked.

I fetched my coat, the old moth-eaten wool looking dingy next to his. I wrapped my scarf around me and waved farewell to Sabrina. She hadn't budged an inch and looked hurt at his total rebuff of her. Hugh was already out the door and in the hall. I felt a pang of embarrassment but sadly little surprise that he hadn't formally introduced himself, or acknowledged Sabrina with even a nod. This was Hugh: he saw people as food, and little else.

He stood expectantly at the top of the stairs waiting for me, his leather-gloved hand creaking as he squeezed the metal banister. The look he gave me stole my nerve to confront him for being rude. He went down the stairs at a fast pace. I had to hurry to fall into step behind him.

Once outside, I saw there was a cab waiting at the curb, idling. I looked up to see Sabrina standing at the fourth floor window as I got into the car. The air was thick with synthetic air freshener, the oppressive scent coating my mouth. My father slid in after me, folding his height into the back seat.

We set off and went over the bridge. Ahead, the city was golden and luminous, the sky a vibrant purple. I finally found my voice and turned to Hugh. His face was in profile, eyes watching the cityscape.

"Where are we going?"

He turned to me slowly, as if waking from a dream. It seemed like a moment more before he even recognized me.

"Dinner." Not much of an answer, but I didn't push further.

On the other side of the bridge, we instantly fell into bright and boisterous Chinatown. The fantastical neighborhood unfolded before us and I eagerly drank it in. The flashing lights, the unfamiliar language on all the signs and the droves of people, bundled tightly to protect them from the cold. Watching them reminded me again how small my own world was.

I pictured my mother walking these streets, coppery hair trailing down her back, paint-smudged hands, and a confident grin. I could envision her hailing a cab on any of these corners in her wild cheetah-print coat. She'd loved this city and her life here. But the city doomed her just the same. As soon as her path crossed Hugh's, she was marked, that art show was a deal with the devil.

I scrubbed my eyes and forced my thoughts away from the past, turning to look at Hugh again, his face multicolored as the city lights reflected off him. He was stoic, so indifferent to me beside him that I might not been there at all. I supposed if I wanted to get to know him, I'd have to ask him something, anything. Harder question was if I wanted to know Hugh McGarrett any more than I already did. After all, it might be the equivalent of peeling an onion: too many layers and bound to end in tears.

Blocks rolled by and my courage shriveled. I dreaded a repeat of our conversation from the night before. The driver slowed and stopped in front of a darkened building, dimly lit from inside by what looked to be red lanterns. It conjured images of a fortune teller, or a brothel seen on TV. He paid the driver who barely acknowledged either of us, and we stepped out into the cold.

My feet crunched along as I followed Hugh to the curb, weaving between trash cans and toward a dark, signless entrance. He opened the door and parted a heavy velvet curtain, vanishing inside. I followed. It took a moment for my eyes to adjust—the space was smoky with incense. The walls were painted a vibrant red, even the carpets were red. The tables were black lacquer, and centered on each was a small red bowl with a candle in it. There were some patrons scattered around, nestled into the various nooks and crannies.

Strange music played softly, discreetly masking the conversations around us. It felt as if we'd stepped into a church—the quiet voices, the candlelight. Everywhere I looked I saw religious objects mounted on walls, or tucked in corners. A life-sized Christ near a small stone Buddha, a Shiva on the other side. A small arrangement of crude figurines of Catholic saints with painted black faces. They were arranged on an altar. Also on the altar, I saw chicken feet, and red powder. Voodoo? I stared at this shrine a long time. A small mirror with a feather on it reflected back a male figurine, the Christ of the group, his face painted red. I was tempted to reach out and touch the arrangement, but didn't want to get in trouble or embarrass Hugh.

From out of nowhere a small dark-skinned woman appeared, her hair cut asymmetrically and dyed an unnatural auburn. She had a long silver earring that dangled to her collarbone. Her lips were painted a dark reddish brown, her eyelids made up heavily with black. Her dress was ankle-length, deep red, and tight-fitting. I imagined if she stepped back against the wall she would just vanish. She surveyed us both for a moment, and I noticed with surprise her reaction was not one of fear but of interest. I turned to my father, and he smiled. Without a word, the hostess led us to a booth that seemed to be carved out of the walls and the shadows. I slid along the wooden bench, settling on a plush burgundy silk pillow. My father did the same on the other side. The woman brought us a sweating carafe of water and two glasses and then disappeared. I tried to check out some of the other patrons.

Unlike the hostess, who matched the space as if hatched from it, the rest of the diners seemed ordinary. A variety of ages and ethnicities, all talking in hushed voices. The loudest noise in the room was the gentle tinkling of forks on plates and the clink of glasses. Hugh was watching me intently as I stared around. I felt out of place, undoubtedly looking like the bumpkin I was. I eased farther into the booth and met his eyes.

"What is this place?"

His eyes twinkled with mischief as he replied, "A restaurant."

"It seems more like a temple or a church than a place to eat," I replied, looking around some more.

"The owner is a unique character. He's an artist as well as a restaurateur. He makes religious art—or as he calls it blasphemous art. This restaurant is his salon, a meeting place for creatives and patrons of the art."

I didn't respond. Frankly, I didn't really understand what he was talking about. I had been raised faithless. My mother had never really mentioned God, one way or the other. I guess she'd done me a favor not raising me to think I was damned. I had enough issues without believing there would be more suffering on the other side once I died. In Hell, forever . . . no thanks.

"The hostess . . ." I clammed up when another woman in a long body-skimming dress with a high collar came to the table holding two black suede menus. She was tall, whip-thin, and lovely in an otherworldly elfin way. Her silver-blonde hair was swept up in a complicated twist, her long bangs obscuring half her face. Her lipstick was as red as the walls and a high contrast to her pale skin. She handed me a menu politely, and as she turned to my father, she gave him a flirtatious smile along with his menu. Strangely, I was finding it off-putting to encounter so many people who weren't scared of us. I'd grown used to being practically invisible. I knew it couldn't be a coincidence—this restaurant was probably owned by another vampire.

"My name is Renee," the waitress said, "and I will be your server this evening. We have a few specials tonight, but first, can I interest you in some drinks?"

My father ordered a bottle of wine and two glasses. Renee complimented his choice and walked away, a distinct sashay to her hips.

I stared after her, imagining her body below me, her throat pulled taut, the smell of her skin, the taste of it before I bit in. I flushed and looked away nervously. The thoughts felt like they belonged to someone else. It was knowing that she was like Sabrina, knowing I could possibly have her if I wanted her, that made her more attractive to me. As if reading my mind, Hugh met my eyes and raised an eyebrow. I busied myself with my menu.

The waitress was already heading back to our table, silver tray balanced perfectly with a bottle of wine and two glasses. She placed them on the table with precision, her eyes fixed on my father the entire time. Her desire plain on her face as she spoke of the vintage and deftly worked the corkscrew. I waited in anticipation for her to comment on my youth, ask to see an ID, or have Hugh say it was all right because I was his daughter. But it never came. Instead Hugh took a sip from his glass and nodded, pleased, and her painted mouth smiled wide, teeth glinting in the candlelight. Her eyes were glazed, spellbound by my father's nearness. After a few moments of this, with me looking back and forth between them, she finally brushed away the fog.

Renee recited the dinner specials as if programmed. Everything she described sounded foreign and fantastical. Quail with cranberry glaze atop a mint couscous. Duck liver pate on ciabatta with truffle oil and shaved fennel. I tried to look blasé, to emulate Hugh's cool demeanor as he leaned back in the booth sipping his wine and watching the woman with the cold eyes of a predator.

Once she had completed her recitation, Hugh dismissed her, saying that we'd need a moment.

"Anything sound good to you?" he asked, skimming the menu.

"Honestly, I don't really know. We're a tuna and hot dog kind of house."

"I can order for you, if you trust me." I didn't see the harm.

"Why did you bring me here of all places?" I asked, after Renee had returned and Hugh had ordered for the two of us.

When she was gone, he leaned forward conspiratorially. I mirrored him, elbows on the table.

"The food is quite good. Though I don't much care for the over-the-top Gothic style. A bit too dark and red for me. Too obvious. But surely you've noticed the staff have something in common?"

I nodded, eyeing the hostess and the other patrons. A few met my eyes and gave me a nod. It wasn't just the waitress and the hostess. They were all like us, or those who liked us. I belonged here—I wasn't an outcast or a freak. I was ordinary in a way. I was tempted to ask Hugh if this was normal, if there were vampire hangouts, if he had friends.

I couldn't take it anymore. "That's odd, right? A restaurant full of our kind of people?"

He pursed his lips thoughtfully. "I have it on good authority that the owner here is one of us. Coming here, it must be what it's like for . . ."

"Regular people," I blurted, a hard-to-name emotion blossoming, knowing that we'd been thinking the same exact thing. He nodded.

We went on in silence. Hugh didn't feel the need to fill the quiet like Sabrina did. But I couldn't help myself.

"I've never been to a nice restaurant like this. Hell, I've never even had a friend until Sabrina. It's like I've been asleep my whole life." I reached for my wine glass and took a deep drink, more for something to do than thirst. Coughing, eyes watering, I felt like a clumsy kid. Hugh was clearly amused and my cheeks felt hot.

"How'd you find out about this place?" I asked, to change subject from my hacking.

"As I said last night, us muses run in similar circles, often with artists and we occasionally overlap. And word of mouth travels in a small community. Since we're all circling the same museums and galleries. It's nice a place like this exists."

"Are there a lot of . . . muses in the city? That you know?" Hugh shrugged, eyes scanning the room. "Not a lot, no. There aren't many of us anywhere, that's why we're special. Rare."

"Are they your friends? Do you like other . . . muses?"

"It's complicated. You recall the feeling when you first saw me last night, right? It wasn't pleasant. We're like big lone cats: territorial. We can be friendly, sure, but I've never found it to amount to much." He sipped his drink, thoughtful. "You're in a better mood than last night. Considering how we left things. I thought we were going to jump right in for round two."

I leaned back. "Please, I had a nice day with my friend, that's all."

"That's good—it's a wonderful city. And have you thought more about my offer to stay here?"

"I don't know. It's a lot to take in. I guess I thought I'd show up and you'd . . . I don't know . . . fix everything. Fix me." I was embarrassed to confess this.

Hugh leaned in, face careful. It was clear he wasn't a man who dealt with emotions much and he was unsure what to do with me. He opened his mouth then closed it.

"You know, it's funny . . . I hated my mother, but she gave me something really special," I said.

"And what was that, Jane?" Hugh studied me.

"Ignorance. It was easier when we were just sick and lonely in our old house." I ran a finger along water drops on the table.

Hugh chuckled humorlessly. "I'm sorry I can't fix you or give you better answers. Ours is a harsh world and it seems a disservice to downplay that to you. You've been lied to enough."

I tried to imagine a Hugh as a child, with his dying mother and bloodsucking father, off in some sprawling English manor house.

"My father sat me down one morning on his knee and pointed to my mother sitting outside in the sun and said,

'Mummy is going to die soon, because you take her blood.' I began to cry, and he told me not to be sad. That it was natural, and that it was life."

"That's so terrible," I said, hand going to my chest.

Hugh's face was devoid of any emotion; he just pressed on. "After she died, we always had nurses and tutors and my father's wives around to take care of our needs. But I knew I'd killed my mother and it's impossible to go back after that, Jane. You have to harden your heart."

I shifted uncomfortably in my seat, eyes on the sculptures. "What's your father—my grandfather, I guess—like?"

"He's a mean old bastard. And a survivor. My father always stressed a certain . . . detachment, with donors. He doesn't like anyone to get too close. I like to think he was trying to protect me by raising me the way he did. He's pragmatic at his core. Then I went to university in America, and haven't talked to him much since."

"You think he would want to know about me? That he has a granddaughter?"

"I don't think he would care much, honestly, but I will let him know in a letter. He's not much for phones and he likes to pretend email was never invented."

I swallowed, wanting to ask him something, but fearing the answer. I steeled myself and met his eyes, so similar to my own. "Why are you doing this for me? I know I was an accident. I know I'm an inconvenience to you. I just need to understand your . . . intentions."

Hugh laughed out loud, long teeth on display. "Here I thought you wanted to get to know your father."

My heart trilled at his use of the word father, and I hated myself for it. He was a user, a killer, a manipulator. But I couldn't deny the power of someone like that being kind, treating you as better or more worthwhile than everyone else. "I do. I just don't want to get hurt." He put his hands together on the table.

"This isn't a trap, Jane. Did I want a kid? No. I've got a nice life here. And if we are being frank, I'm a selfish bastard. We all are. We have to be. But that's irrelevant. You're here. The milk has long been spilled. Do you want to hear more about my life?"

I exhaled slowly, wanting to trust him. "Go ahead."

"Thanks. So, I left my father and came here to study art history. That's when I met Margot. She had this abrasive laugh. She hated it, thought it was ugly. I loved it because it was so . . . unrestrained. She was like Sabrina, like your mother, but unlike them I was attracted to her beyond the blood. I had a college roommate then, like them as well, and he was meeting my needs.

"When she asked me out that first time I knew I was in trouble. You see, I liked her. I liked her a lot. And after the first date, I loved her. I never realized how intensely our kind could love." Hugh paused, lost in memory, a soft smile on his mouth. In that flicker I could imagine him young and in love, far from the jaded creature he was now. "Although she was drawn to me like the others, I loved her as an equal from the start. Barely six months into it and we were living together. Obviously, her family was suspicious of her impulsiveness.

"We married halfway through college. She was enormously wealthy, from an old money WASP New England family. Time passed, and we both finished school, but by this time Margot was starting to show the effects of interacting with our kind. She was tired all the time. My bites had stopped healing and were leaving ugly scars. Her family was concerned. But we were in love, and I was sure that she would be okay." Hugh sipped his wine.

And I watched him, my hand on chin, knowing and dreading how this story would end.

"To protect Margot," he continued, "I started getting blood from others, but it was never as good, because it wasn't hers. It's best to feed from a few at the same time, keeps everyone healthy. You'll learn this with time, to set up a community. But she was jealous of the others. So I would always come back to her, again and again. And no matter how much it hurt her, she let me, because she loved me. I wished we were like the stories then, that I could make her like me with a bite. But we can't, we must be born. And then she died. We lasted four years. And they were the best years of my life." His eyes were sad, but it was an old, familiar pain. Like he wore it around his neck in a locket every day.

"Why tell me this?" I asked quietly.

"Because even if your love is perfect, and you do everything right, you can only get a few years out of Sabrina if you feed on her exclusively. But not much more than that. Even if you are really careful, and have lots of donors. We are a destructive force at our core, no matter how hard we fight against it."

I dropped my chin, looking at my hands intertwined on the table top. I had no counter-argument.

Our food arrived. Renee smiled at Hugh seductively as she slid the plate his way. He reached out, and took her wrist. He thanked her sincerely, and their eyes locked. I watched her pupils expand, her tongue snaking out and moistening her lips. This empty flirtation felt disrespectful after the story of Margot to me. But Hugh had clearly mastered compartmentalization a long time ago.

While he still had his hand on her arm, his eyes slid to me and winked. I realized then he was doing this for my benefit, showing me the control we could have over the willing, showing how easy it was to shut off any feelings. The lesson had begun. And I could not help the twin feelings of repulsion and curiosity. I watched him and took notes as a pupil, without a word. Teaching his cub to hunt. He smiled again, teeth broad and lethal. Renee dropped her gaze demurely, swaying a little on her feet. He let her hand slide out of his and she walked away from us, a bit unsteady.

"It's all in the touch and in the eyes. Then the voice. But the touch intensifies it, makes humans pliable and more responsive."

The waitress had been utterly consumed by my father in that moment. If he'd asked her to open a vein right there, I bet she would have. Was I like that with Sabrina? Certainly not. But I thought of that first night, the alcohol, my hunger for her to touch me. I wanted something from her that I couldn't name, and she played right into that. When I didn't want to fight, she stopped. My fingertips absently went to my lips, the ghost of her blood there.

"It's like she's under a spell. . . ." I murmured, watching Renee from across the room.

Hugh nodded, cutting into his steak and lifting a piece to his mouth. "Most people, we make their skin crawl. But the tradeoff is that those like that waitress, like the hostess, like your mother, and Sabrina . . . they are so receptive. They want to be our prey. You can do practically anything to them if you keep them touching you, close to you, talking to you. The longer they are away, the more strained the connection, the more they think about what actually happened . . . the more they notice the bites."

He gestured for me to eat. I had left my plate untouched. Just like in my mother's journal, as soon as Hugh was away, she'd start to question everything. I tried to not feel guilty that I wasn't defending the human race. I stared down at my artfully arranged chicken, sitting on a bed of poached pears and mashed sweet potatoes. A small decorative flower adorned the side of the plate. I cut into the chicken and took a bite, the combined flavors delicious and complex in my mouth. My father watched closely and was pleased.

"I want you to talk to the waitress when she returns. See if you can get her to be as interested in you as she was in me."

I shook my head, my mouth full. "Uh, I'm a teenage girl, and you're a man. I highly doubt it."

"What's the harm? You need to understand what you are capable of doing, the power you can wield over these people. You use it on your little girlfriend almost daily, so I figured you'd prefer trying it on another woman."

"So . . . you've fed off of men before?"

He laughed, loud enough that a couple a few tables away looked over. "Of course I have. My college roommate for one.

Remember, Jane, I'm an opportunist. I'm not very concerned about the outer packaging if I'm hungry. I think few of our kind are. Although I do prefer women. But it's different for everyone."

"Well, I . . ." My mouth opened and closed like a fish.

"Let me put it this way: do you fantasize about sex or about blood?"

I was uncomfortable with the personal shift in conversation, but he had been my father for approximately two days. What did he know about talking to a teenage daughter? What did I know? And he was right. I'd never thought about sex, never really cared. The life thrumming within Sabrina excited me far more than anything. My lack of response was his answer. He leaned back and crossed his arms, taking the point for himself.

"I don't much fantasize about either," I responded, cheeks hot.

He waved my answer off with a brush of his hand. "What I'm saying is that our biological urge is for blood, using sex."

"What about the others? Regular people? Can you drink their blood?"

He took another bite of his steak, nodding with his mouth full. "You can get blood from anyone, but it will be a very different experience with the unwilling."

"Have you ever done it?" I asked.

He nodded and I stopped eating, fork held above my plate. There were so many people walking the streets that the idea of just anyone becoming prey opened up an entire world of options.

"If you're desperate, you'll go with what you can get. It happens, believe me. I have gone for street people, preferably unconscious. But you have to be ready, since regular people are going to fight tooth and nail to get away from you."

"Yeah . . ." I thought of Hob's Valley. One wrong step and villagers with pitchforks would be on my front porch, I was sure of it.

"Right after your mother left, I was in a bit of a state. There was another woman that I was seeing, but not very often, so our bond was not as strong. She had to go away for business. I was sick, with your mother gone unexpectedly and Barbara—the other woman—away as well. Anyway, there was this homeless man who used to skulk around near the gallery, begging food or change off anyone who passed—all but me, obviously." Hugh leaned in, dropping his voice a notch. "I was sitting there in the shop, my skin itching like crazy, my stomach screaming, and I was watching that poor bastard outside. Finally, I offered him a hundred-dollar bill to help me load stuff into a truck, and even with that kind of money in his hand, he was still reluctant. But I eventually convinced him to come to the back alley, to help with lifting something there. Then I just clocked him with a cinder block and drained him dry. One of the few times I killed someone in one feeding, but it was amazing. I was fat as a tick by the end, so full I had to undo my pants!"

He laughed at this, the memory strangely fond for him. I tried to keep my face free of emotion while he talked. But the idea of him killing bums in back alleys was a combination of horrific and nauseating. Worse still, I hated how attractive the idea of drinking until I had my fill was, the other person be damned.

"After lying there for a while, I realized that I now had a dead body to clean up. It was a whole thing. . . ." Hugh waved his hand and drained the dregs of his glass, filling it back up immediately and topping my barely touched glass as well.

"How did you—"

"Oh, I ended up wrapping him in plastic and putting him in the boot of my van—the gallery's van. Then I drove all the way to Jersey and dumped him in the ocean in an industrial area. Never saw anything about it in the papers, so I suppose I got away with it." He took another sip of his wine and finished his steak. I wanted to ask more, how killing made him feel, how he lived with it. But Renee returned to take our plates. Hugh nodded at me, communicating wordlessly that it was my turn to talk to her. She had eyes only for him though, as she stacked the plates.

"Would you care to see a dessert menu?" she said in a husky voice, her eyes glassy.

My pulse raced. I swallowed it down and cleared my throat. It had the desired effect of breaking her out of the fog. She turned to me.

"Yes, I would like to see the dessert menu." I held her gaze. I tried to pour all of my hunger, all of my need to be wanted, to be loved, to be held, to be understood, into my eyes and into her. I was excited and discomforted by how easy it was to keep her attention on me. I wasn't even touching her yet, but I had the sinking feeling that if I asked her to sit beside me, she'd do it.

Slowly, Renee reached into her black apron and produced the small metallic folder that held the dessert menu. She handed it to me, and I reached deliberately, letting my fingertips brush along hers. She inhaled shakily as we made contact, her body shivering. The connection snapped into place, and I could feel her pulse through my fingers. My sense of smell opened up tenfold and suddenly I could smell her skin, her perfume, the perspiration beneath her deodorant. I could see the thump of her heart in her neck and feel my breathing and heartbeat fall into rhythm with hers. It was as if we stood in a black tunnel together, completely closed off from anything but one another. It was so tempting to stay there, hidden away in a world filled only with her breaths, her scent. But I shook it off and I could see my father in my peripheral vision. He was smiling wolfishly.

"What would you recommend for dessert?" I finally said.

She frowned for a moment before whispering, "Death by chocolate with fresh raspberries."

I risked a glance at my father, he nodded.

"Great. That's what we'll have. Thank you, Renee." As quickly as I had ensnared her, I cut the tether. She blinked hard for a moment, absently wiping the pearls of perspiration that had blossomed on her upper lip. I could feel her searching stare on my face, but I didn't look back at her.

"Uh . . . okay. I'll put that order right in for you." Her training overcame her discomfort as she spun away, frown on her face. As soon as she was out of earshot, I turned to my father, barely containing my excitement.

"Oh my God, I can't believe that worked. I thought it would be so hard, but it was . . ."

"Easy. Yes. I think she would have done anything you told her to. Good girl."

I beamed. Inside, the familiar guilt was rattling around, hollering for me to be horrified, but I ignored it. I felt great, powerful. I hadn't been very good at being a person, but maybe I was good at being a monster. I would be fighting a lot less with Sabrina if I started using that little trick when it was time for blood. I wanted to feel shame for thinking that, but there was no room for it. I was soaring on a feeling of complete control. I couldn't get the dumb grin off my face.

When Renee returned, she placed the dish between us a bit unceremoniously, her composure slipping, making no attempt to look at either of us. My father thanked her anyway as she dropped the two forks on the table surface loudly and pivoted away, hurrying to the safety of the swaying kitchen doors.

XXXI.

After dessert, Renee returned, slid the check to us, and vanished again. My father jammed a credit card into the black sleeve without looking at the total. She didn't look at either of us as she processed payment and left, and it made me a little sad, the euphoria earlier curdling to a more familiar pang of regret.

"Do the people that work here know what we are?" I asked.

"I'd imagine so."

"But what we do to them, is it like hypnotism? Or are we just turning them into slaves? You think she actually likes me somewhere in there? Or just because I told her to? She seems embarrassed about it now."

"I wouldn't overthink it, Jane. I think you woke an interest she didn't know she had." Hugh stood up and asked me to wait. He went to talk to the hostess. She leaned into him, receptive. Money exchanged hands. Then, gathering our coats, he gestured to me. I followed the tall shape of my father through two darkened double doors into a very intimate dining space that had to be for private parties.

The room was also red, a more vibrant shade than the main dining room. The floor and ceiling were painted a dark glossy black. The room had one long table surrounded by tall, gray leather chairs. A round velvet sofa was nestled in the corner farthest from the door. It faced an electric fireplace. The only light in the room came from the dancing flames. Hugh took our coats and hung them on nearby chairs, comfortable with the room, like he'd been in it before.

He gestured for me to sit on the sofa, so I did, comforted by the heat emanating from the fireplace. He stood near the door, affecting a relaxed pose, but I could see the tension beneath it, the hunter peeking out. I wanted to ask what was about to happen, when the door pushed open. Renee came through. She had on her service smile, but it fell when she saw me sitting on the sofa. Waiting.

XXXII.

"*What* are you . . . ?" She started to say to me when my father stepped behind her and immediately put his arm around her.

"We thought you were an incredible waitress, my daughter and I, and we wanted to thank you. Won't you please sit with us a moment?" I watched her go from uncomfortable and tense to completely compliant in the blink of an eye. His arm firmly around her waist, his mouth close to her ear, she relaxed. I watched nervously as he locked the door behind him. She smiled dreamily and sat between us.

"That is really nice of you guys." She said and Hugh smoothed back her hair and shushed her. She basked in the caress, catlike. He cupped her face and locked eyes. They were nearly mouth to mouth.

"I want to kiss you, Renee, would that be all right?" I saw a ghost of doubt, of fear, flicker across her face, but it was pulled quickly under and she nodded, smiling. He pressed his mouth to hers, and she sighed.

There was something strange about watching my father deeply kiss this woman. I looked away, staring at the fire, feeling deeply uncomfortable. In my periphery, I saw his hand move down her neck to her breast, heard her intake of breath as he squeezed. He gestured to me, but I wasn't sure what he wanted me to do. Watching my father and this woman in such a private moment made me squirm with embarrassment. So I did nothing, my hands clasped tightly in my lap, knuckles white. He kissed along her neck, and gestured at me again, this time with force. When I still didn't move, Hugh took my hand and placed it on the woman's. I couldn't help it. I took her hand without thinking about it, running my thumb over the pulse point at her wrist. She moaned, and I knelt into the crux of her arm, rolling up the dark sleeve.

Renee had an elaborate floral tattoo on her forearm, and I hoped my bite wouldn't ruin the artistry of it. I ran my hand over the purple irises, noting how smooth her inner arm was, like silk. I licked her skin. Her perfume was spicy and utterly appealing. Once I felt that enough of my saliva had numbed the area, I bit, knowing that the first sweet mouthful of blood was always the best. I could see my father's mouth on her neck, biting in near the collarbone, his other hand up under her dress. I tried to ignore them as I got my fill, noting how different it tasted from Sabrina's. I thought of wine connoisseurs and their ability to detect all the subtleties of flavor.

I was losing track of time, and I tried to pull myself away. I wanted to drink and drink, lose myself to the feeling of sinking into warm, depthless, water.

I forced myself to stop. I pulled Renee's sleeve to cover her arm and edged myself down to the end of the sofa to avoid temptation. I saw a trickle of blood dribble out her sleeve where her arm hung limp off the couch.

My father was nearly done himself. I stared at the fire, trying to force indifference. He slowly detached from her throat, unceremoniously wiping his face on her dress before pulling it up over her neck. Renee was nearly unconscious, breathing heavily, a half smile on her sweaty, pale face. He pulled her long skirt down and arranged her more comfortably on the sofa, as if she were a ragdoll.

Leaning over her, he stroked her hair away from her face. Her eyes fluttered as he whispered in her ear.

"Thank you, Renee. Perhaps I or my daughter will call on you again. Don't forget us, all right? Have a big glass of juice and a slice of cake and you'll be fine." In a surprisingly tender moment, he smoothed her long blonde bangs back and kissed her temple before straightening up and getting his coat. I did the same and we left the restaurant.

I welcomed the fresh air out on the streets, the incense and heat inside were too intense. I was buzzing with blood. My body felt like it could fly if I willed it, but my soul felt sick. My father was more composed. His cheeks were ruddy, and his mouth was red and bee-stung. I could smell her on him even from a few feet away.

"Let's walk a bit, shall we? It's a nice night and I feel very warm." He smiled down at me and in a gentlemanly fashion, offered me his arm. I stood for a beat, unsure, before finally taking it. My heart swelled in my chest, betraying me.

We walked in silence. The city was interesting enough to steal my focus. I loved all the shuttered storefronts, the beautiful clothes and jewelry on display in the windows. On a cold night like this, the restaurants and bars were brimming, so full that the floors were hidden beneath the press of active bodies. I enjoyed the feel of my arm in his; there was a safety in it. My father's arm. Hugh, my father.

A wave of emotion came over me then, and a few stray tears seeped out, nearly freezing to my cheeks before I could wipe them away. I tried to hide it, feign a runny nose, or a cough. But Hugh was shrewd. Although his gait was casual, his eyes were everywhere. He stopped us short, turning me toward him.

"Are you all right, Jane?" His voice was cool, as if he was obligated to ask. I tried to affect a casual air as I broke contact and stepped away.

"Yes. No. I don't know. I just felt really overcome. I liked that too much. I like how I feel too much. But I feel so guilty. Is she going to be okay? Will she be in trouble or lose her job? Or maybe go to the police? It just felt like we really took advantage. . . ."

"Jane, Jane. She'll be fine, woozy from blood loss, but fine. And she won't go to the police. She was consenting. More than likely, she'll just be confused and probably embarrassed. I doubt that she'd even tell her best friend, or her boyfriend. So don't worry. This is how we get by, especially if you want to give your lover a break. Spread out the love, so one person is not getting all of it."

My senses were sharper than they had ever been. I could hear cars blocks away, rats scurrying in alleys, TV sets playing in a hundred apartments. I felt like I could run for miles without tiring. My body was operating at peak performance. But I hated how good I felt, how shameful it all was.

"I've been so hungry my whole life. . . ." My voice trembled and I felt like a fool, a child. The more I tried to clamp the feeling down, the more it pushed up and out, my eyes wet with tears. I jammed my hands in my pockets and started walking, Hugh following close on my heels.

"If I hadn't found Mom's journal, I'd probably have just wasted away and died. Or gone mad and done something terrible. If I hadn't found you, I would have kept the hope that there was a cure for me. If not a cure, then at least a future that didn't involve perpetually using and exploiting people. And I hate myself right now, Hugh, more than ever in my life. I hate myself because I like how strong I feel. And I like being with someone like me, who understands."

"It's not all bad, Jane. We play by different rules."

"But I don't want to."

"It's what we are designed to do."

"But you kill them!"

He shushed me and began moving again, his hand on my lower back guiding me.

"This is not a philosophical discussion about morality, Hugh. This is real. We destroy real lives," I said.

"I'm getting tired of this conversation, Jane, since it seems we're just going in circles. Here's the deal: you either get over it and do what your body demands, and live, or you starve yourself and start attacking people, or just waste away. Or you could just kill yourself. As you suggested when we first met."

"I've lived with very little blood before. I could do it, or maybe stop entirely. I wouldn't hurt anyone."

"Do you want to go to jail? To a mental hospital? Or even worse, have them drag you under a microscope and try to figure out what you are?"

"Maybe that would be better! Maybe then we could find a cure. Or at least an alternative?"

Hugh swore, and looked at me pityingly. "You don't think any of us have tried that before you? You don't think that others have hated what we are forced to do, day in, day out? The problem is, we're not just biology, we're not just parasites. We need more than blood. We need the life, the love, the soul—call it what you will. But what keeps us going is not just plasma and red blood cells. It's them. We need them to love us, to see us."

"Are you saying it's magic more than science?"

"You should understand more than anyone. You wept because I offered you my arm. You have lived your life more loathed than a stray dog, or a leper on the street. Your own mother hates you, ignores you, and feeds you solely because of the biological lasso you have wrapped around her neck. Sabrina, on the other hand, brings you happiness; her love gives you a reason to go on. Isn't that a sort of magic?"

I squirmed under his hard gaze, regretting the traitorous tears, regretting how wretched I was. I just wanted a moment of peace. For the world to stop whirling past, for my fate to feel less foreordained.

"Yes, fine! You win! And there's something terrible about that, and pathetic. So let me feel sad, at least for a second, let me grieve for the life I thought I'd have someday. I know you've lived this way forever, but I haven't."

Hugh took a few steps, looking into a closed storefront window. "It's not as bleak as that, I promise."

"It's not? Have you ever had a relationship that you didn't use your influence on, at least a little? How do you know anyone's ever really loved you? We can't have friends, we can't be a part of anything real. We can't make anything. Everything we do is an attempt to fill a void. Everything we are is fake. We have nothing of our own. I love Sabrina. It scares the shit out of me to think she might not really love me—not the way she thinks she does."

Hugh sighed, eyes still on the shop window. "I wept for Margot like the world had ended when she died. I wanted to die. I went to my father and begged him to kill me because I was too much of a coward to do it myself. So I understand. But life is hard and filled with terrible choices, Jane. Either deal with it or don't. End of discussion. Come. I will take you back to the apartment. It's been a long night."

I followed him silently. Hugh didn't have the solution I wanted. I was suddenly exhausted to my core.

As we silently rode in the cab, all I could focus on was the idea of stealing love, stealing life. Where did Sabrina's liking of me as a person start, and where did her mindless compulsion to be my victim end? If I didn't know I was doing it, could I still be at fault for the manipulation? And if that was the case, why didn't I compel my mother to love me my whole life?

When we arrived at the dark apartment building, neither of us moved right away. The stillness was unnerving and I thought Hugh was disappointed in me. I cleared my throat as I reached for the car door.

"Thank you for dinner. You've been very generous. And thanks for . . . educating me." I said most of this through gritted teeth, trying to keep my voice even. Hugh wished me a good night. As I stepped onto the street, he stopped me.

"If I could do it over again, I would have found a way to leave Margot. Save her. I loved her that much. So when I tell you to leave Sabrina, it is not to be cruel. And I had a nice night with you as well. I will call the apartment or pop by tomorrow morning."

I nodded and shut the cab door. The apartment building loomed before me, the only light shining down from the fourth floor, where Sabrina waited up.

After a while, I went in. The waitress's blood was still running through me, thrumming with vitality, but my mind was tired. By the time I reached the apartment door I was totally spent.

I went in and found Sabrina splayed on the sofa, a bag of chips in her lap, her eyes glued to an inane TV show. When she saw me she jumped up, eager for details of my night. Her hair was messy from lying down, one pigtail drastically higher than the other. It made her look like a little girl, despite the makeup and garish T-shirt. I wanted to run to her, hold her, but I couldn't move, the knowledge that she couldn't survive me, that she might not even love me at all, kept me rooted to the spot.

"So?" she asked, anxious but smiling.

"I'm really tired and I don't feel much like talking now. I'm just going to go to bed. I need to think about a lot of things." I winced as I said it. I shucked off my coat and shoes at the door.

Sabrina came to me, her face crinkled in concern. "I've been sitting here for hours, waiting for you. You can't leave it like that. Come on. This is the shit that talk shows were made for—long-lost fathers, family secrets . . . so, spill."

I took a breath, my voice low when I did finally speak. "I told you, I don't want to talk about it. I don't have to tell you everything, especially for entertainment. Goodnight."

"Jesus, what is your problem? What happened?"

I closed the door behind me and leaned my back against it. I slid to the floor, pulling my knees up. The floor was cold but I didn't care. I could hear Sabrina on the other side. Angry, moving around, her scent—that familiar combination of vanilla and cigarettes—wafted under the door. With a muttered oath she pounded on the door, calling out a few more choice things, but I didn't answer. I crawled into bed, still in my clothes, but I didn't care. I curled into a fetal position and pulled the duvet over my head. Eventually Sabrina gave up trying the door, and things settled down on the other side of the wall. I assumed she slept.

XXXIII.

When I came out the next morning, Sabrina was awake and eating a granola bar. She glared at me defiantly. But when I turned away from her, she stomped from the room, slamming the bedroom door behind her. I let out a breath I didn't know I'd been holding and crumpled to the sofa. The TV still blared, but under that I could hear Sabrina crying.

My heart twisted in my chest. I wanted to run in there, to apologize, to hug her. But I was doing the right thing. I didn't want to spend my life surrounded by zombies who thought they loved me. I would free my mother from being a perpetual victim. Sabrina could live her life. And no one else would get hurt.

I took a long, hot, shower. My luggage was in the bedroom, so I just wore a towel, sipping coffee and watching the pale, sickly sun rise over the snow-covered city. It was a shame the sun didn't burn me up like in vampire movies. It'd make things a lot easier. I could just drop my towel, step into a band of light, and it would over. Granted, burning alive would be terrible, but at least it'd be fast.

Sabrina eventually came out, head high and obviously ignoring me. I ignored her right back and went in to get a change of clothes. It was for the best. I needed to know where the line was between Sabrina making her own choices and me compelling her. The fact that she was angry at me proved I was making the right choice. Her anger was real. I slid on some jeans and a sweater, leaving my hair down to dry.

Sabrina spent a long time in the bathroom, and when she emerged pink from the shower in a towel turban, I could see the bite marks on her arms and neck, healing slowly, which would probably leave permanent scars. She tried to keep ignoring me, but halfway across the room she finally spun around.

"I'm still so pissed at you, because I like to think we're a team. But you're right—you don't owe me anything. And I was being immature. You have a lot of heavy stuff going on. For what it's worth, whatever Hugh is or isn't, or whatever he's been saying, please don't push me away. You won't hurt me: I'm tough."

"I can't take that chance, Sabrina. We have to stop seeing each other." I started cleaning the counter, pretending not to care.

"God. You want to be a martyr, or something? What options do you have? Really, what are you going to do? Waste away in that rotten old house?"

I perched on a barstool at the kitchen island. "It's over, Sabrina. We leave today. I've learned what Hugh could teach me. End of discussion," I said, chewing a hangnail.

The knock on the door startled us both, and I realized it had to be Hugh. Sabrina huffed and made a production of walking to the bedroom and slamming the door, again.

I took a second to gather my nerves before answering. I plastered a nervous smile on my face and let Hugh inside. He surveyed the apartment, no doubt looking for Sabrina.

"Why didn't you let yourself in again?"

"Figured you'd appreciate the gesture, after last time. Where's your friend?"

"She's holed up in the bedroom. We had a fight. I told her it was over. She's not happy about it." I sat on the sofa. He didn't say much, just raised an eyebrow.

"Would you mind if I talked to Sabrina alone?"

My first instinct was to say no, definitely not. He could see my hesitation, even my hostility, at the idea.

He gave me an exasperated look. "I just want to help her understand all this. Please."

I gave in. The alarm bells clanged but I nodded. He thanked me and went to the door, rapping on it gently. Sabrina opened it a crack. He asked if he could come in and, after looking at me, she let him. He shut it behind him, which left me staring at the door.

I could hear their muffled voices on the other side of the door, and curiosity had me up with my ear pressed to the door.

"I know it doesn't feel like it, but Jane is making the right decision. She doesn't want to hurt you."

"She won't," Sabrina responded petulantly. "She's getting better all the time."

"You're right, Sabrina. She's getting better at being a cold killer. She doesn't want you to be her first kill."

I stepped away from the door not wanting to eavesdrop further, finding the conversation depressing. Hugh must actually like me a little to involve himself. Otherwise, why did he care what I did to Sabrina? She was no one to him. Maybe I should stay in the city with him. Maybe Hugh could help get my mother into a nice nursing home, and then I could come back down, change schools, be with Hugh. Try to make it all work. Sabrina could be healthy and happy and most of all, safe, up north.

They'd been quiet in there a while, enough time to have had the short conversation that would get her to break up with me. I stood up, impatient, and crossed the room to the bedroom door. I raised my hand to knock and thought better of it, and instead pushed in. The room was as I had left it that morning— curtains open, bed mussed. But on it lay Sabrina, swooning and wearing only a bra, Hugh at her throat, drinking deeply.

I reacted instantly, screaming and pulling at his shoulders, digging my nails in and yanking him off. He released her, his mouth a smear of red, the hole at her throat deep, deeper than any I had ever inflicted. Sabrina was chalk-pale but smiling, not caring she was nearly naked. I moaned—at least, I think it was me, the sound seemed to come from somewhere outside my body. I crumpled to my knees, my hands balled into fists glaring at Hugh.

"Why?"

"To show you how easy it is. I know you love her, but look, not even five minutes with me and she was ready to forget you. Do you see? She loves all of us. I was like you, after Margot. I'm trying to protect you from that. She . . ." He pointed to the barely conscious Sabrina, lying on the bed, her blood seeping out wastefully onto the sheets. "She's just like all the others. They're all the same!"

"And this was how you wanted to teach me that lesson? Would you have killed her if I hadn't come in?"

Hugh shook his head, straightening his clothes and wiping his face. "I hadn't planned to do this, Jane. But she was so obstinate. Don't overthink this. . . ." He gestured at Sabrina in the bed. I rushed to her side. Her pulse was weak, and I tried to stop the bleeding with the sheets.

I glared at him. "Get out of here. Now, Hugh. I'll figure this out on my own." I practically snarled this out, choking on my anger. He put his hands up in defense, his face unreadable. He was almost out the bedroom door when he swung back and pulled an envelope from his pocket.

"You may not believe it, but I was trying to help. Oh, I almost forgot. This is for you. I wish you luck. You know where to find me if you need anything. Just lock up and leave the keys at the gallery when you leave."

I was too furious to reply, so instead I just kept my arms around Sabrina and watched him through the bedroom doorway until he was gone. When the front door closed, I allowed myself a breath of relief. I shook Sabrina awake. She stared at me blearily, woozy from blood loss. I rummaged through her bags, finding her first aid kid and bandaged her neck.

It was impossible to ignore her reality staring at the supplies laid out: gauze, ointments, iron supplements. All the essentials when dating a vampire. I sat her up and got her some water and food. As she sipped and ate, her color started coming back. Then her lip trembled.

"Are we still fighting?" she asked in a hoarse whisper. I laughed without meaning to and shook my head no. She finally noticed she was topless and felt at the gauze at her throat.

Her gaze went far away for a moment before it scrunched up on itself, to fight the tears.

"I get why you didn't want me to meet your dad." I nodded and hugged her, our foreheads touching. She got herself cleaned up and ten minutes later, all our things were piled by the door, and the apartment looked like no one had ever been there. Except for the blood-sprayed sheets I'd bundled and tossed in the bathtub.

XXXIV.

We loaded the car with our bags, Sabrina looking terrible. I worried about her driving, but she assured me she just needed to rest and then she'd be ready to hit the road. I sat in the front seat while she dozed in the back, neither of us feeling safe in the apartment.

I opened the envelope Hugh had given me. It was a few sheets of paper. Lawyer stuff, finances, transfer of funds for a few thousand dollars. So Hugh had put together some sort of trust fund for me. A Post-it stuck to the last page where my signature was meant to go caught my eye.

In Hugh's cursive handwriting: Renee the waitress 917 555 8726

I wiped at the angry tears welling and clouding my vision. Why do this? Hurt Sabrina and write me a goddamned check? He really was inhuman.

Sabrina finally stirred. She sat up and began snacking, bags full of junk food in her lap. She was paler than I'd ever seen her. If I'd known how to drive, I would have offered. But she insisted she was fine and crawled into the driver's seat, the bandage visible at her throat. She looked guilty. I knew it wasn't her fault, she'd been manipulated. By both of us.

"I don't know what happened, Jane," she said, so defeated that my heart ached.

"It's fine, really."

"No, it's not. I don't understand why I would do that with your . . . Hugh. It's so fucked up."

I couldn't look at her, not wanting her to know the truth, instead staring at the envelope in my hands. A braver person would tear the financial documents up and toss it out the window. I jammed it into my pocket, instead.

"He was proving a point, Sabrina."

"I don't understand. What point?" she whispered.

"That he could do whatever he wanted to you. That's what I learned the other night. We can control people, make them do things for us. For all we know, I'm pulling the same puppet strings with you, only I didn't know."

"That's crazy, Jane." She swallowed audibly, grimacing in pain.

"Is it? That's why this has to stop. I don't want to manipulate you. I'm not my father." And I wanted that to be true. I remembered the sensation of cutting the connection with Renee the night before, and wondered if I could do the same thing to Sabrina. Though my heart protested even at the thought of it. I understood a little more about Hugh at that moment. It was a lot easier to distance yourself when you felt so little.

Sabrina started to answer but I shut her down. I needed the silence to think. She was too tired and upset to fight me about it and stayed quiet. I directed her to drive to the gallery first. She gawked at me like I'd gone crazy, but I told her she'd be safe in the car.

The gallery was different by day—abandoned-looking, the windows dark and reflective. There were no footprints in the morning snow on the sidewalk in front of the door. I jumped out of the car and walked with determination up to the front door.

Trying the handle, I thought it would be locked, but it opened with ease. Natsuki's paintings were still up on all the walls. I stopped and stared at The Dowry again, the complicated relationship between the white of the surface and the violence of the red all the more haunting now, knowing the "dowry" had been her blood. I wonder how many dowries my father had collected in his life.

My steps echoed in the open space. I was tempted to call out. The lights were off and it was cold, but it felt like someone was there. Before I could say anything, a feminine voice called out from the back, where my father's office was.

"Just a minute . . ." Natsuki. My potential stepmother. She came out a moment later, wearing a black shirt-dress, cinched with a thin white belt. She wore the same red heels and her hair was twisted up into a messy white-blonde knot, held together with gleaming black chopsticks. She wore no makeup and glasses with large oversized frames. I noticed her hands were stained with paint, and a bite was visible in the crook of her arm.

"Ah, the prodigal child returns. . . ." She said this flippantly, almost jealously. I clenched my jaw, fighting a brief but violent urge. She was like Sabrina, like my mother, like Renee the waitress. If I really wanted to stick it to Hugh, I could strip her down and rip out her throat, leave her sitting in the gallery with a note saying "Lesson Learned." But there was no point—he wouldn't care. Natsuki crossed her arms, watching me as the silence stretched.

I cleared my throat. "So, he told you."

That same perfectly shaped eyebrow raised and she smiled. "Darling, he didn't need to. You look exactly like him."

"Apparently so. Is he here? I need to talk to him." I looked past her impatiently. She shook her head.

"No, last I heard he was going to see you and then to a meeting. He'll be back in a few hours, though. Could it wait?"

"No. I really have to get on the road. Just tell him . . ." I held the envelope in my hand, tempted to hand it back and say, "Tell him thanks but no thanks." But I thought of my mother living someplace warm and safe, where she would get three meals and a soft bed. I clutched the envelope tight. The money was too important to us to give back just out of pride.

"Just thank him for his generosity, and for everything." I went to the door. Something stopped me. The curious part of me, the part who that had never met another willing donor before. It forced me to turn back to her.

"Can I ask you something? It's personal."

Natsuki nodded.

"You know what my father is, what I am, and what he does to you?" My eyes shot to her arm, and she nodded. "Okay, well, does that frighten you? Does it make you wonder how long you have? How long before you're bedridden, how long before you're little more than a husk? Before you're nothing at all?"

She smiled tightly. "It doesn't bother me, because your father and I love each other. He needs me, Jane. And besides, he would never really hurt me. Our relationship isn't like that." She spoke as if she was reading it off the wall behind me.

"It's happened before, you know. Many times before, even with my mother."

She continued to smile, unfazed. "It's different with us."

I could feel his influence in her words. The confidence was hers, but the blank, diluted stare as she spoke was all his. She was a pawn, another in the scores of people who had loved Hugh McGarrett and paid for it with everything. There was no point in talking to her further, she was doomed like all the others. I thanked her for her time, closing the door behind me as I left.

When I got back in the car, Sabrina asked: "Did you talk to him?"

"No. Let's get on the road. Can you drive?"

"I can manage. We just need to take it easy. Are you okay?"

I nodded, astounded Sabrina could be so calm. She'd been molested and mind-fucked by my father, and here she sat, concerned for me. What did we do to these people?

"I just want to go home and make sure my mother's all right." I was agitated, wanting nothing more than the open road and the city at our backs. I took her hand tenderly, forcing her eyes to mine.

"We should talk about what happened in the apartment," said Sabrina.

"No more questions. Let's just be quiet and go. Now." I squeezed her hand and I pushed, hard, harder than at the restaurant, harder than that first night when I didn't know what I was doing. I pushed her to listen to me, to comply, to just do whatever I fucking said.

Her brows furrowed for a moment before smoothing out. She smiled, glassy-eyed, and nodded obediently.

Something twisted so deep inside me it nearly snapped, and a whispery voice said I might not be as cruel, but I was just like Hugh. I was creating my own world where making people bend to me was normal.

I watched her placid face as Sabrina drove. It was rush hour and the snowstorms had left the roads in bad condition. I kept worrying if it was safe. She gnawed her lip, eyes locked to the taillights in front of her, focused.

She was much thinner than when we first met, her skin sallow, hair dull. She'd lost so much blood over the past few days. My eyes went to the gauze at her throat, a small bloom of blood had seeped through. He'd coerced her just to prove his point. They would do anything for us, including die. We were programmed to be their muses, and they were programmed to die for us. And if I could see Sabrina as just another one, then maybe I wouldn't feel so conflicted about what I had to do to survive. I knew that in his inhuman way, Hugh was trying to help and protect me.

Didn't make it feel any better.

An agonizing hour later, we got out of New York City's limits and into Connecticut, inching north with agonizing slowness along the narrow roads and bridges. We eventually spilled out onto the emptier freeways. It was a relief when the car's speedometer finally crept up to sixty-five. The snow continued to fall, and Sabrina remained silent as the miles flew past.

Evening came, and we stopped at a rest stop for food and fuel. We stood in the long line of commuters, all looking harried and frozen. Sabrina swayed on her feet, her skin waxen under the harsh fluorescents.

This is the price for my love, I thought bitterly.

The wall menus showcased nothing that was remotely appetizing to me. I stared at a large man in front of me, hypnotized by the flannel pattern of his shirt and the sweat stains encircling his old baseball cap. Finally, it was my turn, and the woman behind the counter was made visibly uncomfortable by me. I ordered a yogurt and a coffee. She slid me my change and receipt with relief.

We sat at a plastic booth in the corner. I watched Sabrina pick at her fries, her lank black braids swaying. "How are you feeling?" I asked.

"Terrible. I am so, so sorry about your dad." Sabrina whispered, her voice shaking. "I don't know what happened. It was like one second we were talking and he's telling me how much he appreciates that I'm there for you, and that I'm so important, and the next . . ." Fat tears ran down her cheeks, and she mopped them up with the sleeve of her sweatshirt.

"It's not your fault, Sabrina. He can influence people, mess with their minds and he was . . . proving a point." I felt dead as I said this. Our table faced a playground outside. One older employee, on break, smoked out there, moving around to stay warm.

"You said that before. What point?" Sabrina asked.

I laughed. It was an ugly sound. I couldn't look at her. "Basically that you're disposable, that you love me because you're programmed to. That you could easily enough love him, or anyone . . . like us. We're your muses. He was proving that what you and I have is nothing special and I shouldn't feel bad about eventually killing you."

She scowled, her face folding in on itself. Tears plopped into her sad value meal. "I don't want that to be true, Jane. I don't believe him."

I handed her a napkin and sipped my coffee, needing to occupy my hands. "I do believe him, Sabrina. I've spent the weekend trying to find a way to keep you in my life. To prove to myself that I'm not compelling you to love me somehow. But I can't."

"What does that mean?" She looked afraid.

"I don't know. It means let's just get on the road and go home. I need to see my mom, and we need some space to think about things. I'll be fine for a few days. Hell, maybe some hunger and discomfort will let me see things clearer." I tried to smile supportively and pat her hand. It felt fake, even to me.

The rest of the ride passed in near silence, but it was a tired, lonely silence this time. The silence when there was nothing left to say. We were just circling the same issues over and over anyway. I even allowed myself to doze, but the dreams were strange and upsetting, so I forced myself awake. The snow finally let up, and the sunset was a brilliant show of pinks and purples. The sky turned clear and starry as we drove, and I marveled at its remote beauty.

After many more hours and a few more rest stops that all looked exactly alike, eventually the sights became more familiar, and soon enough we arrived at my old gate. It had only been three days, but it felt like an absolute lifetime had passed. It was the same old pink house, only now covered in thick snow. I wasn't the same person that had gingerly gotten in this car just a few days ago, who was afraid of roads she didn't know.

I took Sabrina's hand as she slowed in front of the driveway. Her lip was already trembling. She knew what was coming.

"You are an amazing person, and you will have an amazing life. I refuse to take that away from you, because I really do love you. And because of that, I don't want to see you again."

And then I kissed her, pushing, pushing, all the pain, all the hunger, all the sadness, into my command. I cut the tether with everything I had. I willed her to go and leave me.

And she did.

PART III: Memento Mori

And some, they said, had touched her side,
Before she fled us there;
And some had taken her to bride;
And some lain down for her and died;
Who had not touched her hair,
Ran to and fro and cursed and cried
And sought her everywhere.

—Conrad Aiken, "The Vampire"

XXXV.

The gate wouldn't budge. The snow had piled up since we'd been gone. It was deep and heavy enough that I couldn't move the gate more than the foot we'd left it open. So I had to toss my bag over the top and wriggle through the gap. Once on the other side, I turned to watch Sabrina's taillights fading into the night.

I willed myself not to cry. I probably didn't have any tears left, anyway. The wind was sharp and cold, and at that moment, a great gust hit me, a few leaves skittered loudly over the crisp frozen snow. The icy flakes stung my exposed face and hands.

I began the long, arduous trudge to the house. The driveway was completely covered. The heavy snow had forced down the weeds and the brambles that had been taking over the property for nearly two decades. And beneath that snow, cities of insects slept in their nests, animals hid snuggled into their dens and warrens. All dreaming of spring. The serene white spread out, undisturbed, glistening in the moonlight. It was easily two feet deep, and by the time I reached the sunken porch, my thighs and lungs burned from wading through it. My boots were soaked through and my toes were numb. I stamped my feet and shook off my clothes as best I could. The house was dark inside. I opened the old door with hands numbed into claws.

The lights were out and it was darker inside than out. At least outside, the stars and moon had reflected off all the whiteness. In here the air was cold and musty, the shadows deep and treacherous with debris. I could see my breath in the air. I let my bag drop at the base of the stairs, slipping off my wet shoes and socks and putting my old sneakers on my bare feet. The floor was too cold to go without them. I called out to my mother and fumbled a bit, finally hitting the dusty foyer light. The darkness scampered away, hiding behind stacks of canvases and old boxes. One of the bulbs flickered and dimmed, and the shadows slithered back out, regaining ground. The orange light, artificial and sickly, illuminated the peeling wallpaper and stained floors.

I first checked the front parlor. It was empty. I went to the sunken club chair, discolored where my mother's head and hands had lain for a decade. The blankets I'd tucked her in were pooled on the floor beside half-eaten bread scraps. The stove was cold and looked like it hadn't been used in at least a day. I filled it with wood and got the fire going.

My teeth chattered as I went to the kitchen. It hadn't changed much since I'd left it three days ago. It was all so still and dusty, I could have been gone for years. Like the sitting room, there was a strange feeling of vacancy. There were no new crumbs or dishes in the sink, and the table was bare. I tested the taps and was surprised and relieved to see the pipes hadn't frozen. To be safe, I left the faucet running at a slow trickle.

Tommy, my cat, burst from under the table, rubbing frantically against my legs. There was no food or water left in his bowls. I rubbed his head, welcoming his purring attention, and fed him. Once he was happily crunching, I stared up at the main stairs and exhaled, a tremor of fear running through me. I knew I was dawdling.

Up the stairs I called out again, feeling afraid now. I reached the top and walked to my mother's room. The door was ajar, but it was dark inside. The air, while cold, was heavy with the smell of urine and sickness. It was strong enough that I covered my mouth as I stepped into the room. I whispered her name, my hands shaking as I went to the lamp. I tried to swallow the scream that had lodged in my throat but I couldn't. My senses practically throbbed as I tried to reach out, to see an outline in the bed, to hear her breathing, any sign she was here.

"Mom?" I said louder, but there was still no answer. My fingertips found the lamp's knob and turned it. The room was suddenly cast in dim, pinkish light. It was all exactly as I'd left it. The blankets, the curtains, the ornate bed. The paintings, photos and books cluttering the corner, all where they'd been left three days ago.

I approached the bed, holding my breath.

XXXVI.

My mother wasn't there. The blankets were rumpled and unmade, but no one was beneath them. I called out, frantic, and searched the house, room by room. She was nowhere to be found. Outside, the snow lay untouched outside each door, except for my single path from the gate. Whimpering, I settled on the floor in the center of the living room. My house was completely still, my breath the only thing to keep me company. I looked at the phone, even debated calling the police, but it all felt so futile.

Somehow, miraculously, my mother had left. She'd regained enough mobility and had left. It was the only explanation. I was devastated. I never thought that even if she could leave, that she would. I wished she'd left a note, at least, or that there were some clothes taken from her closet. Some sign that she didn't wander out into the cold to die.

Because that was what it meant wasn't it?

My body crawled with dread at the thought. Where else could she have gone? No car, no friends, the snowstorm, freezing conditions. I moaned, fists pressed to my eyes until I saw starbursts. That made my choice a lot easier, I supposed. Fewer loose ends.

I crawled on my hands and knees to the phone, debating calling the police for a brief moment, before pulling it out of the wall and gathering the now full, happy Tommy to me. Sitting on the floor, I snuggled him, staring up at the ceiling. I remembered finding him as a kitten in the back field when I was just a little girl. Small furry ball of orange, and while he'd been somewhat feral, eventually, with some effort, I got him to come to me. My mother let me keep him with the promise that I would take care of him, a promise I had kept. For almost ten years. He purred and I wept, squeezing him tightly, grateful for the warmth.

I must have cried myself to sleep, because it was early morning when I woke. Stiff and cold, still on the floor. I stared around blearily until it all came rushing back.

I got up put more wood in the stove and then, stupidly, searched the house again. Then I went to the back door and I screamed out for my mother. The scream tore from me, unbound, a concentration of grief bursting from my chest, splitting me open down the middle. I screamed out my emptiness, my loneliness.

But there was no answer, except frightened birds taking off from a tree they were roosting in. I gave up and closed the door. My body was stiff from sleeping on the cold floor. I went to the bathroom and started the shower. Watching the water spiral down the drain I felt my sanity dangling on a fraying thread. I was losing myself. Without my mother, without Sabrina, and strangely, without Hugh, I was nothing.

I got into the shower and sunk to my knees, crying again without realizing it. I stared at my wrists, fantasized slashing them. Angrily, I bit into my skin, my sharp teeth easily parting flesh. I tasted my blood. Watery, pinkish, lacking the vibrancy and life of Sabrina's, but the taste was still soothing to me. Calming. I lay in the bathtub, suckling at my wrist until the water turned cold and the wound stopped bleeding.

Shivering so badly I was doubled over, I shuffled to my room, pulling my drawers out with abandon to find clothes that were warm enough. I found my thermals, put on my jeans over them, and a thin sweater, and over that another sweater—a moth-eaten, heavy fisherman's sweater. I slid on two pairs of wool socks. I mindlessly wandered down the stairs, and mercifully the living room was warm. I put a few more pieces of wood in the stove, and crawled into my mother's old chair. Tucking my feet beneath me, I bundled up in her blanket. The smell, once so repellent to me, had become soothing and familiar. It kept the emptiness at bay. I watched the flames dance in the fire and slowly warmed up. My head ached from crying. I sat like that for hours, dozing, empty. Totally alone.

Life was small, and cruel, and meaningless. It soothed me to think about it that way, to embrace the emptiness of it. I thought of the insect kingdoms in my front garden. All striving to survive and breed and die, never stopping to ask why. I thought of big cats, watching herds of gazelles go by, stomachs empty, waiting for a weak one to separate. I didn't want to play the game of hunter and hunted.

Finally, I built up enough nerve to go down to the basement. I went to the terrible room that held my mother's deepest secrets. I tested the lock on the outside. It was firm after all these years. This would work, this would be good. I slid my hands along the painted sheetrock, the stained cement. I felt a sense of resolve.

XXXVII.

It was nearly dark, and I was ready. I did a walk-through of the house again, making sure it was as presentable as it could be if someone came by. I wanted it to lie. To show it housed two beloved women, who cared for their home and each other. So I went from room to room, touching things, letting nostalgia flood me. I made the beds, I washed the dishes. I left the window in the kitchen open enough that the cat could get out once he'd eaten all the food I put out for him.

Finally, I felt as ready as I ever would, so I went back down to the basement. I felt the same revulsion as the first time I'd gone in. I laid out the blanket on the dingy, horrible sofa. It was too grotesque for me to let my skin touch directly. It smelled of sweat and old blood even now, all these years later. I set out my supplies on the floor before me.

I had a bottle of my mother's sleeping pills and a jug of water. I let my hand fiddle with the knob before taking a resigned breath and slamming the door shut. Locked. There was no way for me to lock the deadbolt on the outside, but the doorknob lock was firm. Once closed in, I was overcome with the finality of my choice.

The small room was miserable, the stains peeping out through the clumsy, manic whitewash.

My face felt hot, my hands icy and numb. I eased down onto the sofa, and with little to do and the small window blacked out years ago, I committed to taking the pills and going to sleep, forever.

The store brand sleeping pills were difficult to swallow, even after flooding my mouth with water. They hit my empty stomach with a splash. I took them all. Then I sat and waited.

From the low angle on the floor, I could see the carved words peeping from behind the sofa: hidden words, prayers, pleas, ghosting through the walls. My victims' words.

Eventually the pills took effect, the creeping drowsiness pulling at my hands and feet, then my eyelids. Before I went under, I dragged out my grandfather's straight razor. This was the very one that my mother used to stare at and contemplate her own death. There was something poetic in that. With a clarity of purpose, I put the blade to my wrist and dragged it up to the crook in my elbow, as deep as I could. Pain, hot and immediate. The skin slid open with ease and blood welled up, thick and dark. Teeth gritted, and with my stomach threatening to purge the pills, I did the same to the other arm. Moments later, I was pulled beneath the undertow.

XXXVIII.

"I'm sorry you had to die for me," I said aloud, startling myself out of sleep. I sat up, woozy and surprised I was still alive. My head was screaming, my heart beating erratically. Blearily, I looked around my tomb. I was covered in blood, my arms raw and horrible.

I moaned, a piteous sound. I picked up the razor and slashed again and again, above and across the other wounds until my hands were too slick with blood to grip the blade. I screamed aloud as the pain lit my body on fire. I dropped the knife and it fell with a clunk to the cement. I lay back down, curled up, the smell of blood everywhere maddening. The blood loss acting fast, numbing my limbs, turning my vision soft and furry. With little protest, I succumbed. My last thought was more of a prayer: I never want to wake again.

My prayers went unanswered. Eyes crusted, I woke again, crawling through cobwebs and blurry vision, staring disoriented around the cell. My shoulders were stiff from sleeping on the cold dirty floor and my gut was pinched with hunger. How was I still alive? My forearms were a tracery of deep horrible slices, skin bloodless and waxy. My stomach felt like it was filled with barbed wire, the pain so intense I couldn't take a deep breath. The floor around me was covered in congealed blood, encircling me like a vile red island.

I woke. I woke. I woke. I don't know how much later.

I could feel the flesh burning off me, my body ravenously stealing what energy it could still find. I saw it in my skeletal wrists, carved and scarred by the blade. I lifted myself from the ground and every joint creaked. I felt delirious. Had I been sleeping and starving for days? Mere hours? Time ticked away differently down here in my cell, or maybe it never moved at all, maybe I was forever trapped in a circular moment. Or maybe I was dead and this was limbo. Forever and ever.

Strange dreams, red skies, fat goldfish with hard bodies, writhing against my legs, nibbling my skin, gnawing holes. Things getting inside, moving underneath my skin like a cat under a sheet. I scream and they crawl out my mouth, choking off my cries.

I woke to find myself clawing at the door. My fingernails were jagged and bloody. Splinters of different sizes protruded cactus-like from my hands. The door was covered in gory furrows. My sleeping self was trying to get out. It was no surprise. My inner monster had been keeping me alive all these years. My hands throbbed and I slowly dragged myself back to the couch to pick out all the slivers.

Each jagged piece a reminder that regardless of my efforts, I lived on.

XXXIX.

Sleep was becoming easier as time passed, though the more I slept, the more I tried to escape. I found myself precariously balanced, clawing at the sealed window, trying to dig out a hole in the sheetrock. My fingers were sprained and broken. I had gashes from nails and electrical wire that were bloodless and ugly. I didn't want to be awake, but I feared my sleeping self and its survivalist autopilot.

I was floating, weightless. Bodiless in a velvet blackness. It was neither warm nor cool in that middle place. It was utterly silent and peaceful. I was dangling on the precipice of non-being, fraying at the edges.

Wait.

Something called to me. It was so far away, all the way back down in my body, in that world of pain. I didn't want to return, I begged to be released, but my wishes went ignored and instantly I was in my pain-wracked, crumpled form again.

I heard something.

I felt the pass of air under the door. Heard the knob turning. My eyes wheeled around in my stiff skull, searching the cell for a place to hide, but there was nowhere, and I was too weak. I remained there, prone. By the time the door whooshed open, I had nearly passed out from anticipation.

XL.

The basement doorway was dark, and the gust of cold, mildewed air strangely refreshing. I took a deep breath without realizing it, and there was more to the smell than old laundry soap and mold. There was life in that air. The figure stepped in and gasped. As soon as she crossed the boundary into the light, I moaned.

My mother. My mother who couldn't go down stairs on her own, my mother who wandered into the woods to sleep. My mother, the horrible old crone who only swooped in to torture me. The mother shape stepped farther in and clasped her hand over her mouth. She was dressed in real clothes: jeans, a coat. And she had tears in her eyes.

Don't cry for me, Mother, I don't deserve it.

She came to me. I tried to roll away from her, but all I could manage was to raise one of my crooked and mutilated hands to halt her.

"Oh, God . . ." She reached out to me, touched my cheek. I flailed then, using my last reserve of strength to knock her away. I didn't want her coming an inch closer. I could smell her, through the cold, through her clothes, through the short distance that divided us. She smelled like food, like life, like salvation, like home. My dry tongue scraped along the top of my mouth. I knew my teeth were bared, shriveled lips pulled back. Sharp teeth. My eyes, so dry they could barely blink, just burned instead.

"Get out . . . of here . . . please." My voice gurgled through my ruined throat. My mother shook her head. She lowered herself stiffly, knees popping. She was too near, too alive. Her hands fluttered over and around me, as if wanting to touch me but afraid to. I would have laughed, if I had I the strength. Was this all I had to do to get her to touch me? She gasped at the floor she was kneeling on. My blood was everywhere, congealed and sticky.

"What a terrible life I gave you." Her eyes were screwed shut. I was so confused. Where had she gone? I had searched everywhere for her. Was she hidden away? I wanted to ask her but I was too weak. Did she leave and come back? Was this a dream? It had to be a dream.

My mother could move, she was being kind, she spoke clearly. What a strange hallucination. The sight of her leaning over me, moving, talking, touching me as I lay dying was confusing. I thought of the sculpture in Hugh's gallery—the mother looking down at her dead baby. I coughed.

"I was in the attic. When you came back I hid. I wanted to leave, leave you, but . . ."

"You shouldn't be here," I gasped out, my throat ruined.

She reached out and ran her hand along my face. The warmth from her palm left tracks of sensation, it was like an antidote. But I was greedy for more than a kind touch, and I wanted what was beneath her skin so badly my teeth ached. With a shaking breath, I squeezed my eyes shut.

"It's not safe . . . please, just go."

"I can't."

I turned my face as far away from her as my ruined neck would allow. My hands clutched tightly to my chest to keep them from reaching out to her. I heard her fumbling behind me, the sound of fabric, a hissed breath, and suddenly the air around me exploded with the smell of blood. I turned back, snuffling the air like a dog. She was on her knees, her coat sleeve pushed back, a streak of red blossoming where she had just cut her wrist with the knife. The cut was deep enough that I could watch the pulse in the fount, feel the heat. I keened, like an animal in a trap.

"Why are you torturing me?" A harsh whisper, my gaze staying riveted to the dripping laceration. A drop of blood, then a few more hit the floor. I could have wept for the waste. The desire to lick the cement was overwhelming. I whimpered.

My mother brought the offending wrist closer, my resistance leeching away as the distance closed between us. She lifted my head to her lap with her other hand.

"It's not your fault." Her other hand reached out and stroked my hair. The touch was so soothing, so kind. My whole life I'd yearned for such affection from her. I let out a wretched sob. I followed her gaze to her painting in the corner. Her eyes were hard to read then: guilt, maybe? Grief?

"I can't . . ." I finally said, leaning closer to the blood. Eyes on the wound.

"It's all right. I want you to." Our eyes met and she smiled, and she was in that moment the most beautiful person in the world. A divinity made flesh, brought down to my basement hell to offer salvation.

"I love you, Mom," I whispered and she nodded, bringing her wrist to my mouth.

PART IV: Epilogue

Some things are more precious because they don't last long.

—Oscar Wilde

𝒥 lived alone my whole life: friendless, loveless, isolated, but despite my solitary existence, I wasn't selfish. A successful life demands that you become selfish, that you must take care of yourself. Rapunzel was weak because she was waiting to be saved. She could have lowered herself down on her own hair anytime, hacking it off at the base. She could have run away from that tower a new woman, a free woman. But she didn't. Instead, she waited in her prison. Sabrina could never have saved me. I wasn't living in a fairy tale, and no one could save me from myself.

When I finally woke in that basement cell, I felt peace. My unnatural body, while still very hurt, was mending, and I got up without too much protest. My peace dissolved when I noticed the body of my mother. She lay in a fetal position, her small hands in tight tiny fists, her skin slack and yellow, corded blue veins standing out in high relief. Empty and desiccated. I dropped to my knees, scooping up those brittle hands. They were cold and stiff. Her cheeks were hollow, her closed eyes bulbous. The skin covering her eyelids was nearly transparent, reminding me morbidly of a baby chick in an egg. I let a shaking hand touch her head, her sparse hair.

My mother was dead.

My fist was in my mouth, choking off the scream in me. I threw myself onto her body. It was bony and unresponsive, all angles, but I clung to it as if it was a life preserver. I wrapped my arms around her and I squeezed, getting the embrace that she had never given me in life, until the very end. I cried, and pulled the blankets up to her chin. I left her curtains wide open, the pale light giving her the illusion of sleep. I kissed her forehead. It was still a bit damp. I let my hand rest on hers for a moment.

"You did your best. I know that now."

With a final squeeze I left the room, closing the door behind me.

When I left my mother's house for the last time, there was a Rapunzel feeling of escaping the tower and cutting off all that hair, losing all the weight dragging behind me. I stood outside the gate, watching the dark smoke mingle with the night sky and blot out the stars. I was hypnotized by the vibrant flames hungrily devouring the old wood of the house and melting the snow. The smell of fire in the air cleansed me.

I walked along the lonely, snowy street, dragging my suitcase and the one painting I'd decided to keep. Tommy yowled in his carrying case, precariously balanced on the wheeled suitcase. I was still weak and heavily bandaged and it was a relief, after what felt like hours, to reach the high school. It was dark and locked up tight this late at night, so I didn't feel the need to sneak as I crossed the parking lot and sat on the main steps, obscured from the road by some dormant busses and a large tree. I let my fingers wriggle around inside the cat box, petting the cat's soft fur, coaxing him to relax.

I sat for a long time. My backside was frozen and stiff with cold by the time the car pulled up. It was a rental, nondescript, white. It parked in front and killed the engine. I rose with a creak and moved toward it. She was smiling when the window slid down and I welcomed the burst of heat that escaped from wracking sobs dragged painfully from my hunched body. I rocked my mother back and forth, kissing the dead skin of her face, wishing for so many things I couldn't name. I wished she was alive, I wished that I could have known the red-headed painter she was. I wished I knew what her laugh sounded like. I wished she had loved me the way I had wanted.

But . . . she had loved me more than anyone else in the world, as much as anyone could. That truth quieted me. I stayed on the floor, holding her tight, spooning her small, brittle body to my own. And over time, I began to feel . . . lighter. I didn't murder my mother. She had given herself to me, as a gift. That love was bigger than life and death, her love living on in me, in my body, in my memories. It didn't give me peace. But it gave me resolve. I couldn't let her sacrifice be for nothing, and I couldn't ignore what I really was.

I stared at her body a long time.

I got up, returning with a bucket of warm, soapy water and a sponge, and I meticulously bathed her on the floor. I nearly broke when I caught myself testing the water to make sure it was just right—like I had for her a thousand times before. She didn't care.

I carefully washed and dried every inch of her shriveled, scarred body. In the harsh basement light, her body was a galaxy, constellations of shiny pink scars everywhere.

Once clean and smelling of roses, I slid her into a crisp white nightgown, this one ornate with lace and embroidery at the neck. When I lifted her, she weighed next to nothing, and I carried her all the way back into her bed, tucking her in lovingly and carefully. I put her hands on her chest, one over the other, the car. She was similar to when I saw her last: pale skin, blonde hair, freckles, and a nice smile.

"Thanks for coming to get me, Renee. I know it's a long drive."

She unlocked the door and I loaded my gear in the back. Once inside, she smiled widely at me, her eyes loving but also a little vacant.

"It was no problem. You can phone me any time. I had the night off at the restaurant, and besides, you should thank your dad for paying for the rental. . . . Hey, what's that painting?"

Looking into the back seat, I smiled. "It's called States of Being. It's a self-portrait of my mother. It was her favorite."

"She's an amazing painter."

"Yeah. It was her life."

We pulled away, speeding down the road in the opposite direction of the screaming, clanging fire truck. I squeezed my eyes shut and thought of what a tinderbox my house was, with its horsehair plaster and ancient insulation. The house took to flame as if it had been waiting for it all along.

I pictured my mother in her bed. I thought of that painting curling up in the basement. I imagined my old canopy bed a brilliant sight, all aflame. It felt like I was closing a chapter. Freeing all the ghosts inside once and for all.

Sabrina inevitably filled my mind, and I touched my lips. She would have a wonderful life; she was too wonderful not to. I understood the nature of love now, and a large part of it was sacrifice. My father only took; my mother only gave.

I could be more than both of them. A new creature entirely, I had to be, I owed it to my mother and her sacrifice. A second fire truck, from the neighboring town, barreled around the corner, and we had to move onto the snowy shoulder to let them pass.

"Gosh. I hope no one's hurt," Renee said, watching the truck fishtail, turning down the narrow street in her rearview. I patted her hand, lacing my fingers into hers.

"It'll be fine. How long will it take us to get back to the city?"

She turned to me and beamed, forgetting the burning house and the small town we'd just left. The car climbed the winding mountain roads up and out of that dark, craggy valley.

I didn't look back.

AUTHOR'S NOTE

Parasite Life is a work of fiction dealing with suicidal situations and fantasy creatures.

If you or anyone you know is depressed or suicidal, please contact:

US Suicide and Depression Hotline 1-800-273-8255

Kids Help (under 20) in Canada 1-800-668-6868

http://www.spsamerica.org/ (USA)

https://suicideprevention.ca/ (Canada)

https://www.samaritans.org/ (United Kingdom)

https://www.suicidepreventionaust.org/ (Australia)

http://samaritans.org.nz/ (New Zealand)

http://www.suicide.org/ (links to global hotlines and information)

ACKNOWLEDGEMENTS

This book could not have happened without the support of my husband, Phil. You inspire me to take risks and be brave every day, and I love you for it.

Thanks also to Bram Stoker, Anne Rice, Sheridan Le Fanu, Poppy Z. Brite, Nancy A. Collins, Tanya Huff, Charlaine Harris, and all the rest. You've made monsters that are real and complicated. This book is the result of countless hours reading vampire books and wanting so badly to jump into the fray. I'd be honored and humbled to share a bookshelf with any of you.

And a huge thank you also to ChiZine for taking a chance on my strange little book and for my early readers whose support and feedback got this project over the finish line.

ABOUT THE AUTHOR

Victoria Dalpe was born in the wilds of New England. She's an artist and writer whose short stories have appeared in various anthologies. She lives with her husband, writer and filmmaker, Philip Gelatt and their young son in Providence, RI. This is her first novel.